EMOTIONLESS

amie mccracken

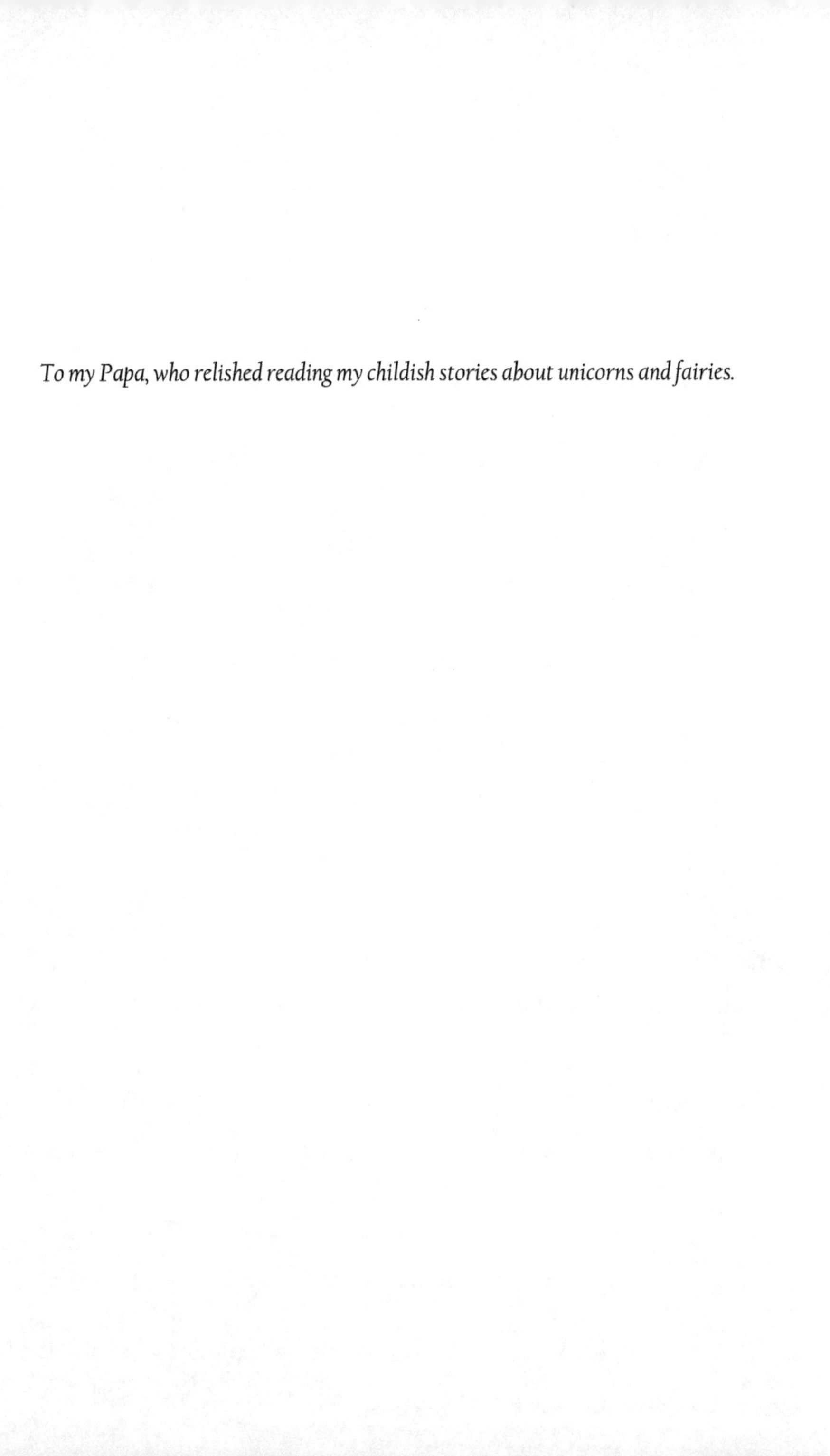

To my Papa, who relished reading my childish stories about unicorns and fairies.

CHAPTER 1
elias

Bright lights, tiny flashes of emotion, burst across the wall screen behind the murderer, lying prone in the body-forming, gel chair, one wire protruding from his head and his muscles twitching. The controller at the back of the room, bathed in the flashing light, watched his smaller screen with intensity. I turned from watching the murderer, Torin Moray, to move behind the controller and view the scenes that played from the brain scan.

Through the fuzz of what looked like an ancient black and white film, we watched the sidewalks pass. The rail yards stood to the left of Torin, the shops to the right. The sky seemed to be gray and cloudy, but that could have just been the absence of color from the scans. A moment of indecision, where Torin stopped at a street corner and turned one way, then the opposite. I glanced up to see his body motionless, paused mid-thought. His stillness was eerie. It was a point of no return; an obvious change in his chemical makeup; the exact moment in time when his body betrayed itself. As he made his choice on the vid, the wall behind him flared a deep indigo.

"Interesting," the controller mumbled.

"Excuse me?" I said, bending down to be closer to him so I wouldn't disturb the murderer's memories.

"That color is not common for changelings." He looked up at me. "Sorry, EMT patients." With a blush, he put his elbows up on the table and settled his chin in his hands.

We kept watching.

And as we viewed, things became even more interesting. The colors on the wall grew from monochrome and dull, to brilliant and variegated. An entire rainbow and so much more from the entire spectrum of light danced across our faces. As each choice was made, the murderer seemed to find more and more emotion rising in his system.

He walked through the door of an old building and climbed creaky stairs that had chunks missing. Down a hallway, and through a door, he found a woman. A glimpse at her face gave us the briefest of flashes of a buttercup yellow. It lasted only a millisecond, but it had been blinding. When our eyes refocused, we saw the woman yelling. She stood in a derelict room with a hole in the wall and a mattress on the floor behind her that still held the imprint of a body. As she continued to yell silently at Torin, he charged at her and raised a brick from the floor to strike her in the head. The room we actually stood in turned a brilliant purplish red, and the murderer's body spasmed in the chair uncontrollably. The medical professional standing by to help rushed forward and supported his head in the chair to keep him from biting his own tongue.

I snatched my tablet from the table and left the room. When the brain scan finished, they would send the entire folder of information directly to me. For now I needed to find Dr. Rooken and relay what little I knew. This could be a problem for our system. If people couldn't trust changelings anymore, could they trust anything?

I reached the hospital after a bus ride and a short walk. I found Dr. Rooken leaving surgery, outfitted in a silicon bodysuit and preparing to wash up and change.

I handed him my tablet with the vid cued. He ran a hand through his scraggly hair. He pinched his cheek between thumb and forefinger. Then, he stopped all movement, just like the murderer had at the street corner. Dr. Rooken rewound the vid and played it again, this time his jaw gradually opening in amazement.

"Blue? The wall was blue?"

"Yes. The controller thought it was odd too. I didn't know we could produce such color."

"Normally you can't."

We began to walk. Dr. Rooken's silicon bodysuit squeaked with each step.

"Do they have distinctive evidence linking him to the murder?"

"Besides the brain scan they have fingerprints and DNA mixed with her blood."

"The brain scan confirms it. This is going to be a disaster. Can you start the preliminary research and see if we've had any other crimes from an EMT patient?"

"Certainly."

I veered off from Dr. Rooken, his back still bent over the tablet as he walked, and made my way to the lab. I stepped in and the clinical lights slowly brightened to show me the wall screen and large work table. I asked the computer to pull up all files of acts of violence reported about an EMT patient.

"I have a robbery that was unsolved, where the owner of the store claimed it was an EMT patient. No evidence."

"That won't work. No true crimes?"

"No."

"Broaden the search. Look for acts of passion."

"I have three reports of EMT marriages to humans. Would you like to see those?" the computer asked.

"Yes, please. Anything else unusual?"

"I also have three live births from the same couples."

"Were the children norms?"

"At birth, yes." She displayed the newspaper clippings on my personal screen.

"The fathers must be EMT. I don't believe the mothers would be capable of carrying to term if they were EMT."

"Confirmed."

"Ok. I'll look these over." I scrolled through the photos and articles. In each the mother smiled and the father didn't. In two cases the women had been impregnated artificially. In one, the baby had been grown in an artificial womb. I looked up the clinic one of them had used and vidcalled.

"Hello. I'm an assistant at the EMT Clinic in Denver. I have a question about one of your clients?"

"That's confidential," the secretary said. She studied something on her desk.

"What paperwork would I need to get the information?"

"Signed allowance form either from the parents or from their personal doctors."

"Ok, I'll have that sent right over. Thank you."

"You're welcome, have a good day." Her voice was cheery. I didn't attempt to mimic it and hung up. That part about norms always confused me. Why did they feel the need to lie to make me more comfortable?

I sent the allowance form to Dr. Rooken's account with a small explanation. I saw that he accessed the files through a tablet, and then I turned back to my work. Dr. Rooken walked into the lab, no longer wearing a silicon bodysuit but instead a pair of slacks and a doctor's coat, his head still bent over my tablet.

"I've signed those, but what did you find?"

"Those men from the forms married human women and had children." I spoke while moving files around and sending them to the proper places.

"It would take surgery for EMT patients to provide their half of the DNA."

"Yes. I want to find out if that's how it happened. I need a signature from their personal doctor."

"Good thing you know me." Dr. Rooken laughed and shouldered me. I looked at him, eyebrows raised. "I'm just saying it was easy. Lighten up." He sighed.

Within a few minutes the screen blinked and new files appeared in my database. I worked my way through the other two men until I had all of their information up on the screen in a visual formation.

In each case the men had provided their own DNA. Dr. Rooken settled on a stool, crumbs falling from his lips as he munched on a sandwich. A tiny vacuum cleaner sprang to life in the corner of the room and zipped under his chair.

"I wonder if maybe these women fell in love and coerced the men into it." A piece of lettuce landed on the table and Dr. Rooken picked it up to eat it, his eyes focused on the wallscreen.

"That's possible," I said.

"Should we talk to them?"

"They would never disclose that information. If you speak with the women they would deny it out of the need to feel loved, and if you speak to the men they would deny it because they believe it. It is pretty simple to dupe us, Doctor. When it comes to feelings at least."

"That's true. So how did the alleged murderer feel? Was he coerced?"

"Why do you say 'alleged'?"

"Because I don't believe it." He took another bite of his sandwich.

"The brain scan—"

"The brain scan only shows that he murdered her. That doesn't mean there wasn't someone else behind it. Was it premeditated? Or was it a plot where he was only a pawn? Someone telling him what to do and why."

"He is still the murderer."

"Yes." He turned to the tablescreen and sifted through research until he reached the newspaper clipping for the murderer. Then he mumbled, "But that won't bode well for us."

They had not identified the man in the newspaper. He was an insignificant rail worker, having kept his job and housing after the therapy. Torin Moray had been one of the first batch to receive EMT. Living and working near the point of origin, after treatment, had always been taboo, but it had become illegal shortly after Torin was changed. That meant the people around him were familiar and possibly a danger to him. It's why I had needed special paperwork to come back to Denver to work for Dr. Rooken. In the case of the murderer, the police would have plenty of character witnesses to back everything up. The girl was unrelated to him as far as anyone could tell.

"I understand a random act of murder in an unmodified human. But a man who has no hormones, why would he kill a girl he doesn't know? The system has been proven. There has to be something else behind this," Dr. Rooken said.

"How would we ever find it?"

"We'll have to try. Otherwise the EMT project will go down the drain. It can't survive when the whole purpose has just been set on a ledge."

"I'll start looking into it, Doctor."

Further research into Torin's background required a lot of reading, so I took my tablet and went into the doctor's office to sit down. As usual, his desk was covered in different tablets containing different sets of files and correspondence. He could never keep it all organized on his personal tablet. I began to clear the desk when I spotted a physical, instead of digital, button I hadn't seen before. It was made of wood, like the desk, and fit level so it was nearly hidden. The varnish had been rubbed shiny. I pushed it. From the side of the desk popped a little drawer, and inside sat a paper journal.

I left the tablets and messy tablescreen as they were and picked up the journal. Sitting in the doctor's chair, I opened it.

> *"They had not gone far before they saw the Mock Turtle in the distance, sitting sad and lonely on a little edge of rock, and, as they came nearer, Alice could hear him sighing as if his heart would break. She pitied him deeply.*
>
> *"'What is his sorrow?' she asked the Gryphon, and the Gryphon answered, very nearly in the same words as before, 'It's all his fancy, that: he hasn't got no sorrow, you know. Come on!'"*

I closed the journal and pondered what the passage from *Alice in Wonderland* meant. I couldn't form an opinion, but that was normal. I could never form opinions.

I put the journal back in its hidden drawer and closed it. Turning back to my job, I gathered my tablet, looked over the room, and sat on the couch.

"Doctor," I called across the hall.

"Yes, Elias?" He strolled into the office.

"Can I ask you a question?"

"Of course."

"Why haven't you made the choice?"

"My family. I love them and don't want to leave them."

"I left my family," I said. I watched his face go from sleepy to sad. "Did I say something wrong?"

"No, I said something wrong. I'm sorry for mentioning family. I don't mean to make you feel bad for the choice you made. As you said, it's a choice."

"You didn't make me feel bad." I turned back to my work and started transcribing pieces from one document into another. The doctor poured himself some coffee from the machine in the corner.

"Elias?"

"Yes?"

"Do you miss them?"

"I vaguely remember feeling happy. It's like when I wake but am not fully awake. I remember that I made the choice so they would be happier. I just hope they are. Other than that I don't miss them."

Dr. Rooken pondered my words then walked back out of the office and into the adjoining lab. I went to his desk and pushed the little button to pull out the journal. I looked in the back and found a name and quote.

Sebian Wolff

"Do not give in too much to feelings. An overly sensitive heart is an unhappy possession on this shaky earth." Johann Wolfgang von Goethe

Sebian Wolff had been Dr. Rooken's mentor, the man who had invented Emotional Modification Therapy.

I opened the journal to the first entry after the *Alice in Wonderland* excerpt.

"Without feelings of respect, what is there to distinguish men from beasts?" Confucius

The passion of violence, love, insanity—they all evoke powerful emotion in a human being. Yes, we must have respect to distinguish ourselves from beasts, but how are we better than beasts when our passions move us to kill and maim each other? That is not a form of respect. It is our conscience that distinguishes us from beasts. We must have a clear mind to make decisions, and how can we with all the emotions bombarding our systems? Remove that and you have a human who will function better. A human who can make decisions that won't hurt others.

Dr. Wolff believed that without hormones we wouldn't perform random acts of violence. Perhaps what the murderer had done wasn't random? Perhaps he hadn't been taking his Hormone Stabilizing Serum?

Over the past fifty years the governments of the world had slowly been turning to EMT as a means of making more logical, safer decisions. Dr. Rooken worked closely with the government and our projects were mostly government funded. We provided research; they provided the means. But if this man was capable of murder, what did that mean for the leaders of the world? What did it mean for our research?

I put the journal back in its drawer yet again. I didn't want to show it to Dr. Rooken. It might upset him to know that Dr. Wolff had kept something secret. Or so I rationalized. I would make a choice later.

CHAPTER 2
aloisa

It was all over the news. The murder of an unmodified human by a changeling. I sat on the bus, my eyes glued to the screen on the seat back. Thelia, my employer, reported from her news desk.

"We don't have word on why this has happened, but police do have the killer in custody," Thelia said.

"That's a relief," a random woman broke the silence on the bus. She clutched at her chest, her eyes bulging and her other hand gripping her purse.

"We're going to hear from John now. He's at the scene of the crime. John?" Thelia said. I stopped watching as the rest of the people on the bus broke into chatter. Outside my window, on the wall of a run-down building, someone had graffitied a man circled by flames. It was a childish and sad attempt at the symbol most people attributed to the rebels.

"Well Thelia," the newscaster continued, "This is a very unsavory part of town. As you can see behind me, I'm at the rail yards. The woman's apartment was near here and, as far as we can tell, the EMT man worked just down the road. We've been trying to get in contact with his employer, but the police got to him first. So now we will have to wait for the report," John said.

The bus moved from my neighborhood through a gate into the protected areas of the city; retinal scanners on the bus catalogued the crowd. Here the sidewalks gleamed with tiny diamonds and microfibers, the cars were all shiny, and the houses were triple the size of our apartment building.

"Were there any witnesses, John?" Thelia asked.

John adjusted his tie and cleared his throat. "We don't know. We don't know much at all. Just that an Emotional Modification Therapy man murdered an unmodified human woman. The question is: why? Or even more so: how? If he doesn't have hormones, how can he feel enough anger to kill someone?"

That really was the question. And the reason everyone on the bus was freaking out, probably everyone in the city. It wasn't a pretty day when changelings started attacking people.

A changeling walked down the sidewalk, her step even and her face blank. I always envied their posture. They didn't seem to have a care in the world—well, honestly, they didn't. She saw me watching and turned her head, looking me straight in the eye. No smile, no wave, nothing. Chills crept down my back, and I swiveled back to the screen in front of me. My fellow travelers were once again quiet.

The woman on the bus who had spoken earlier gasped. A man next to her leaned in, and they started whispering. The bus filled with hissing and spitting. Not everyone on board was unmodified. A man across the aisle from me kept his eyes on the screen in front of him. The world around him erupted in chaos while he sat still. Heads turned, tongues wagged, and he watched the news as if the story were that of a kitten having been rescued from a tree.

Soon, others on the bus noticed we weren't alone and furtive glances over their shoulders shut them up, or tiny 'tsks' from others' mouths quieted the noise. The bus was silent again when I got off and walked up the mile-long driveway to Thelia's house. She was still sitting at her desk, fluffed hair and red lipstick, reporting the news, while I got to come here and spruce up her garden.

After hours of being knee-deep in fertilizer and wrist-deep in weeds and seedlings, the pathways were beautiful once again. They had looked just fine before I had started, but daily maintenance was my job so I maintained with vigor.

The house towered above me, throwing a shadow as the sun sank. Footsteps on the gravel walkway alerted me to the presence of someone else, and I turned to find Thelia barreling toward me. Or maybe she was striding. Either way, she always walked on stiletto heels with complete determination. I hadn't even seen her walk any other way. She continued right on by me as if I wasn't there, even though I offered a tiny smile, and she went to get lost in the labyrinth. It was a typical routine for her. I saw a changeling following in her wake with a tray of tea and cookies. He left them sitting on the bench just outside the labyrinth, ready for when she decided to come out from her hiding place.

I shook my head and started tidying my tools. But a voice stopped me.

"Hello Aloisa."

I whipped around. Thelia sat on the bench next to the tray.

"Hello." I felt at my face to see if I had any dirt on it, only to realize I had my gloves on and there was now definitely dirt smudged across my forehead.

"You're not a changeling."

"No."

"What do you think of this murder business?"

"I don't know. It's scary?"

"Is that a question?" She plucked a leaf from the shrub next to her. The yellow veins mirrored the blue ones on her hand.

"No?"

"Again, a question. I'm considering firing all of my change-lings. Good thing you aren't one. At least I'll continue to have a beautiful garden even if I won't have food to eat." At this she swept a cookie from the plate onto the gravel walkway. We both stared at it sitting on top of the rocks.

"Thank you?"

She waved her hand at me, sweeping me away as she had the cookie. I gathered my tools and hurried down the path, cringing at every crunch my feet made on the rocks.

The apartment smelled like fish. The instant I inhaled, I ran for the bathroom and threw up in the toilet. I dragged my hand across my mouth and looked at my pale face in the mirror. Rubbing my fingers along the greasy skin, I molded it into strange shapes. I rinsed my mouth of the acrid taste.

In the living room, Jordan was already asleep on the couch. Dinner sat on the coffee table, a single rose cut from my plants on the roof among the plates. I had missed our anniversary dinner. Stripping down to my shabby underwear, I slid under the blanket and snuggled up against his solid form.

He mumbled into my back and started running his hands over my body. I shivered. The feeling of his calloused hands rubbing my sensitive skin was arousing and painful all at once. I smelled him; his Jordan-sweat, wood, and glue. The chemicals he used every day to clean the hospital lingered under the clean sawdust. I placed one of my hands over his and followed it all over my stomach and down my thighs. He had a bandage on one finger, probably a cut from working on a sculpture. I turned to him.

We made love in the slowest manner possible, staying calm and quiet. He seemed to want me so badly that instead of being sweet he was urgent, making the feelings last forever but taking what was his when he was ready. The digital clock in the security panel blinked 3 am when he pulled away and sat up next to me. I let him cool off and then put my head in his lap, hoping he would hold me.

"I love you, Aloisa."

"I love you too, Jordan. I'm sorry that I wasn't here."

"It's all right. We can go out to lunch tomorrow."

"We can't afford that."

He rolled out from under me and walked to the bedroom.

I stood and pulled the blanket around myself, making my way to the stairs and up to the roof door. It was supposed to be locked, but the super hadn't fixed it or the hall lights since before we had moved in. I pushed the door open and was bombarded with the smell of smog and a tiny blip of fresh air. In one corner of the roof my oasis sat waiting. A tiny garden built of random bowls and tins filled with dirt and plants filched from the burn pile at my various jobs. In the center of this hodge podge stood one actual pot. Inside that pot was a white rosebush. And inside that rosebush, entangled among the vines, stood a gryphon rearing on its lion legs. A beautiful wooden sculpture Jordan had made for me when we were married.

I plonked down on the bench he had built me, curling my feet under myself and looking up at the stars. I breathed the freshness my plants offered me. I worried that life would only get harder.

elias

Walking home that evening after work, I followed my normal path. But just before my apartment door, a hand grabbed my arm and yanked me into an alleyway. The alleyway was much darker than the street. I couldn't see the person who had pulled me aside.

"Can I help you?" I asked.

"There's nothing wrong with wanting things," a distinctly male voice said. The shadow that stood before me was taller than me and was cloaked in a long coat. His voice had a husk to it.

"If you want something and I can help, please let me know," I said.

"I want you to want things. There are reasons changelings should go back to wanting things."

The idea of wanting something was so foreign, so unnecessary, that I dismissed it immediately. Yet I wondered why I had been accosted. Why would this man bring me to a secluded area to talk about wanting things? Did he have Rolexes hanging in his coat? Was he a nudist getting ready to expose himself to me? Whatever his intentions were, I knew one thing: This man was only speaking to me because he was scared of EMT patients. He had heard about the murder.

"Again, can I help you with something?"

"You are dangerous. Until you become normal," he said.

"If I can ask, what is normal? Unmodified humans are dangerous as well. How do I know you aren't going to pull a knife on me right here?"

"The level of danger I present is nothing compared to yours. At least I'm predictably unpredictable. Don't you want to be normal again? I can help that happen."

I looked at the people walking by in the street, most headed home from work but probably some of them wandering or going to dinner or any number of things. This man was trying to get information. That or feed me information on the murder and the flaws of EMT. The question was, did he know Torin Moray or was he not quite sane? How had he known who I was?

His finger pointed to my chest where my hospital badge hung. He pinned it against my shirt, poking the sharp metal tag into my skin and muscle.

I had one answer to my questions.

"I can make you want things. I can bring you back from the dead," he said.

"I don't need that. Thank you very much. But do you have information about the murder? Do you know the murderer?"

"You are so juvenile," he said and swung around to pace the alleyway. There wasn't an opening at the other end so he had no way to leave without pushing beyond me. I wouldn't block him.

"If you know something about the murder, it would be very helpful to us. I can take your information or just have you come by the EMT Clinic to speak with the—"

"I would never go to that place. Don't even ask. I have needs too, and the number one is to stay alive. But beyond those needs I have wants. I want to fondle beautiful women; I want to drink alcohol until I can't feel my toes anymore; I want to ride roller coasters and feel my stomach drop out from under me. What do you want?"

At that he shoved me aside, avoided the retinal scanner on the corner of the building, and joined the throngs on the sidewalk rushing by. I put one hand in my pocket to find a card there that he must have slipped in. It had an address printed on it and nothing else. An address that would be located down by the rail yards. Very near where the murder took place.

Back at my apartment, I looked up the address on my tablet.

An image of a red brick building with a large oak door and iron studs, like a medieval castle, showed up on the screen. Not the same one the murdered woman had lived in, but in the same general area. The building was listed as an abandoned warehouse and had recent records from police searches stating that nothing was inside. It was owned by a numbered company that didn't trace back to anything specific. It didn't seem to be connected at all, and logically it didn't make sense to pursue a lead from a random informant.

I set the tablet aside and threw the card in my paper receptacle. Then I proceeded with my normal routine before bed.

CHAPTER 3
aloisa

Coming in the door of our shabby apartment after another long day in the sun, I heard Jordan pounding away on some project of his.

"Jordan?" I hung my purse and coat by the door.

"I'm in the living room. Just finishing up. What are we doing for dinner?"

"I ordered from the guy downstairs, hope that's ok." I walked into the living room and fell into our old, purple couch.

"Don't see why not," he said. He lifted the goggles that protected his eyes and came over to kiss me. "This one is almost done."

I looked around him at the sculpture. It was coming together as a pegasus. I could see the curve of a wing extending above the creature's head, reaching for freedom. It wasn't fully formed yet, but it was definitely there. That little grasp for a chance to fly.

"Aloisa, did you hear me?"

"Sorry, what?"

"I talked to Dr. Rooken some more."

"Great." I crossed my arms.

"I think it would work."

"You're talking about leaving me."

"Only to help you," he said.

"I don't want money; I want you."

He plopped down next to me and a cloud of dust burst from his clothes.

"What good am I? You're working yourself to the bone just to survive. We'll never be happy at this rate."

"I'm happy." My arms fell to the couch, palms up and fingers slightly curled.

"No. This isn't happy. Living in this crappy old apartment and working for some rich woman. I want you to *be* that rich woman, and have changelings working for you."

"I don't want changelings. They're strange. And I don't want you to become one either!"

I jumped up from the couch and stormed out of the room, knocking his bottle of glue to the floor. In the kitchen I leaned against the counter, weaving back and forth to relax my spasming muscles. I heard the tiniest snap of plastic when Jordan's goggles went back over his eyes, and he started chiseling again. It was the argument we couldn't settle. The one he didn't understand. His parents were still human.

I went back into the living room. Leaning against the doorway, I crossed my arms again.

"Jordan?"

"Yes?"

"Can't you understand that I love you?"

He stopped hammering.

"Aloisa."

"Do I need to bring Miles over here so he can explain what it's like to lose people you love?"

"I don't need to talk to your brother. I know the money

they left is worth nothing now. Besides there are no other relatives this time to help themselves to the honeypot. It will all be yours."

"If you do it now I'll have nine hundred thousand dollars and a letter explaining what happened to my husband. But inflation is crazy. It won't be that much in just a few years."

"The economy has been improving."

"It's not about the money! I. Want. You. Do you think I preferred having money to having my parents? Do you think any child would want that? I don't know how I can make you understand."

"You can't. Because you're not a child anymore. Because you do need money now. Because your life could be so much better than it has ever been. We've been in this circle of work, eat, sleep, work, survive. I want more for you! I know I can give you more!" Dust flew into the air as he paced the floor and swung his arms about.

"Yes. You can give me more. By being here. By starting a family with me. By loving me. My life is already more than work, eat, and sleep. Because of you!"

I walked up behind him and slipped my hands around his waist. We stood like that until the sun set and the lights came on.

"Come on, let's go get our dinner," I said. "We only have two hours until the lights go out." He took my arms from around him and led me to the door.

Downstairs we greeted Mr. Dao. He sat us down in our normal corner and brought us the dinner I had ordered. Jordan had a beer, and I had green tea. It was so normal. But my feelings were on a roller coaster, and I couldn't find the stop button. I barely ate my noodles and said goodnight long before I should have. Jordan stayed down there chatting with Mr. Dao and his wife.

I trudged up the dark stairs. There had to be a way to convince him. There simply had to. I wasn't a little girl anymore, but every time this argument started up again I was thrown back to feeling like a helpless child, shoveled from home to home, always wondering if I would get to stay with my brother until I was old enough to care for us both. I stopped in the stairwell, the darkness soothing my nerves. Until the sounds of the city broke through, startling me. Suddenly the dark was no longer my friend, and I booked it up to the apartment where I shut the door and leaned against it, happy to be in a place that I understood, that understood me. A place that smelled of Jordan and I, that was stable and comfortable and easy.

Tomorrow I would bring Miles over. He would tell Jordan that I couldn't handle any more of this. His voice would be the voice of reason in this never-ending battle.

The next day I found Jordan sitting in a chair reading his tablet. Miles was already sprawled on the couch. I had called him earlier.

I walked over and sat on the edge of the couch so I could get a closer look at my baby brother. His face was relaxed and slack. Drool trailed down his cheek. He had been gone for months and here he was like the permanent fixture I was used to. I sincerely hoped whatever adventure he had been on hadn't done any lasting damage, to his body or psyche. I swept a piece of his hair out of the way, waking him.

"Hi."

"Hi," I said. Jordan turned a page. "What do you want for dinner?" I stood and took off my coat. The wool scratched against my bare arms, and I felt the seam in the back stretch and nearly split.

"You need a new coat," Miles said.

"I'm fine." I hung it up by the door and turned back to them. "How was the trip?"

"Eh. Same old, same old. Found an old heirloom in a restricted zone. Brought it back to the family. Got paid. They're still rich. I'm not."

"I still don't get why you do it. Or at least increase your rates. You put your life in danger for tangible objects." I sat down next to him and ran a hand down his stubbled cheek. He pushed me away, but I saw a blush creep onto his face.

"What're you reading?" I sat on the arm of Jordan's chair. He was engrossed in a news story. "Anything weird in the paper?" I asked.

"They have a changeling on trial."

"I heard about that on the bus. What else have they found out?"

"He'll be tried for murder," Jordan said.

"No," Miles said. He sat up.

"The man on trial, name undisclosed at this point, had Emotional Modification Therapy many years ago. He is being held on two million dollars' bail and will be tried for the murder of an unmodified human. The police will not comment," Jordan read.

Miles stood and began to pace. His face was made of stone and the air held his anger like an electric charge. My little brother, the hothead—especially when it came to a sore subject like changelings. He had never forgiven our parents for leaving. I had less spice in my blood, but so many of the feelings from my childhood had been flooding my system since the arguments with Jordan had begun. I understood Miles's flare of anger.

Jordan on the other hand stared blankly at the paper in his hands. Then he shot to his feet and snatched his coat.

"I'll run to get dinner."

He was gone.

CHAPTER 4
elias

Dr. Rooken had all of the murder info up on the wallscreen when I came into the lab. Dr. Xanther, the CEO of Emodiant, the company started by Dr. Wolff and Dr. Rooken to control Emotional Modification Therapy, stood next to him. I brought them some coffee. Dr. Rooken mechanically drank, keeping his eyes on the mess of files across the screen.

Dr. Xanther nodded to me and sipped.

"What are you working on today?" Dr. Rooken asked. Neither of us answered. I finally understood he was asking me.

"I need to catalogue the first generation. They've made some leaps in learning lately. Plus I need to run through their physicals and make sure they continue to maintain good health without growth hormones or hormones at all."

"Good," Dr. Xanther said. "Those children are the future of this system. I would much prefer to stop paying EMT patients' families."

I stood silent. Dr. Rooken snorted.

"Really Xanther? That's a bit cold. The whole point of this company was to help people find balance," Dr. Rooken said. He moved some files around on the screen while he spoke.

"It's wonderful that people come to us to find this balance you speak of, don't get me wrong. It's just a drain on our resources to support so many widows and widowers, let alone orphans. The EMT children are the way forward."

"True," Dr. Rooken said. A tiny smile flickered across his face. "I need to speak with the police about Torin Moray. He confessed. Elias, can you also call the EMT men who were married and set up interviews? I'd like to understand more about their reasoning."

"Of course," I said. But he didn't hear me as he left the room with Dr. Xanther, still discussing the beauty of the EMT babies and the advantages to not having to pay for EMT patients.

Within an hour I had appointments with all three families, including the children who were hybrids of norms and EMT patients. They were still very young, but we could watch them during the interviews and see any marked behavior.

I waited all day for Dr. Rooken to come back, but he didn't. So I went home to my small, one-room apartment. I made myself a ready-made protein and vegetable meal. While that was in the oven, I flipped through the available books on my tablet. Relics that had been recommended to me by others. A few novels I could never read more than a page of; too many innuendos and small details that blurred before my eyes as I read.

I sat down with my dinner and the tablet—news articles and a non-fiction book on the Kings of England, back when they had kings.

I went through the routine of cleaning my plates, rubbing down the counters, brushing my teeth, turning down my bed, having a glass of water, and checking the locks and lights. Every night I did the same thing. It was fulfilling and comfortable. There was a tiny bit of satisfaction in it. No happiness, but certainly satisfaction.

Lately, I had to include a massage on my knees before bed. Age was catching up with me. Though most effects of age weren't as pronounced for my kind, this and graying hair were still prevalent.

The next morning I did the routine over again in reverse: pulling up the shade to let in light, finishing my glass of water from the night before, making my bed, brushing my teeth, and cleaning the counters again before making breakfast.

I consumed more news articles while crunching through a complete-nutrition bar. I would leave having my coffee until the office because Dr. Rooken's machine made the best coffee. Or so he said.

I came into the lab and he was sleeping, arms and legs in all directions with his head lolled back in the chair. He was snoring. I shook him.

"Huh? Oh, Elias. Where did you go yesterday?" He rubbed sleep from his eyes and sat up.

"I was here until eight. You didn't come back."

"I must have just missed you. I found out they didn't do a drug test on Torin Moray, of course. They didn't suspect an EMT patient of drugs. In fact, they didn't do much accept politely bring him in to jail. They even gave him his own cell and thought they could let him go. But then a lawyer came in and set them straight."

"Did you get anything then?"

"Yes. He admitted something on the night they brought him in. They have it on tape. He had stopped taking his serum five days before and was trying a new pill that someone had given him. They told him it was better than the serum."

"Does he know this person? Can we get in contact with them?" I asked.

Dr. Rooken took me to the office while we talked. "He has no contact info but he remembers the look of the person.

After I watched the tape I went and asked him why he would take pills from someone unknown to him. He said the man was not unknown. That he had seen him in the neighborhood many times."

"Someone taking revenge?"

"This is why we require people move away. We'll keep looking into it. Did you contact the three men?"

"Yes, all three and their families are coming in for interviews today."

The first couple arrived. The man had brown hair, the woman blonde. But I don't think it was natural—tiny streaks of brighter blonde didn't blend well. Her fingernails were long and painted purple, and her outfit was tight and brightly-colored. The baby had brown hair too and sat passively in his father's arms. They set him down on the floor of our unused conference room in front of a set of toys. Then they sat in chairs across from me.

"Would you like some coffee?" I asked. I would give the interviews while the doctor monitored in another room. He wanted to see their reactions to me.

"Oh yes please, I would love that," the woman said. "Do you want some, hon?" she asked her husband.

"No thank you." He stared straight ahead, not even looking at me but studying the wall behind me.

I got coffee for the woman and sat down with my tablet to take notes. I would ask the same set of questions for all three couples.

"What are your names?"

"I'm Marlane and this is Mattias. Our son's name is Michel. Isn't that the cutest thing ever? We all have M names."

I didn't smile.

"When did you meet?" I asked.

"Just two years ago, oh it seems so much longer than that." Marlane grabbed her husband's hand and cradled it in her own.

"Mattias, when was your EMT surgery?"

"It was five years ago, in September," Marlane answered. Mattias kept studying the wall.

"And you mutually decided to have a child?"

"Oh yes, we knew it would be the most wonderful thing to have a child together."

"Who does what in your household? If you don't mind my asking."

"Of course not! I work and Mattias takes care of the house and the baby. He's so good at keeping everything clean, and I'm such a mess. Besides, I had the higher paying job when we decided to have Michel so it just seemed logical. I didn't even carry Michel; he was developed in an artificial womb."

"Really? What was that experience like?"

"I couldn't be bothered. I love my baby," she leaned down to pinch his cheek, "but I needed to keep working, and I didn't want to go through the pain. You can't imagine how afraid I was of it." Her shoulders shuddered. But then the smile plastered back on her face, and we jumped right back into conversation.

"Mattias, do you love your son?" I asked.

"Of course he does! What kind of a question is that?"

"I'm sorry, but I asked Mattias."

"You have no right to ask that kind of question. I think that's enough." She swept Michel into her arms and pulled Mattias from the room.

I found Dr. Rooken to consult before the next couple arrived. He was replaying the interview.

"Computer, zoom in on the baby please."

"Sure, Dr. Rooken."

"Do you see that Elias?" He pointed to the screen, sitting forward in his chair.

The child played with the wooden puzzle. The other colorful toys were scattered about. I didn't see the pattern until I stepped back a little.

"The toys," I said.

"Yes. What has he done with them?"

The soft teddy bears and colorful computer games and toys that made any sort of noise formed a circle around him, a large circle. Inside that circle were the wooden toys, the ones that weren't animated or soft but calculating and too old for him. They made another circle around him, as if to protect him from the baby toys. He was putting together a puzzle on the floor. A puzzle that I don't think even the doctor could have figured out, but this one-year-old was placing pieces and finishing the puzzle easily.

"Is he that smart?" I asked.

"No Elias, I think they bred an EMT baby without knowing it. We need to get our hands on his medical records. If they don't feed him the hormone stimulants, he won't grow any more than he has. HSS isn't just to keep your emotions in check, it's to keep your body functioning. Humans can't survive without hormones. Well, we couldn't until Dr. Wolff figured out a way." Dr. Rooken started searching through the files on his tablet. I left to get the room ready for the next couple.

"Elias, please mess up the toys again so we can see if this baby is different," the doctor called to me.

The second couple came in. The woman was wearing a baby-blue sweater over a white shirt with slacks. Her long blonde hair was pulled into a neat ponytail. Her daughter had curly blonde hair and was mesmerized by her mother's necklace. The woman, her name was Saeri, bent to set her daughter down. Holding the baby hovering above the floor she said, "Do you have a blanket?"

"I assure you the floor is clean," I said.

She smiled. "Rane, please get a blanket."

Her husband reached into the overstuffed baby bag and pulled one out. I helped them take the toys out of the way and lay the blanket down. When I started to put our toys back down, she stopped me.

"We have our own toys, thank you." Her smile was strange to me. I understood that it was a smile, but somehow it made me uncomfortable. I took the armful of toys to the other side of the room and put them on the conference table. Saeri unloaded a few toys from the bag and left them with her daughter.

I asked the same questions. Saeri answered; Rane sat quietly. Though from time to time I noticed his hands clench together and his eyes bounce from object to object. With this couple, Saeri was the stay-at-home mother and Rane worked. Just when I asked Rane if he loved his daughter, the baby was crawling toward us and bonked her head on the table leg. It was so loud I thought she might have injured herself. She was sitting up, facing the table leg, looking at it with wonder and curiosity, but no tears.

"Oh sweet baby," Saeri said and went to her. She still didn't cry. Saeri picked her up and kissed her head. "We should be going. She probably needs a nap now."

"Thank you for coming in." I stood and shook their hands. Saeri gave me another smile that made my fingers tingle. Rane had a tiny bead of sweat running down his temple.

I followed them out of the room and diverted into the lab to confer with the doctor. As soon as the door slid shut behind me he said, "Why didn't she cry?"

"I don't know. I wouldn't have cried."

"My point exactly. She's just like our EMT babies. I really need their medical records. They'll stop growing if they don't get the right hormones soon." He rubbed his hands together in glee. "I hadn't thought of something like this being possible."

"I'll get right to it once this last couple leaves. Anything you want me to do before they are sent in?"

"Put the toys back," he said.

"Ok."

I was seated and ready when the third couple walked in. This time the father introduced everyone to me. The wife sat down and looked at her lap. She had glasses and fluffy hair that covered her face.

This baby was noisier than the others. He cooed and bubbled at the toys, willing them to talk back to him. The father, Henry, spoke like a businessman, which is what he was. He spoke of his work like it was his second child or perhaps even his first. The mother never looked at me. When I asked Henry if he loved his son, he said of course and went on to give me an anecdote from work that proved it. I didn't pay much attention, scribbling notes that weren't notes. I was watching the baby. Observing as he set the computer toys in a circle far from him and built a wall of the wooden toys between him and the computers. He would make noises that sounded like scolding when he moved a computer and gurgle softly to the wooden toys.

Nothing I said could offend this couple. At one point Henry ran his fingers along his wife's arm. She smiled into her lap. Though Henry wasn't emotional about anything, he seemed truly in love. They seemed to be a happy family. Until the wife brushed her hair back when she stood, and I saw a bruise on her cheek. She picked up the baby, and they left. I walked in a daze into the computer room and asked the computer to zoom on her face and enhance the picture.

"Is that what I think it is?" Dr. Rooken said.

"Yes, Doctor. But we can't conclude that there's abuse."

"He's a dominant man."

"But he should not be capable of that kind of anger. Unless he's not taking his supplements," I said.

"Maybe we should request blood tests?"

"I don't think that's legal. The most we can do is get medical records. I'll get to work on finding those right now."

I searched and searched. Dr. Rooken kept absentmindedly bringing me coffee while he read through reports. For hours I looked, but I couldn't find anything.

"Doctor?" I said.

"Hmm?" He looked up from his paperwork.

"They've never been to the doctor. Not since birth."

"Impossible."

"Improbable. Not impossible."

"All three of them?"

"Even the parents."

"That is just strange," he said.

"How will we get the information? They could be in danger of stunting their children's growth and possibly causing premature death."

"We'll have to get a court order from the evidence in the interviews. I have a psychologist friend who can look them over and order the blood work. I'll take care of it." He touched my shoulder on the way out, pausing to tap it and probably reassure me. I knew those children were in danger, but it didn't worry me.

CHAPTER 5
aloisa

My fingers buried deep in dirt, the wind whipping my hair into my face, and the light sounds of footsteps coming across the rooftop. My tiny piece of heaven. I sat back on my heels and turned to see Jordan with two half full wine glasses in his hands. He set one down on the bench next to me and picked up a trowel with his now free hand. He went to the raised bed on the other side of our little square and started milling the soil. The sound of a bluesy guitar came across the air to us from another apartment, and I sighed, shoving my hands back into the dirt. The presence of my husband was palpable. Like a blanket around my shoulders, or a fire crackling in a hearth.

Jordan came up behind me, his hands snaking around to find mine. They followed my motions, massaging this new home for my plants. His lips touched my neck, grazing the skin ever so gently and raising the hairs to attention. He started using the shovel again to release the plant. I leaned back into him, my eyes closed, and took a deep breath. His strong shoulders supported me, but I felt a tenseness there.

The sounds of the city—trucks rumbling by, shuttles

gliding overhead, horns honking and tires squealing—were interrupted by his throat clearing. The clack and whoosh of his shovel had stopped, but I hadn't noticed in my bliss.

My hands paused their movement; a bolt of adrenaline shot through my system. I was ready for it. I knew the air had been tainted with something. I had ignored it. And here it came.

"We need to talk," he said.

Still facing my plants, and away from him, I considered my words carefully.

"I'm not so sure we do. This was so pleasant until you said something."

He grunted.

"I'm done arguing," he said. I whipped around to get a scan of his face. Did this mean he was giving in to me? Or did this mean he was resolved? His stony appearance said it was the latter.

"Then I guess we're done," I said. My body gave in to the stress. My shoulders drooped, my head sagged heavy on my neck, my hands dropped into my lap, spilling dirt clods across my pants and the rooftop tar. A tiny plop landed in my wine glass, and I watched it sink slowly to the bottom, tingeing the pink liquid with a cloud of brown on its way down.

"I've said what I need to say, Aloisa. This is the best decision for you. I won't have you living like this anymore."

I rose slowly to my feet, my shoulders and head coming up strong, my hands in fists at my sides.

"Like *this*?" I looked at my oasis. "*This*? What is *this* to you Jordan? Because to me this is perfection. This is heaven. This is beautiful and incredible and everything I've ever wanted in life and so much more beyond that. You don't seem to understand that I don't need more. There is no more. Nothing more exists in this world. People with more money don't have *this*.

This is not a thing you can acquire with money. And the fact that you don't understand that just tells me that you do need to leave. I don't want you here anymore. You are not welcome. Get out of my garden." I turned and walked to the edge of the rooftop that looked over the city. The blood rushing in my ears didn't allow me to hear if he walked away or not, so I stood still and silent for what felt like hours. But before the sun even finished setting and bathing the skyscrapers in golds and fuchsias, I turned back to my planting and found myself alone.

I went to the contaminated wineglass and flung the alcohol as far as I could over the edge of the building. Then I threw the glass too.

I woke on Monday morning to an empty bed. Usually he kissed me and then made breakfast and then said goodbye before going out the door. It was our routine. He the cheery morning person; me the grumpy, need-my-space person.

But that morning I woke up on my own when my alarm went off. Jordan wasn't in the bed or in the house; it didn't even smell like he had showered or eaten breakfast. His janitor's uniform was gone so I shrugged it off.

That night, after a hard day's work, I told Mr. Dao we'd be down for dinner. I was much too tired to cook anything, and I was sure Jordan was working away on some sculpture. The apartment was again empty.

It wasn't right. I took the coat I had just flung to the side of the door and put it back on, sweeping out the door and down the dark stairway. I didn't take the time to let Mr. Dao know we wouldn't be eating. I just rushed to the bus stop and hopped from foot to foot until it hovered in front of me.

At the EMT Clinic I asked for Dr. Rooken, head of Jordan's department, and was taken to his office.

He wasn't immediately available so I sat in one of the perfectly-clean reception chairs. I expected to see blood or guts spattered, but they looked brand new. A nurse brought me coffee and asked if I was adopting an EMT child.

"No. They're up for adoption?"

She sat on the edge of the chair next to me with her elbows propped on her knees and her chin resting in her hands. "Someone has to take them."

"They don't have parents?"

"They were donated cells from sperm and egg clinics so the researchers could figure out how to grow an EMT child. It's fascinating really. They don't require HSS, only growth hormones until they are fully grown."

"That's just a little strange." I sipped at my coffee.

"Oh, here comes Dr. Rooken," she said and stood.

I greeted Dr. Rooken. His hand enveloped mine. His smile radiated across the space to me, and I realized he wasn't a changeling.

"What can I help you with Mrs. Riodan?"

"I'm Jordan's wife—"

"Yes. He's a bright man."

"You say that like he's a child."

"I'm sorry, I didn't mean it that way." He motioned to the seats.

"Do you happen to know where he is? He hasn't been home or to work."

"I have found Jordan to be a stimulating companion. I tend to be here at all hours, so when he comes to care for my office we chat while we work. He has told me about his hard-working wife. It's wonderful to finally meet you. You have a love for gardening, if I'm not mistaken?"

"Yes..." My shock at the subject change was so complete that I couldn't form thoughts.

"I have also heard that he's interested in carpentry."

"He's an amazing artist," I said. Then I shook my head, unable to believe I was making small talk. "But that's not why I came here."

"Yes. You haven't seen him. That's common in today's world, is it not?" He gave a slight chuckle. "Let me check the records to see when he last had a shift." He pulled a tablet from under his arm. "I hadn't asked him before, are you planning to start a family?"

Before I could speak he jumped in again, "I'm sorry. That is much too personal for a first-time chat. Tell me more about plants? I've always been fascinated, as plants were the beginning of genetic work. Peas and all that." The smile that again crossed his face was brilliant and radiating. I cringed. Then he looked back at the tablet and said, "We did have a chemical fire this morning."

"But he never clocked in. I made sure to check." I started to stand. If Jordan was hurt and they hadn't told me, I was going to get very violent very fast. My hand fluttered against my thigh, the adrenaline was pumping so fast it felt like liquor traveling through my veins.

"Let's check with the nurses, shall we?"

He held a hand out and led me in the direction of the desk. I stood to the side as he spoke with the nurse. My mind was elsewhere, trying to think of why they wouldn't tell me that Jordan was hurt. Trying to stay away from why he would disappear. In the middle of Dr. Rooken's conversation with the nurse, I walked out of the door without a goodbye. I ran to the bus and hopped on.

The next morning I found myself on a different bus line than usual, headed for the inner city. It hadn't been a conscious decision; my feet had turned the street corner and then reversed and gone back past the apartment to a bus stop that serviced the downtown area, and specifically, the main police station. Sitting on the bus and listening to the chatter of the people around me, along with the commentary on the days' news across the vidscreens, I sucked in each breath with difficulty. Jordan had still not come home. I had spent the night alone. And in my heart I knew.

The bus glided to a stop outside the police station, and I sat glued to the seat for a moment too long. The bus began to move again until I jumped up and collided with the door. The bus jerked to a halt, the people around me mumbling and groaning, and the door opened to expel me onto the pristine walkway.

Inside the building, I walked up to the bullet-proof window where a changeling secretary sat.

"My husband is missing," I said.

"I need a name and ID number."

I rattled them off, watched her type on her desk, and waited for a reaction of some sort—anything in that blank face to give me an indication that she had found him.

"I will need to have an officer speak with you."

"Can't you just see if he's been reported in a hospital or jail?"

"We have not had a report of his retinal scan."

"Ok. Then he's truly missing, right?"

"According to the privacy article 51645235 I cannot give you any more information. I will have an officer come speak with you." She still hadn't looked me in the eye. She read through the files on her tablescreen, and when she did finally look up at me her eyes blurred and stared into the distance over my shoulder.

My hand came up to the glass, much harder than I had intended, and the bang attracted the attention of everyone on the other side. The changelings in the room all stopped to stare at me. Witnesses but non-activists. They simply took in the information. The entire room was on pause, and it was beyond eerie.

I spotted a police officer with carrot-colored hair and a look on his face that registered with feeling. I frantically waved at him and called out, "Hello? Can you help me?" The changelings followed my shout like puppies watching a tennis match. The ball bounced to him and back again to me. He strode to the door to my right and came through to the lobby.

"Ma'am please step back from the counter." He approached me with his arms rising slowly.

I backed away.

"I only wanted some information. My husband should have come home. He's been gone for a few days."

The officer glanced at the secretary and she repeated, "According to the privacy article..." I tuned her out. My eyes pleaded with the officer, my hands out in supplication. He continued to approach me like I was a ticking time bomb. That or a scared gerbil who might run at the slightest hint of aggression. If anything I was definitely the bomb, not the gerbil.

"Ma'am, we can't help you with that issue. We're not allowed. You know there are laws in place to protect EMT patients. Is there anything else we can do for you? We'll log your retinal scan in the computer and keep an eye out for anything strange. Is that ok?"

My hands flew to my face, trying to cover my eyes while still watching him. "You took my retinal scan?"

"Scans are always recorded the moment you step foot in a municipal building."

I backed my way out of the glass doors, feeling the difference in the air outside that enveloped me in smog. Then I turned and walked briskly away.

Down the street I stopped and pulled out my ancient tablet to attempt a vidcall. The signal was weak but it went through. I called Jordan's only other contact—his art dealer Angelica. She answered almost immediately with a cheery, salesperson voice.

"This is Jordan's wife," I said.

"Oh. It's nice to see you! What can I do for you?"

"He hasn't been home for a few days. Have you heard from him?"

The pause was pregnant—too long to think that she didn't already know his plans. But that meant nothing. Many people had been disappearing for years with no trace. It was no longer strange. It was the new norm. My search for him was the out-of-place oddity making her feel uncomfortable.

"Well. Um. I haven't spoken to him in a while. He said he had a big project and would call me. But he also, well..."

Yet another silence. The crowd of businessmen and swanky ladies circled me, threatening to trample me in their workday stampede. The only thing holding them back was a thin, invisible border. The only thing holding my tears back felt like an even weaker wall of glass. My hand reached to pinch my other hand.

"Yes?" I said.

"He asked me to sell everything." She stopped looking into the screen. Her eyes traveled from her lap to something behind the screen to her hands to something to her left. Anywhere but to me.

"Did you?" I said.

"It's almost all gone." She seemed to be looking at a list on her tablet. "I still have a few pieces in the storage unit. And the project he was working on. The one I wasn't allowed to sell."

"I need to see it."

"Um."

"Now Angelica."

"Ok. I can meet you after lunch, does that work?"

"Yes." I hung up. I could hear the solid hum of the empty line. I could hear the pounding of feet around me on the sidewalks. I could hear the murmur of voices around me.

I wanted to call my brother, but he was on a plane to some dangerous destination to retrieve some rich man's artifact.

I slumped down to the sidewalk. The smell of piss wafted up at me from the cinderblock corner. I closed my eyes and let my mind wander into that box that I had held apart. I opened it slowly, letting the feeling of it overtake me, letting my mind and body absorb the fact that my husband had probably gone through with his threat. Out of this box in my mind popped the idea that Jordan had promised he would make my life better.

And before I knew it, the sun was high in the sky and I was late to meet with Angelica.

The storage facility was a labyrinth. We were directed into a room and told to punch in a personal number into a pad on the wall. Then a specific elevator was sent to the specific room to pick us up. Since there was more than one person in the elevator, we had to tell the elevator so, otherwise it would not go to the destination. Then that elevator went to our vault and nowhere else.

Jordan's space was not one of these. But to get to his, we had to follow the procedures to get to the back of the building and into some old garages that housed old cars and were mostly full of junk.

Angelica took me to his garage and opened the door with an old-fashioned key.

"I told you, eight hundred thousand. Isn't that amazing? I don't know why he was holding these pieces from me. I could have used them earlier."

"I know why," I mumbled. The door swung open to reveal a room lit only by windows high in the wall. They dumped sunlight into certain places on the floor, like god-made spotlights. In the middle of the empty concrete floor stood an enormous gryphon, rearing up on its hind legs. It was made of all different colors of wood so that it looked like marble, but when I rubbed my hand along the taught flesh of its thigh, I felt the warmth of the wood. Jordan meant this for me. He knew I would love it. He knew my dreams, well, the ones before he left.

I consistently dreamed of flying on the back of a gryphon. Long, coarse hair gripped in my fingers; the wind whipping my hair around my head; the sensation of my stomach floating and plummeting with each change in elevation. We flew over a lake surrounded by mountains. The great wings of the gryphon pumped up and down, and he cried out in ecstasy just before diving down toward the water. I wore a white, flowy tunic and held a bunch of white roses in one hand, contrasting against the golden fur of the beast. The dream had been Jordan's inspiration for my tiny gryphon in a rose bush.

Jordan must have intended this one for me too.

My tears dripped onto the concrete floor. One fell on the paw of the giant beast and darkened the pine wood. Angelica continued to blabber while she walked around turning lights on and talking about the other statues she had found there.

"Angelica, please turn the lights off. It's more beautiful with just sunlight."

She continued chattering and retraced her steps.

The sun streamed in, dancing through the dust and separating around the gryphon like a curtain. He loved me. No matter what he had done, it was out of love. I knew it now. It didn't feel any better, but I knew it. Jordan had gone to the EMT Clinic, and he was lost to me. It had been done with good intentions, but intentions weren't good enough. My heart started to pound, and I felt my tears dry on my cheeks. Anger flared in my belly.

A flash of nausea jumped up my throat, and I turned away from the sculpture to vomit on the floor.

CHAPTER 6
aloisa

The wind penetrated my wool coat, but I didn't notice. My mind was focused on the little device inside my bag. I had just bought it at the store, and supposedly it would give me the answer to what was going on.

Miles was flying back in the next morning, still no sign of Jordan, and a worry in the pit of my stomach, eating holes through my insides, was absolutely relentless. I tripped up the stairs to the apartment because the lights were still not fixed.

I went into the bathroom and pulled out the metal box. I let it take my retina scan. It beeped. I pulled up my shirt, reclined back on the toilet, and lay the funny little scanner on my lower abdomen. I had to let it sit there for ten minutes and move as little as possible. About two minutes in my back started to protest and a sharp pain shot up through my left hip. I held steady, my teeth clenched, and thought of my fluffy, comfortable bed in the other room. But I held still and let the strange blue thing do its work.

Even before ten minutes were up it beeped and then a little voice squeaked out, "You are pregnant. I am 99.8% sure.

You are fifteen weeks into gestation. The child is male. He is currently excelling on all tests, but a doctor will confirm at twenty weeks if your pregnancy is still advised for completion. Please contact your obstetrician."

"No," I said.

The machine didn't answer.

I let the anger grow inside me until it bubbled over the top, and I threw the blue monster at the wall. It shattered and died. I curled in on myself and slipped to the floor. My back up against the cold porcelain and my face glued to the tiles with my tears, I let my mind shut off. My husband was missing, my life was in shambles, and I was going to bring a baby into the world.

I didn't sit like that for long because the thing inside me had me with my face in the toilet bowl within minutes. I stood up and rinsed my mouth. Crackers were what I needed, but I didn't have any and there were no vouchers left for anything. I went into the living room and sank into the couch. I thought back to my last period. It had probably been months ago, but the arguments with Jordan and the stress over the rest of life had overwhelmed my senses.

The lights went off. I sat in the dark until the sun came up. I probably dozed a few times, but it felt like the longest night of my life. I waited in the same position until Miles got home.

He came in the door expecting to be alone. I could hear him whistling and scattering his things behind him as he walked into the kitchen to search the fridge. He stopped dead as soon as he headed for the couch.

"Aloisa? What are you doing home?"

I couldn't stop the torrent of tears or the awful sobs coming from my throat.

"What is going on?" He rushed over to me.

"Jordan—" I sobbed some more and sucked in a breath.

"He's gone. I can't find him. He went to work three days ago, but they say he never clocked in. I have nowhere to look. The police won't do anything."

"Anything else? Jordan is gone. But what else?"

"I'm pregnant."

"Oh, Aloisa." His groan was so pitiful. He tried to pull me onto his lap. I resisted. "What?" He looked at me. "What's wrong?"

"You just sounded like it's my fault. Like it's a fault at all."

"How could you let that happen? You knew Jordan wanted the EMT."

"I went to visit Dr. Rooken. Jordan has spoken with him about the EMT. He is Jordan's superior at the hospital. He was pretty vague. Never answered when I asked if he had seen Jordan. Just mentioned some chemical fire at the hospital."

"Aloisa! What if he's in the hospital?"

"Wouldn't someone have contacted me?"

"People do disappear all the time..." Miles looked out the window. "Let's start with breakfast. Then we'll figure out what to do."

He went into the kitchen, and I heard the suck of the fridge as it opened and the banging of pots. I stood up, retied my hair in its perpetual bun, and pulled out my tablet to check the daily mail files.

Bill, bill, ad, large file with important seal, bill, personal letter. I touched an ad. It was a little postcard-sized screen that showed a two-minute vid on the environmental impact of certain industrial equipment, particularly the automated systems. I threw it to Miles's tablet. He watched it twice. While he did that, I scrolled back to the list of mail and clicked on the seal.

"Miles?"

"Yes?" He was focused on food now.

"This letter is from the EMT Clinic."
"What?" I heard the spatula clink to the stove top.

Dear Mrs. Aloisa Riodan,

We regret to inform you that your husband, Jordan Riodan, perished in a chemical fire on Monday June 20, 2067. He had just arrived at work when the fire broke out. He showed exemplary courage and helped right away. He ran into the building to save some of the patients who were confined within, coming out with a large amount of burns across his entire body but still walking and leading other wounded through to safety. He went into surgery to attempt to repair the damage and save his lungs, but he died on the table.

We would like to extend our sincerest condolences and tell you how proud we are of what Jordan Riodan did for others. He has been given a medal of good citizenship from the city of Denver.

We have enclosed the paperwork for signing his body into the cremation and disposal facility. We just need a signature, and you can scan it into our database.

We have also included the paperwork consisting of Jordan Riodan's life insurance policy with the hospital. You will receive $200,000 upon the cremation of his body. He had the highest level of insurance available to him pulled out in case of his death.

If you have any questions or would like to talk to somebody, please call the number provided. We are happy to help with anything.

Miles watched me read it. "This is so déjà vu. 'Your parents died in a car crash...'" he quoted from memory the letter about our parents dying on vacation. "What a load of crap."

I handed my tablet to Miles; the letter couldn't be sent to

other tablets. I slumped into one of the chairs and slammed my head onto the table. My mind went so many different directions, like a dandelion blown to the wind.

Miles flipped through the other mail and handed me the tablet back, open on the personal letter.

Dear Jordan Riodan,

Your uncle, brother of your father, has passed away. He left behind $900,000 and had no heir. The money will transfer to you as closest living relative. Please sign the enclosed paperwork and scan it back to the lawyer listed at the bottom of this letter.

I stopped reading.

"They don't care anymore. Too many people have had EMT. The letters about Mom and Dad were definitely more legit than this. I believed it, until you told me not to," Miles said.

"Jordan's not dead."

"Aloisa." He put his hand on my shoulder.

"I would feel it. I would know it. Something would break inside of me. He's not dead."

"You're rich. And no, he's not dead. But he's lost to you."

I signed with my fingerprint the two letters that required it and emailed them off through the system. The eggs on the stove were beginning to burn, but Miles continued staring at me. I set the tablet down and stood up to go to my bed.

CHAPTER 7
elias

Dr. Rooken requested that I watch Jordan's surgery. I hadn't seen EMT before, but he wanted me to take notes. He said it was time I witnessed how it worked.

I sat in the box above the doctor's. The room was like an amphitheater, with the surgery robots and Jordan on the first floor surrounded in an oval by control booths and witness stations. Above the first level there were three seating levels—the first to directly control the robots, the second for the doctors to virtually mimic the movements the machines would perform, and the third to witness and observe.

Jordan looked so small among the massive metal structures, which were nearly as tall as my observation deck. I looked across to the first level and saw men inside control booths, watching and tapping screens. Their faces glowed green in the light from their workstations. Above them sat some doctors undergoing training. They would watch Dr. Rooken and play with their own turned-off virtual control suits.

I felt sweat trickle down my brow and wondered if it was hot in the room. There was no other reason for my body to be reacting the way it was.

I couldn't see Dr. Rooken, he being directly below me, but I could see the Emodiant witnesses across from me on my level. They weren't even looking at Jordan, just enjoying a spread of delicacies and chatting. Their job was to witness the EMT. Each and every surgery.

The robots began to move; I crept forward in my seat. The doctors across the way swept their arms in great arcs, smoothing invisible curtains out of their way and dropping invisible instruments into invisible trays. They directed an eerie army of metal and grease. Below them, the machines were doing nearly the same thing, only a few minutes ahead. They must have been copying the doctor's movements. A dance between man and machine, melding the two as one without a shred of sensuality.

The robots hovered over the floor and gathered around Jordan. Like a gathering of ants ready to feast upon their meal. Their arms stretched and whirred in preparation. Then one took up an instrument from the tray, flipped Jordan onto his back, and plunged the sharp, hollow needle into his brain at the base of his head. Jordan's body didn't even flinch, he was so well drugged.

I did.

That machine stayed immobile while another moved around it to get another instrument from the tray—a very long pair of tweezers. With extreme precision, the second robot fed the tweezers through the large needle. It pulled out a short but visible string and placed this in a jar. The first robot pulled the needle out of Jordan's head. I looked across to the witnesses, who were still ignoring the process.

The first robot plucked a syringe from the tray and fed this slightly smaller needle in under and behind Jordan's ear. It pushed a large amount of blue liquid through to what I knew was Jordan's pituitary gland. It looked like a lot of liquid, too much in fact. But the robot pulled the syringe out and nothing leaked. The inhibitor would allow the organs and glands of his endocrine system to stay intact but lie dormant, not only the pituitary gland but also the pancreas and testes as well as the adrenal gland and thyroid gland among others. The constant administration of Hormone Stabilizing Serum would keep Jordan functioning while allowing him to live without emotion, emotionless.

A third robot turned Jordan onto his back and started kneading his skin with silicon fingers. All the way from his head down to his toes it plied his muscles and skin, helping his body relax after the strain, giving the inhibitor time to work. His lungs pumped harder to allow more oxygen. The nanobots that had been inserted into his body before surgery were doing their job to keep him asleep and alive. The control room on the first level controlled their processes and watch that the larger machines were in good condition, while Dr. Rooken conducted his symphony of gore.

I went to visit Jordan the next day. He wasn't awake yet; his body wouldn't wake for weeks. Not only would the machines keep him asleep for two weeks, but for another two after that most people stayed in a coma from the trauma. The doctors could wake them, but it was better to let their body decide.

I checked all of Jordan's vitals and input information into the computer. He looked like a normal man asleep in a bed. There were no wires or mechanical devices around him. The only thing different was the slightly blue hue to his skin because of the millions of nanobots swimming in his blood.

My hand reached out to touch him; I looked at it like it wasn't my own. Why did I want to touch him? I let it happen anyway. His skin felt like rubber. I could smell the oil that the machines always reeked of. My traitorous hands reached out and rolled Jordan over. I placed a finger on the spot where the spike had entered his brain. Then I touched the same spot on my own neck.

"Elias, are you all right?" Dr. Rooken said and startled me. I dropped Jordan and flipped around to face the doctor, my hands behind my back.

"You're not in trouble. I just want to make sure you're all right. That was your first surgery."

"Why wouldn't I be all right?" I asked. I looked him in the eye. But something in the back of my mind was niggling at me. I wasn't all right. And I didn't know why.

"I've never asked you," Dr. Rooken said, "but do you know why I had you transferred to work with me?"

"No."

"You were studying to be a genetic scientist before your change. Even after your change there were reports about you that you knew and understood more than could be accounted for. Now that I think about it, I'm not sure if I wanted you here because you were brilliant and would be an asset to me, or because you would make an interesting test subject."

"What do you mean by that?" My fingers tingled, and I wiggled them. Dr. Rooken looked down at my hands and smiled.

"Maybe one day you'll understand," he said, then he left the room.

With my shoulder against the door jamb, I studied Dr. Rooken's movements. He worked over Jordan like a man dressing a mannequin. Jordan was still under the influence of the nanobots; he lay peacefully on the bed. The doctor checked his vitals, twisted his joints, flexed his muscles, and proceeded to dress him. Jordan's body flopped around while Dr. Rooken grunted and groaned, ripping Jordan's pants off from under his dead weight.

"I can do that," I said and stepped into the room. Dr. Rooken smiled at me and left, with Jordan half-dressed, completely limp, one leg hanging over the edge of the bed and one arm bent at an odd angle. I lifted one hand and slid his arm through a sleeve. Circling the bed, I did the same on the other side. Then I cradled his head and pushed it through the neck hole. Slowly tugging on each side of his body, I pulled the plain, brown, cotton, long-sleeved shirt down. It was the same style I had hanging in my closet, only mine were usually gray or white.

Then I worked underwear up his legs and over his hips, and again with a pair of plain pants. I gently pulled socks over his feet, taking special care when he involuntarily jumped at a tickle to the bottom of his foot. He was fully dressed, my job was done, but I stayed where I was. His pale face had no wrinkles; it was completely slack. There was a bit of stubble coming through, but he would never grow as much hair as an unmodified human, especially as soon as he began his HSS treatments.

I picked up his chart to see where he was headed. First it would be a boot camp to keep an eye on him and make sure everything was working properly. There they would feed him and retrain his mind a little to understand what certain cues meant, like bleeding and sweating. Things that he would be confused by or that wouldn't trigger any reaction and might therefore cause health issues.

Scrolling my finger down the screen, I found where he was being placed. A logging camp in Oregon. So he would also be on muscle enhancers to compensate for the lack of testosterone, something to help him build enough muscle to do his work. Calisthenics were also in order. Dr. Rooken and I would vidcall him there after a month or so, to check on his progress. Then he would be gone from this area for good.

I replaced his chart and glanced at his chest. It rose and fell in a steady rhythm. In just a few hours, the nurse would deactivate the nanobots and a new Jordan would wake to this world.

The monitor above his head started blinking yellow rapidly. Then text rolled across the screen.

Emoxapraline low. Replace cartridge.

The drug that allowed Jordan's body to function without hormones. The same drug that came in much smaller doses in my HSS. The nurse came bustling into the room and started messing with the box of drug cartridges in the corner behind Jordan's bed. She took out a nearly empty one that showed a slight, bright green film on the inside. Slipping a new, full cartridge into the box she tapped some commands on the screen and it ceased flashing. I followed her out of the room.

I walked down the hallway to Dr. Rooken's office. I went to the desk that was still a mess, something I had been meaning to clean. I left the tablets scattered and pushed the worn, concealed, button.

"I do not think there is any thrill that can go through the human heart like that felt by the inventor as he sees some creation of the brain unfolding to success... Such emotions make a man forget food, sleep, friends, love, everything." Nikola Tesla

There are ways to make what you want to happen, happen. Well that sentence was terribly worded. If you want it badly enough, you can make it happen. There, that's better. But wanting something is not the only essential ingredient; you must know the truth. You must have felt something. But to feel some-thing means that it can hurt. In ways that are beyond human capacity, ways that our nerves could handle ten-fold but from which our minds simply collapse.

That is why. That is exactly why.

In order to not feel this pain anymore, I can eradicate it. I have the truth, I have the soul-searching experience, and I have the need. So I'll take all of my ingredients and mix them together to create a concoction that eliminates feeling. Then my unhappi-ness will no longer plague me. Then I can truly be content.

I raised a finger to my brow. There was a tightness there. Something I hadn't felt as long as I could remember. Dr. Wolff's journal was affecting me in ways I hadn't foreseen. It was time to either put it away for good or give it to Dr. Rooken. But as I placed it back in the secret drawer, I couldn't bring myself to slam the casing shut. I also couldn't bring myself to leave it sitting on top of the desk for Dr. Rooken to find later. I gently closed the hatch and told myself I would take care of it another day.

CHAPTER 8
elias

I was knee-deep in research when I heard a voice. It squeaked in my ear like an irritating bug. I kept going with what I was working on until the voice came again: "Is Dr. Rooken here?"

I looked up. Standing in the doorway was a woman. She had long, silky brown hair and beautiful sky blue eyes. She took my breath away. It felt like I had been punched, except that I had never been punched before (that I could remember). She kept staring at me while I attempted to get my breath back. Then her eyes fell to the counter, where my hands were.

"You're bleeding," she said.

I looked down. My bright-red blood trickled from my finger where the scalpel had slipped. I rushed over to the sink and started rinsing it. "I'm sorry, who were you looking for?" I asked.

"Dr. Rooken. May I sit?"

I nodded my head and looked back at my hand. Out of the corner of my eye I watched her settle in, filtering through the files on the tablescreen with her eyes.

"So where is Dr. Rooken?"

"He'll be here shortly. He had an appointment." I rubbed a towel over my hand, ripping the cut open again.

"You're being too rough. Let me help." She dropped off the stool and came over to me, taking my hand and applying pressure to the cut so it would seal. "You have to be gentle or it will open again." She wasn't looking at me but was talking to my hand. As if my hand would know what to do. I wanted her to look at me. I wanted it so badly it scared me.

Finally, she did. Our eyes met. There was something familiar about her. She smelled like lavender, lavender and vanilla. I wanted to touch her cheek, just brush my hand across it. I wanted to put her on my knee like a little child and rub my hand through her hair while I told her stories. My mind was in such a whirl. I flung her hands away and went back to my work.

"Stupid changelings," I heard her mumble.

Then Dr. Rooken walked in. I left the room.

I felt so out of sorts that I left the EMT Clinic and walked home to loosen my tense muscles. I needed the air and the movement, but I had absolutely no idea why. As I power-walked down the street, I saw a woman holding the hand of a little girl. I couldn't see the girl's face, only her brown hair as she bent down to look at an insect on the ground. My throat started to close, and I gasped for breath. I clenched at the concrete wall of the building next to me, my vision glazing and the little girl no longer visible. A man going past glared at me, his hand out to ward me off. I vaguely heard a voice ask if I was all right. And suddenly, I felt tired. So tired that I wanted to lay down where I stood.

Home was only a few more blocks, so I continued on. I saw the blues and grays of the walkways and the overcast sky, the blur of color when a person passed me. I found my building and went up the stairs—a never-ending tunnel of brown— and finally reached my own door. Inside, I collapsed on the couch and let my heavy eyelids do as they pleased.

But I couldn't sleep. Instead I stood and went back out the door, down the street, to a park where children played. The sun was bright and intense, forcing me to squint to see clearly. And clearly I did see—a lone girl, with brown hair. I felt that another presence was on the playground, a little boy, younger than the girl, running to and fro among the rocks and trees and piles of sand. But when I looked for this little boy, there was no one there. Only the girl. She was swinging back and forth, back and forth. I no longer felt tired. I no longer felt afraid. I sat down on a burm below a young tree dotted with flower buds and neon green leaves.

The girl, who hadn't been looking at me but had been watching the sky and singing a song, stopped her childish chatter and snapped her head up to show me her eyes. A stunning blue. Like mine and yet softer.

"Daddy?" she said.

I sat bolt upright, no longer reclining on the grass but tangled in blankets on my own couch. Sweat poured down my forehead into my eyes. I was completely drenched. My mind immediately registered that as unhealthy. I needed HSS. Sluggishly hauling myself upright, I made my way into the kitchen and wrenched open the fridge. In a slotted shelf on the door sat a row of syringes filled with neon green liquid. I tugged one out, snapped the locked top off, and plunged it into my shoulder muscle. The kitchen came into better focus. Outside my window the sky was again cloudy and raindrops began to splatter. My heart eased, and my lungs filled. I turned to the syringe lying on my counter, dripping the last bits of neon liquid. I set about cleaning it up with a sponge before making my usual dinner of protein and vegetable.

aloisa

Dr. Rooken took me into his office.

"Aloisa, what can I do for you?" Dr. Rooken motioned to a chair.

"I heard something about EMT babies. I want to volunteer."

"Excuse me?" Dr. Rooken set down the cup he was about to sip from.

"I would like to help with the EMT babies."

"That's a bit difficult. You are a norm."

"As are you." I started chewing on my nails.

"But I don't work directly with the EMT babies. The EMT nurses do that. The babies can't handle coddling; it actually seems to infuriate them." His eyes traveled to the window. His hand crawled along the desk surface to find a pen and begin absentmindedly clicking.

"I won't coddle them."

"Aloisa," he cleared his throat, "Why do you want to do this?"

"You know why."

"He's not here."

"I know that." It came out in a whisper. I couldn't get the words past the tears, and I wouldn't let the tears fall.

"All right." Dr. Rooken stood. "Let's get some paperwork in, and I'll figure out a position for you."

"I'll take anything." I leaned forward, eager to have a connection with my lost husband. Anything that would make me feel like he was still beside me, living this life with me. We went out into the hallway and into the restricted area.

We came into what Dr. Rooken called the womb. I didn't like the idea of going in, but I followed him. Inside felt, well, like a womb. The temperature was rather warm, the air was humid, and the noises that permeated my entire body with hums and vibrations sounded like a heartbeat, lungs breathing, blood swishing. Two walls, besides the glass door we had come through, were also made of glass, the other was solid white to hide the womb from view of the hallway. We had walked into what looked like a giant fish tank. On the far wall were a few monitors with lines constantly traveling across them.

I looked at the two men in front of me. Sitting at glass desks, they were watching the monitors. Anytime a line on their screens spiked they would type on the glass keyboards to correct the problem. They turned to face us when Dr. Rooken called their names. It wasn't until then that I noticed they were robots.

"Hello Dr. Rooken. What can I do for you today?"

"Aloisa, this is Dee and Dum. He's not dumb, that's just what Dr. Xanther named them. They work as one so they refer to themselves as one being. You'll get used to it.

"Dee and Dum, I need paperwork for Aloisa to fill out to help us out here in the lab. Can you get that for me?"

"Of course," they said in unison and swiveled to face the screens again.

I walked up to the glass before me. Inside was a blue liquid with bubbles floating around. At least they looked like bubbles until I got closer. They were embryos. Set loose in the liquid to settle where they would grow. Some floated, others sank to the bottom. One came particularly close, and I could almost see the child inside the pink film. I lay my hand against the wall, waiting for the tink of glass hitting glass, but when the bubble landed it molded to the side and then stuck there. Inside was a baby. A tiny human. One that was probably the age of my baby. I laid my other hand on my belly.

"Please don't touch the glass."

Startled, I pulled away. Dum had spoken.

"The heat from your hand may be different than what I am trying to regulate. Thank you." He went back to his monitoring.

"Isn't it amazing?" Dr. Rooken asked. "We can grow up to one hundred children in here. They can range from brand new to the full gestation of eleven months."

"Eleven?" I asked.

"Yes. If a woman's body could handle it, it would be better for the baby to stay inside until eleven months."

"You don't think there's a reason we have children at nine months?" I asked.

"Studies have shown—"

"Dr. Rooken. I don't care about studies. If my baby wants out at nine months, I'm going to let him out."

Dr. Rooken's eyes widened and then traveled to my abdomen. He smiled. "Yes, I suppose you're right."

I turned back to the liquid. The baby that had attached to the wall was floating away.

"Here is the paperwork." Dee handed a tablet to Dr. Rooken.

I took the tablet from him and started answering questions. Dr. Rooken went to the main monitors in the room and did something with the computer. Once I had finished, I handed the tablet to Dee. I could have sworn the robot smiled at me. He looked human enough; it was his eyes—optical lenses— that gave it away.

"Let me show you the newborn room. We also have our first generation room but that isn't observable. That's where our older children are; the first batch we managed to grow," Dr. Rooken said.

In the hallway outside was a window like any other hospital nursery window. Nurses tended to hundreds of bassinets, lined up in grids and extending deep into the room. The monitors on the wall showed the temperature being maintained perfectly and the scent of lavender pumped through the vents because it was nap time.

"The babies grow faster than normal, so we work hard to keep them calm," Dr. Rooken said, motioning toward the monitors. "We feed them a hormone supplement to encourage growth. Other than that they subsist entirely without hormones."

The babies closest to the window rolled around in their bassinets. It was uncanny to watch a newborn looking at its hand with so much intensity, or to see another newborn roll from front to back, something an unmodified human couldn't do until at least four months of age.

A few seemed to be crying, but without tears. Teardrops contained hormones, and these babies didn't have those at all. I shivered.

"Can you come in on Mondays?" Dr. Rooken interrupted my stunned study of these alien children.

"That will work," I said, my eyes still locked on one particular baby who seemed to be looking back at me.

"We'll see you then." He walked away, leaving me to watch and ponder or maybe just escaping any questions I might have had.

CHAPTER 9
elias

The next morning I went directly to Dr. Rooken's office and the desk. My fingers found the well-worn button, caressing its concave smoothness. I hesitated a moment, and then pressed it. Out popped the little drawer and the diary that sat within. It was like a drug, calling me back for more. I still hadn't told Dr. Rooken, so I looked furtively over my shoulder to be sure I was alone, and grabbed the diary.

"There are moments in life, when the heart is so full of emotion / that if by chance it be shaken, or into its depths like a pebble / Drops some careless word, it overflows, and its secret, / Spilt on the ground like water, can never be gathered together." Henry Wadsworth Longfellow

There is nothing so special as a child in this world. The moment you hold that precious thing in your arms for the first time is the most beautiful and the most terrifying, the most intense and the worst. It's something that all of us find we want, at some point. But is it something that all of us need? There is an inherent biological requirement to procreate. Especially when we are witness to death. How many times have people turned to sex after a traumatic event? The children created out of this chaos cannot be expected to live a life that isn't tainted by their beginnings. Of course there are some children borne of planning and practice and consideration. But a lot of children are brought into this world because of rash decisions and passion. We could cut down on the overpopulation simply by eliminating these instances. And with EMT, I can do that. I can make people not care about sex. They will not have traumatic experiences, so they will not turn the other direction and cry out for love and affection to make them feel more alive. It's something that we can prevent, this birthing of people we don't really want.

It was like his every word sank deep into my soul and pierced it. I had never felt like this before. That moment the woman had walked into my lab, she had startled me. I was not used to being startled, but this woman had an effect on me. I would need to ask Dr. Rooken about it.

I put the diary away and went to the break room to shoot a dose of HSS; something to calm my nerves and return my system to normal. As I pulled the syringe from the fridge, the bright green liquid illuminated my hand and showed me the angry red cut. It reminded me of the woman, touching my hands, caressing them under the water. She was so kind and gentle. Yet she hadn't enjoyed touching me.

All of these thoughts forced me to jab the needle in too hard. The green liquid slid into my muscle like sludge.

The syringe jumped from my hand, crashing to the floor and shattering, splattering the tile in a sickly neon. My hands shook.

I sat down on the couch and closed my eyes. I waited for the HSS to take effect. I was instantly calm as soon as I sat down, there was no wait period since I had no adrenaline coursing through my system. I just needed to have patience, so I waited. And waited. And waited.

Walking into the womb after my HSS took effect, I found Dr. Rooken speaking with his boss. Their low tones seemed to be constant and monotonous, but the looks on their faces showed frustration and even anger. I worried they were talking about me, but as soon as they saw me they both smiled and then shook hands. Dr. Xanther left the room with a nod.

"How are you Elias?" Dr. Rooken asked.

"I'm good. Is everything all right? Things didn't seem normal."

"Things are never normal with Dr. Xanther." Dr. Rooken turned to the desk next to Dee and Dum and sifted through some paperwork. "Let me ask you something, what do you think of the new volunteer?"

My throat constricted. Reaching up with a hand to smooth out the skin, and hopefully understand why my body had done such a thing, I swallowed.

"Why do you ask?" I asked.

"Just wondering." He peered up at me, his hands still on the files on the table.

"I'm...well, I'm not entirely sure. There's something strange." I looked around for a chair and decided to instead fall onto the edge of the table behind me.

Dr. Rooken came over to me and looked directly into my eyes. My breathing was shallow. There was nothing I wanted more than another shot of HSS. My body craved it, called for it, desired it. I hadn't felt—well I hadn't felt anything at all—but I hadn't felt a feeling like this in years. I didn't even remember feeling. And this had me frightened, which just made more feelings come through. Bombarding me with adrenaline and emotion and fear and so much more.

"Elias?"

"I'm fine. I just need a little more serum."

"Did you miss a dose?"

"I had some a few minutes ago because I felt strange. Things are strange. Everything so strange."

At that point Dr. Rooken took me by the shoulder and steered me out into the hall and around the corner to the break room again. He pushed me onto the couch and pulled more HSS from the fridge. He held the needle out to me and then bustled around the room, shifting things from place to place and mumbling.

"I should report her. They need to know what she's trying to do. She could be dangerous if she uses her connections here to find her husband. It's just not safe. I'll let her keep working, not let her on to the fact that I've told anyone. I need to keep her here, in sight, but this just isn't right." He paused and looked back at me.

Then he left the room.

He left me.

I leaned back, letting my head fall and smack the wall. The shakes dissipated. The feelings ebbed away like mist on a hot morning.

CHAPTER 10
aloisa

I sat in the warmed chair. The fact that the gel and silicon molded instantly to my body and wasn't cold on my bare backside didn't help me relax one bit.

The doctor came in and set her tablet down.

"Hello, Aloisa."

"Do we see the baby today?" I asked. My legs shook with the need to get up and move.

"I'm sorry about your husband," she said.

The sweat trickling between my breasts sent a shiver through me. It wasn't so much the frigidity of her voice, more the bland disregard and lack of true empathy.

"Is there anything I can do?" she asked.

"Yes." I looked directly in her eyes. "Tell me how the baby is."

She coughed on her own spit and went to work.

Next to my chair was a wall of medical equipment: a hologram projector, a probe, a screen cataloguing my vitals from the medical chair, a few ominous objects hung from hooks and I glossed over them. The gel chair beneath me formed into a bed. The projector flickered on, drawing my eyes when the hologram popped out from the wall and displayed above my stomach. I stretched out my hand, letting my fingers dance through the pixels.

"That's your baby," the doctor said. A fully-formed human, curled tightly in a ball, eyelids twitching in sleep and fingers grasping each other. I wanted to feel his velvety skin, tickle his tiny feet, see his eyes gazing back into mine.

I looked at the doctor, my fingers still trailing through the digital representation of my child.

The doctor's cold, calculated face caused another jolt to my system. The hologram child rolled and kicked out. I felt it, the movement of a fish in a bowl. Then I knew. He was mine, and I would keep him. This tiny, problematic creature.

"Miles, I refuse to let them keep him from me. Dr. Rooken won't look at me straight. It's all wrong."

"I know. But there's nothing you can do about it." He wrapped his whole hand around my upper arm.

"I will do everything I can." I ripped away from his grip and kept going down the stairs.

We split outside the apartment without another word.

The whole day I trekked from office to office. Asked nurses at the hospital questions. Tried to get in to talk to Emodiant—their large marble lobby intimidated me, but their changeling receptionist didn't. When I got heated and tried to slap her, she sat passively. I stopped my hand just as it grazed her skin; her head held steady and true.

I stormed out of their building, running down the sidewalk weaving in between businessmen and wealthy women. My bag hit one woman, knocking her shopping bags to the ground.

"Oh I'm so sorry," I said and stopped to help her only to

find that it was Thelia. I hadn't bothered to show up to work after receiving my blood money. After the few days of hunting for Jordan and then losing all track of time in my spiral of depression, I figured she would fire me anyways. I missed the soil and green, but I didn't miss the changelings.

"Aloisa. What are you doing on this end of town?" She said it with such disdain that I turned to walk away. I owed her nothing.

"I heard about your husband," she said. I stopped, staring at the skyscrapers towering above me. Why did everyone know? Why did everyone *have* to know? Disappearances were commonplace. This was nothing new. Our world had become a revolving carousel where people hopped on and off at random.

"How?" I asked.

"Miles."

I swiveled to face her. "Miles?"

"Yes. He did some treasure hunting for a friend of mine. I'm very sorry." She bent to pick up her bags. "Would you like to get some coffee? There's a great place around the corner."

We sat down with coffee and her shopping bags littering the floor. I still didn't know why I had agreed. I tapped my cup with my fingers, inhaling the aroma of coffee and cinnamon.

We sat in a bubble of silence. The coffee shop around us hummed and buzzed. Suddenly, Thelia tilted forward, crowding my personal space.

"I can help."

"Excuse me?"

"I can help you find him." She had whispered it. As if someone would hear her and arrest her. "I've done it before."

"Done what?" I sipped my java.

"Found an EMT of course."

"Don't tease me. I don't need that from someone like you."
My mouth said it, but my body leaned eagerly in.

"I'm not stupid, Aloisa. And I'm not teasing you. I have sources."

"That do what?"

"Find things, people. Like your brother, only more secretive. It's not against the law, but it's certainly not smiled upon." She sat back. I watched her cup as she pulled it to her ruby-red lips and drank. "But if you don't need 'someone like me,' I'll just be going."

She stood, gathered her things, and was nearly out the door before I woke up and called, "Stop!"

We set up an actual meeting in the privacy of her home, and I made my way onto the dusky streets. The smells of humans and smog overpowered the area. My head was down so I didn't see the sun reflecting in the sky scrapers. I also didn't see the man behind me until I turned the corner.

At the coffee shop, he had ordered a latte right behind us in line. I remembered his beaky nose and hairy hands as he had scanned his tablet. Now those hands casually swung by his sides, and he looked abruptly away from me when I spotted him. But his gaze didn't settle on anything in particular, and his gait didn't slow. He just kept coming; turn after turn, weaving through the people on the clean and sparkled sidewalks. I stepped into a store to lose him in an aisle of electronics, but he didn't follow me in. After wandering the aisles and hoping he had lost interest, I went back outside and nearly bowled him over on the edge of the doorway.

"Excuse me," I huffed.

"Sorry," he mumbled, tipping an imaginary hat and ducking out of my way. His sleeves were rolled up, showing the hair on his hands that crawled up his arms.

"Can I help you?" I asked.

"Waiting for a friend."

"Right. Ok. Stop following me." I turned and hopped on the next bus that pulled up to the curb. But instead of climbing the stairs to find a seat I simply stood in the door until the bus driver shut it, ensuring my tail couldn't get on behind me. I peered over my shoulder as the vehicle pulled away and watched him watching me through the windows. He grinned and kept staring at me as he vanished from my sight.

CHAPTER II
aloisa

I called Miles and had him meet me at Thelia's house. She was already making calls to contact people when the doorbell rang. I let Miles in and went back to making myself a cup of tea. It needed milk.

I went to the fridge, but before I grabbed the milk I spotted syringes filled with the changeling juice. It glowed neon green in the fridge and made everything around it look radiated. I touched it, pulling my hand away when I felt how cold it was. I snatched the milk and shut the door.

"Anything?" I asked Thelia.

"I'm still calling people. Miles, how are you?"

"I'm confused. What's going on?"

"Thelia found me outside Emodiant. She said she could help me," I said.

"Aloisa, this isn't what you want," he said through his teeth.

"It's not?" I wasn't sure if I was confused and innocent or if my face was hard as a rock. This was what I wanted. I wanted my husband back no matter what. I would do whatever I could to find him. He had left me, but I wouldn't let him stay away.

"No. Can we go in the other room?" He glanced at Thelia, who turned back to her tablet.

"No. I want to find Jordan."

"He doesn't want to be found. He left. He left *you*."

I sank down onto my stool, sipped at my tea. "Miles. Oh Miles."

"What?" The question had such bite it pierced my skin.

"He thought it would create a better life—"

"And you explained to him over and over again that it didn't work with our parents and wouldn't work with him. You told him you wanted him to stay, but he left anyways. You said you would work three jobs for the rest of your life if you could have him. But he didn't listen. He didn't love you enough to stay. He went the easy way. Now he's somebody's butler or a car mechanic in New Hampshire. Aloisa, you have a baby to take care of—" He choked on his spit.

The monotone of Thelia's mumbling in the background halted. Now I wished we had gone in the other room. I hadn't known he was going to tell her my life story.

"Miles. I think it's time we left. Thelia, thank you. I'll call you." I pulled my baby brother from the room and out the door.

"How could you!" I said, once we were out of earshot.

"What?"

"She used to employ me. Do you think she wanted to know everything, every single detail about my life? No. She didn't. And now I've lost my chance to find Jordan. Thank you." I stalked down the sidewalk.

"She'll need to know every detail in order to find Jordan. That's how the rebels do these things," he said.

"Rebels?" I said without turning around.

The door behind me opened.

"Aloisa?" Thelia said. "Please come back in. You're pregnant?"

"Thank you Thelia, but I'll figure it out on my own. Miles, you're not forgiven, yet." I kept walking, but Miles stopped me. He pulled me to the side of the path while Thelia looked at the sky, giving us what privacy she could.

"The rebels are dangerous. But they might be your only chance. I have people, but they have no allegiance. They work for money," he said. "I shouldn't have said all that about the baby, but obviously she doesn't care. Or maybe she cares more because of it. I don't want to find him, and I don't think you should. If you're going to do it then this might be the way." He had conceded. It had been too easy. I searched his eyes for why.

"This worries me. Why do you suddenly trust it?"

He shrugged. "I don't. I know my big sister and how stubborn she can be." I shoved him, and he grinned.

"I don't know if I can now. I don't need her looking at me with those pitiful eyes." I tucked flyaway hair behind my ear.

"Then don't look at her."

I laughed.

Back in the house Thelia continued making calls. She would turn every once in a while to smile at me or to make sure I had enough tea and cookies.

"I've called everyone I know." Thelia plopped down onto a chair. "We'll hear from somebody soon. I hope."

"How does this work?"

"They look for signs of new EMT patients first. Then they narrow it down with information from you. Typically, things that he did before he had his hormones removed, he will continue to do, because they are very close to his heart. I know that sounds weird, but it's a trend among EMT patients who were very passionate about something."

"Who is this 'they'?" I asked, glancing at Miles.

"I will be completely honest with you throughout this, Aloisa," Thelia said. "I have no reason not to be."

"Why not?" I interjected.

"You're a charity case," Miles said. Thelia's head whipped in his direction, but she didn't contradict him. "The only thing she cares about is feeling like she's made a difference in this world. Am I right?" he asked her.

"I suppose so." She looked up at me. "The rebels are who I work with. They want to eradicate EMT. They think Emodiant has dangerous ideas to take over the world, and I believe them. Which is why you're more than a charity case to me. You're a step in the right direction."

"Ok." A tear plopped into my tea, making ripples. Thelia reached for the mug but didn't pull it away. She stayed still, stayed silent. She let the moment take us over and a calm settled over the room.

CHAPTER 12
aloisa

"Aloisa?" Miles called as he walked in the door. "Aloisa!"

"Yes? What's wrong?" I spoke in a sarcastic tone. "How can I possibly help you with your issues, dear brother?"

Miles found me in the living room, sorting through paperwork. It just kept coming in: people looking to be my accountant, people looking to "use" my money in ways that made absolutely no sense. It was a nightmare. I just wanted to have Jordan back and be working three jobs again.

He stood in the doorway, his arms crossed, his eyes lasers into my soul. Once I finally stopped sorting, he spoke.

"I have some news."

"Is it about Jordan?" I stood up. The tablet flew from my lap and crashed to the floor.

"No." Miles's face scrunched up like he'd bitten a rotten apple.

I sat back down.

"I have a job," he said.

"What does that mean?"

"Someone looking for family paperwork in South America. I have a few weeks to prepare."

"But that's in the radiation zone. Not to mention all the rogue militias that could randomly attack you. They say there are men living down there who can crush your skull with two fingers." I slapped my hands over my mouth.

"It's not that bad. Plus it'll just be me and one other guy. No reason to cause a ruckus. We'll be in and out in no time. No need to worry."

"Worry? Oh, I'm not worried." I stood again and started pacing.

"Seriously, sis. It's ok." He stretched a hand out to me. I batted it away and kept walking in circles, breathing through my nose and telling myself this was bad for the baby. My belly had long ago popped and things were obvious now.

"Everything will be all right. I need to go get some supplies, and we can stock you up too. And the baby isn't due for a while yet, so there's no worry there."

"I'm not worried about me!" I screamed, whipping around to face him. "How can you think I'm worried about me!"

"Calm down. I'll be fine, just leave it alone," he said.

He snatched my coat from the rack and placed it firmly over my shoulders.

Then he walked out the door.

We went from supply store to supply store—clothes, climbing gear, radiation protection. Then we headed to a street market, one I hadn't heard of before. Men in trench coats manned empty tables, women with knotted hair and rotting teeth haggled with customers who wore baseball caps and had their collars flipped up. The street was narrow, more like an alley. I put my hand on my belly protectively.

"What is this?" I whispered to Miles.

"Black market."

"What, as in an actual place?" I said it a little too loud. The man to my right jerked around and opened his one eye wide. Miles grinned. He walked me down the shadowy, dingy alley until we reached a fat man. This man looked like he belonged in an ice cream truck, making kids smile. His rosy cheeks and pot belly were jolly, not sinister. Miles grabbed my elbow and kept me close to his side while he chatted with the man. I heard snippets of the conversation: "guns" and "knives" and "transport." My mind couldn't focus, and what little did creep in, I wanted to keep out. This was not making me feel as if my baby brother would be safe. I started to hyperventilate.

Miles started rubbing my back; his attention was still focused on Santa. When he was finished, he turned to face me and we pulled even farther back into a dank corner.

"I wanted you to know. I needed you to understand that I was protecting myself. There will not be a problem, but when there is, I'll be ready."

"Great," I said between heaving breaths. "I need to sit down."

Miles rushed us out of there, to a bright park on the other end of the alley. Children were running around the trees, chasing flying balls and yelling. I didn't even make it to a bench, just the grass, before I plopped down.

"Breathe," Miles said.

"Oh that's helpful. Thank you." He continued rubbing my back while I settled my heart, lungs, and mind. I didn't want him to go, but I knew there was no way to stop him.

Miles went to find me something to drink. In the exact moment I finally felt calm, a child ran up with a pile of paper and shoved one into my hand.

It read:

Our world is crumbling

Our leaders are corrupted

And it all comes down to one thing

Help us

Eradicate changelings

Bring about justice

Save the world

There was a tiny burning man in the corner that when scanned was probably the invite to some rebel rally. I tossed the paper into the wind and watched it dance and float away into the bright sunlit sky.

elias

We vidcalled Rane at work. Dr. Rooken spoke with him. He didn't want Saeri to interfere.

"Hello Rane. This is Dr. Rooken. I was wondering if you could come in after work today?"

"I'll just call Saeri," he said.

"That won't be necessary, it's really quick and we wouldn't want to bother her. You can just drop by on your way home."

"I suppose, but I should call Saeri."

"If you feel the need to report to her, have at it." Dr. Rooken looked at his nails then flicked his eyes back up to Rane. Rane looked at his desk. "We'll see you later then."

"Goodbye," Rane said.

"Why did you do that?" I asked.

"We don't want Saeri. I couldn't think of any other way to get him to come alone."

"But I thought this was about the children and the fact that they aren't being treated properly for their medical status?"

"I'm hoping I can get him here alone so I can pinpoint what made him marry and have a child."

"Do you have a theory?"

"I love how analytically you think. Most people would have been angry at me for that."

"I physically can't get angry, Doctor. Do you have a theory?"

Dr. Rooken laughed. "Yes. I think something triggered his memory."

"Is there a reason?"

"The murderer. He was sentenced to prison but had to be kept in isolation because normal humans would certainly harm him. He started talking to himself. They recorded it all and found that before he murdered the woman he had been traveling in the state where he grew up. He had a few encounters in his home town with people, in particular an old girlfriend. We looked up the girlfriend and found she looked very similar to the woman he murdered."

"What about the drugs?"

"That was a dead end. We found the guy. He was giving sugar pills. He just wanted to make money."

"No ulterior motive to putting EMT patients on placebos?"

"Elias, the word gullible is written on the ceiling." Dr. Rooken looked me straight in the eye while he said it. I looked up.

"No, it's not."

"My point exactly. An EMT patient will do what anyone tells them. Makes me wonder if it's a good thing that our world leadership have had the procedure."

"I still don't understand."

"Never mind. The money was the only reason he was giving the pills."

"So now you think it might be a memory trigger? Along with the HSS withdrawal?" I breathed a sigh of relief, rubbing the bruise on my arm from the badly aimed jab.

"Yes."

"Anything I should do to prepare for Rane?"

"No, I'll give the interview this time."

Rane came into the lab, clutching his briefcase with both hands. He settled on the very edge of a chair, his eyes darting around. I left him there and went back to the observation room. Dr. Rooken sauntered in and slouched into a chair opposite Rane.

"How are you today?" I heard his voice come through the speakers with a tinny echo.

"Fine."

"Did you have a good day at work?"

"I always do," Rane said.

"Would you like something to drink?"

"No thank you. Why am I here?"

"I wanted to hear more about you and Saeri."

"Then I should have called Saeri."

"No. I want to hear it from you. Have you known each other long?"

"Since high school."

"Really? When did you have your surgery?"

"Seven years, two months, and five days ago."

"Did you date before then?"

"No. We never dated. We met after my surgery at a coffee shop. I remembered her from high school."

"Remembered her? Did you like her in high school?"

"I don't think so."

"What are you doing! How dare you!"

I looked up at the screen. I had started to catalogue more embryos on my tablet. Saeri had burst into the room and was yelling at Dr. Rooken. She had her baby in a sling and looked ready to slap both men.

"Rane, we're leaving," she said.

"Yes, Saeri."

"Saeri, please. I need to speak with you about the baby. Please." Dr. Rooken stood and straightened his tie.

"What about my baby? I can't believe you did this behind my back. Rane, this is not over."

"I think your baby may have been naturally born without hormones. I can't get medical records; they don't seem to exist," Dr. Rooken said.

"That's because we don't use a doctor. She sees a naturopath. But why should I believe you?"

"She doesn't cry. She hit her head on the table when you were last here, and she didn't cry."

"She cries. She's perfectly normal." Saeri wrapped her arms around her baby, protecting the sleeping infant. "Wait. I'm not talking to you anymore. We're leaving."

She snatched for Rane's hand, missing a few times in her frustration, and then whisked him out of the room. I turned the cameras off and waited for Dr. Rooken. But he didn't come in. I went to his office looking for him and stumbled upon something much more interesting. Saeri and Rane stood in the hallway, whispering fiercely. I pulled back around the corner. The things they said didn't match their demeanor. I expected scolding; this was conspiring.

"Grab a tablet. That's all we have to do," Rane said.

"No. If I don't get into the computer system while we're here, the tablet will do us no good."

I decided to interrupt, see if I could be of assistance.

"Can I help?" I asked, striding around the corner.

Saeri squeaked.

Rane gripped the tablet in his hands until his knuckles turned white.

"We got a little lost," Saeri said. She snatched the tablet and put it in her baby bag. "That's just my personal tablet, but there's no signal in here. Can you point us the way out?" She took Rane's hand and walked past me without even waiting for directions. Rane glanced back, and I saw the tiniest smirk on his face before he was tugged out of sight.

The tablet Saeri had been holding certainly looked like a hospital-issued device, but I was disinclined to think her a liar so I continued on my way.

I found Dr. Rooken on the couch in his office. His arms were hanging between his legs, and his jaw was slack. It looked like he had just had a stroke.

"Doctor? Are you all right?" All thoughts of Saeri and Rane in the hallway disappeared.

"I'm fine Elias." He sat back and covered his face with his hands. "I'm just a little shocked."

"You found the answer to your theory," I said.

"What?"

"He had a memory trigger to make him do the emotional things he did. He knew her in high school. Perhaps she had a crush on him in high school and used his EMT to her advantage. Without better treatment he will continue to find new emotions." I suddenly realized the reason for Rane's smirk. He was losing control.

"We'll never know now. There's no way to prove that theory without testing. And that baby will never grow up. She won't even develop her brain further. Though this is a new option to move forward with."

"They'll go to a doctor when they see she's not developing further than six months. We need to speak with the other men. We need to prove your theory. I saw something—"

"One track mind, Elias. I'm going home."

"But—"

"No. I'm exhausted, and I'm going home to be with my family. I'll see you tomorrow."

CHAPTER 13
elias

Having forgotten my lunch on the kitchen counter that morning, I made my way to the hospital cafeteria. I selected a sandwich labeled "protein" and a water and sat at a table alone. As I munched on the stale bread and crumbling mystery meat, the voices of the EMT ladies at the table adjacent to mine traveled across the air to my ears. I could hear every word. And they continued to raise their voices until most of the room had turned to watch. There was no anger, no elevation to their voices. Simply volume. As if someone had turned a tiny knob on their voice boxes up to eleven.

"I said that I don't want to know anything about it."

"But you don't understand. They can help."

"I don't need help. Things are as they should be."

"You sent word."

"No I didn't. You must be thinking of someone else. I've never seen you in my life, and I never contacted anyone."

"It's right here. Your signature on this tablet. Right here." She pointed to a file open on her tablet. The first woman, the one with a hospital uniform, jumped back. Her chair crashed to the floor, getting the attention of anyone who hadn't already been listening.

"That is not mine." She walked away. Quickly.

The second woman finally noticed the audience she had and started gathering her things. But before she left she paused at my table and held my gaze for a few seconds too long. I swallowed my soggy mouthful of sandwich.

"Can I—"

She slapped a card on my table and walked away before I finished.

I glanced down at the card to see the same address of the abandoned building that the man in the alley had given me. I shivered.

The room had turned its view to me. No one followed the woman as she left. Their eyes burned into me from all sides. I felt my skin begin to heat. I gulped and realized I needed, absolutely needed, more HSS. I jumped to my feet and practically ran.

The hallways back to our department seemed a maze of white and gray and bright lights. I shoved past people in my way, causing more disturbance than was necessary. My heart started to speed up to match the cardio I was forcing on my body. But it was more than that. It was also a mixture of emotion that I felt spilling through my bloodstream like liquid across a table top. After four wrong turns and hitting my knee on a short medicine tray, causing it to hit the floor with a loud bang, I found my way to the break room. I dashed to the fridge and snatched an HSS syringe.

It didn't help.

My heart still raced.

My face burned.

I threw the bottle in the sink.

Then I went to Dr. Rooken's office. I shoved my finger into the hidden button. I yanked the journal out. I paced back and forth as I flipped pages. I searched for something to calm myself. I hoped for words of wisdom. I wanted a way out.

A word. A single word lit up on the page and dragged me in.

Escape.

There is nothing quite like a good escape. A place one can go to rid themselves of excess baggage, people, thoughts, worries. A place to be alone and get away from it all. To be able to hear oneself think again. To breathe.

My escape, my oasis, is this cabin. Oh how I love it. I loved it when my family came with me; I love it now when I'm here alone.

These Montana mountains surrounding this flower-filled valley with the mountain stream running just beyond the porch where I sit in a rocking chair and sip coffee, this is where I like to be. Hidden back at the end of a tiny road called Serenity I truly find myself. Here is the one place on Earth I can rid myself of emotion without having to use the process I devised. And here is the one place I don't feel the need to perform EMT on every single human I come into contact with. I am serene. At home. Comfortable. One might even say that I'm content.

But the world can't be held at bay forever. I must go back, and I must continue my work. If I don't I think I'll be shut away in an asylum for the criminally insane. Because I will murder. I will kill for the pleasure of it. People are incredibly hurtful, and I am going to eradicate that.

For now, though, I will sit here and sip my coffee and allow my thoughts to wander as I so rarely do when I am in the city among my species.

aloisa

A woman with a red handbag, a man in a suit, a young girl with tattoos, and what looked like a homeless man all piled into Thelia's kitchen. She refused to let them farther than that. We stood, or sat on the stools, around the island. Miles came with me as moral support, but he stood in the doorway to the living room and didn't participate.

"Just stay quiet please," Thelia said to me.

"But—"

"No. You don't talk. They shouldn't even see you."

"Who are these people?"

"Shush, we'll talk later."

"Thelia, why are we here?" the woman with coiffed hair and pink nails asked.

"We need to find something. Someone."

"Why would you need to do that?" the girl with purple hair asked. She grabbed for a cookie and nibbled on it.

"Don't play with me," Thelia said.

"Why can't we have some fun?" the homeless guy mumbled from somewhere under his beard.

"You've got to be kidding," I said. "Thelia, what is this?"

"Is this the lady we would be finding for?" the man in the suit said.

"No."

"Against the rules, Thelia. Stop bringing the clients to us. Or I suppose, bringing us to the clients," handbag lady said. She was studying her nails instead of looking at Thelia. In fact, none of the people were looking at Thelia or anyone else.

"I thought you wanted to change the world," Miles said.

All four of them turned their heads in unison to face Miles. I clutched my hands in my lap under the table, terrified they would jump him.

"We'll do it," the suit said.

"Good. Because I'm tired of playing games," Thelia said. "What do you all need to know?"

"Do you have the list?" tattoos asked and popped the last

piece of cookie into her mouth. When she raised her arm to eat the snack, her sleeve lifted from her wrist, and I glimpsed a man wreathed in flames tattooed there.

Thelia slipped my packet of paper across the table to the gentleman. He picked it up and felt the heft in his hand. Reams of paper had been difficult to find in our digital world, but the rebels required it.

"A tad much, isn't it?" he asked. "Anything else we need to know?"

"There's plenty more," I said. The homeless man's eyes pierced mine for the briefest of moments.

Thelia opened the door, and they marched out. Miles and I followed without another word.

I went directly to the EMT Clinic afterward to start my shift, hoping for distraction. The babies creeped me out so much. I strolled into the nursery, snapping my bubblegum, arms swinging. I started humming the instant the door sealed shut because the eerie silence of a hundred babies lying awake and watching from their cribs set my nerves on edge.

Counting down the rows, I found EMT 14, or Fred as I secretly called him, and wheeled his crib to the feeding room. When I had first started volunteering I had tried to coddle and swoon each child when I fed and changed them or gave them shots. Against Dr. Rooken's advice, of course. Now I tried to avoid Fred's eyes as I ordered a bottle from the machines and took his temperature. He stared at me. His eyes followed my every movement. He made no noise. He reached for nothing.

I sat in the chair and handed him the bottle. He was old enough to feed himself, and I didn't want him in my lap.

When he was done, he dutifully burped and lay back in his crib with a sigh. He smiled. Instantly the computer pushed a smaller bottle of purple liquid into my hand—the growth hormones.

I gave him the second bottle. This one he tried to refuse and started to whimper. I placed my hand under his back as support, leaning over his crib and finally looking directly into his eyes.

"It's ok. Just drink this one and we'll be done. I promise," I said.

As he opened his mouth to protest, I shoved the nipple in and a bit of the liquid dripped out onto his tongue. He stopped everything, his legs going rigid and his face blank. Then he sucked hungrily at the bottle, as if I hadn't just fed him. I watched as his eyes unfocused and dulled.

I wheeled him back out into the nursery and went to find Dr. Rooken. I couldn't do this anymore. But as I passed the womb on my way to the lab, something fluttered in my stomach. My own baby, making his presence known. I stopped in the hallway and looked down at my abdomen. I smoothed my shirt over the bulge. I couldn't stop coming here. I needed to understand.

CHAPTER 14
elias

Dr. Rooken and I studied Moray's case, files strewn across the screen. We reread everything, looking for any clue. There wasn't much help in looking it all over again. It was already catalogued in my head. The computer had also compiled my findings into a nice and neat report. But Dr. Rooken trusted in human instinct and wanted to read it all again for anything that might not be obvious to a computer, or me. So I was rereading, though it was tedious and repetitive. In fact, it felt like routine.

"I haven't found anything." Dr. Rooken yawned and stretched back in his chair. "How about some coffee?"

"Sure, how would you like it?"

"No, Elias. I meant how about you and I go to a coffee shop and grab a coffee, together."

"Oh. Ok." I closed all of the apps on my tablet. I asked the computer to reorder the files and—

"Elias," Dr. Rooken interrupted.

"Yes?"

"Leave it be. Let's just go."

I glanced one last time at the mess in my lab and then turned to follow the doctor. He took me outside of the hospital and across the street to a diner that the hospital staff frequented. I had seen something like this in a movie once, but I had long since stopped watching movies as they seemed like two hours of wasted time. But I remembered that scene, a diner full of doctors chatting and eating in a hurry. Most of them just waiting for a call to an emergency.

As we sat at the bar, sipping on terrible coffee and watching the people in the diner, Dr. Rooken's tablet rang. It felt like déjà vu.

"Yes. I'll be right there. No, it's not a problem. Ok."

Dr. Rooken hung up and looked at me with a very large grin on his face.

"The nanobots are done. Jordan has woken. Let's go welcome him to his new world."

We scanned our tablets and swiveled our chairs around. Dr. Rooken walked much faster and with a bit of bounce. It confused me. It was so drastic a change from just a few minutes before.

We reached Jordan's room, and Dr. Rooken peeked through the doorway. I couldn't see past him, just his back and the light spilling from the room beyond. The nurse had opened the curtains so Jordan could get some sunshine.

When Dr. Rooken finally walked through the doorway, I was able to step up to the door but I didn't look in; just listened from the hallway. I had to strain to hear over the other hospital noises of nurses checking in, machines beeping, footsteps on the linoleum, and groaning patients.

"Hello, Frin," Dr. Rooken said.

We had to change names; it was all part of the process, separating from our previous selves to remain indifferent.

"I'm a little confused," Jordan said.

"That's all right. We'll get you figured out soon enough.

We've made a lot of changes in your body and it needs some time to settle in. But in just a few days you'll be going to a place where there are others like you. You can relearn everything you need to know. You'll be a whole new person. Isn't that exciting?"

"But who was I before?" Jordan asked.

I gulped.

"That doesn't matter, my dear man. Let's get you checked out and then we can talk some more."

I looked around the door jamb and saw the doctor giving Jordan a checkup. He looked healthy, his skin glowing and his eyes bright. He sat up in bed while Dr. Rooken maneuvered around him and lifted limbs, tested reflexes, and checked his heart and lungs. The doctor glimpsed me and waved me over.

"Jor—Frin, this is Elias. He's going to help you get ready for the boot camp."

I widened my eyes and stared at Dr. Rooken. That wasn't part of my job description. What did he expect me to do? This wasn't the order of things.

"Don't worry, Elias. You'll do fine. It's just a matter of explaining things to Frin. I've even got a manual for it that Dr. Wolff put together."

The mention of Dr. Wolff perked my attention. Something else he had written? That was something I wanted to read.

I looked at Jordan then, for he was staring at me. My face stayed blank, as did his. He looked exactly the same as he had when he worked at the hospital, and I wondered if my and Dr. Rooken's presence was a bad idea, seeing as we knew him before. But I was reassured by his continued confusion. Perhaps we were not enough of an emotional connection to create any triggers.

A nurse walked up with a cartridge of HSS under one arm and a tablet which she handed to me. The only file on it was a manual written by Dr. Wolff. I sat at Jordan's bedside to read things I hadn't heard in over twenty years while Dr. Rooken left.

"You are a different person now. You might have flashbacks or memories come up, but they should only be glimpses and once you are on Hormone Stabilizing Serum those feelings should go away. This is a transition period. Don't have any fear; it will all turn out for the best. You are a better person now."

"But who was I before?" Jordan asked. I looked up at him and saw his nose turning pink but his eyes stayed dry. His breathing was slightly elevated. Dr. Rooken had warned me about these emotional outbursts. The nurse was finished connecting the HSS and motioned to a button by my left hand. I pushed it. Within minutes Jordan was laying back comfortably against his pillows, his face a healthy pale again.

"Don't worry about that," I said. "May I continue?"

"Of course. Thank you," he said.

"You will be sent to a boot camp of sorts to learn new things. These may be things you knew before, so your body will have a sort of automatic memory, but your brain is functioning like a child and needs to be retaught. You will be in a comfortable room filled with others like you. You will learn to eat again, as your body will not have a trigger for craving food. You will learn to take care of your body. You will also learn—"

"What does that mean? I know I am male, but what does taking care of my body mean?" Jordan interrupted.

"Cleaning it. May I continue?"

"Certainly."

"You will also learn how to perform a trade of some sort. For some people that means becoming a helper for others. For you specifically," here I was supposed to fill in the blank, but Dr. Rooken hadn't told me what he would be doing. "I'm sorry, Frin. I need to find out what you will be doing. We'll come back to that."

He sat forward on the bed, his legs nearly over the side, and his heart rate monitor beeping faster. "But I should know that. What do I do if I don't know that? I'm a little frightened now. What is frightened? What is this thing my heart is doing?" He looked at the monitor and reached a finger out to it, staring with wide eyes and a partially open mouth. I thought he might start drooling. Since his heart rate didn't calm, and he looked back at me with terror in his eyes, I pushed the button again.

"Go ahead and sit back, Frin. I'll continue?"

"Yes, sorry. That won't happen again." He put his legs back on the bed and smoothed the comforter.

I took him through the rest of the manual with no more incidences until we came to the final words. "If you have any fear, just speak with someone. There is no need for fear, and we will teach you how to deal with the world when you are ready to join it again. This also means being very regular about taking your medication. That is the end of the manual." I closed it. "Do you have any questions?"

"No, I don't think so. Questions. I'm not sure. What would I ask?"

"Anything you like." I folded my hands over the tablet.

"Do I have a family?"

"Where did you hear that word?"

"On the television." He pointed to it.

"That shouldn't be on. Don't turn it on." I didn't even know why there was a television in his room.

"Do I have one?"

"Not anymore."

I turned and left the room.

But the next day I was back again. There was more to explain to the new patient. I walked up to the nurses' station.

"I need Jordan's file please."

"You mean Frin. Don't forget that."

"Yes, sorry." Both of our voices were as flat as a calm sea. There was no hostility, but also no cheerfulness. It was business as usual. Though it was beginning to wear on me. Why had we chosen to do this? And why had Dr. Rooken chosen to have me induct the new patient into his new world?

She handed me the tablet without a smile or a nod and went back to typing. I looked over the charts before going in the room. Jordan hadn't slept very well the night before. He had needed a dose of anti-anxiety medicine to help him sleep after tossing and turning and calling the nurse in several times to ask questions. My job certainly wasn't over. I needed to alleviate his fears somehow, or he wouldn't have a smooth transition into this new universe.

Stepping through the door, I noticed first the rumpled sheets. The dull, placid look in his eyes transitioned to a brilliant sparkle when he saw me. He didn't smile, his lips didn't remember how, but he perked up.

"Hello Frin. Are you all right this morning?"

"Yes. I think so. I didn't sleep too well. I have so many questions."

"Let's see what we can do about that." I pulled a chair over and sat down.

"I still want to know if I have a family. I just want to be certain. I need to take care of them."

"No, Frin. You don't have a family. And even if you did, you can't go back to them in this state. They wouldn't understand. You are very different now. That's good."

"Are they being taken care of?"

"You don't have a family."

"But is someone providing them with money and food and things?"

"A one-time transfer of funds will be provided."

"Oh." Then the dullness crept back in, like the shadows lengthening by the setting sun.

"Any other questions before I finish explaining your new journey?"

"I suppose not."

"Then, after boot camp, you will be placed in a job. Typically this is something you have an affinity for since that will make you most content and the most productive. You are being sent to a logging area to work with wood. Once you are there you will be allowed to find your own house or apartment and set up your life. There are people in every area that can help you. You will be given a contact to check in with and this person will also provide you with your HSS. They'll also perform physicals and check-ups as needed to be sure your body is healthy and running well."

"Ok," he mumbled.

"This is the last time you will see me, Frin. Are you sure there's nothing else you want to ask me?"

He looked up and gazed into my eyes. There was pleading there, something akin to a child asking for sweets. He twirled his fingers in the sheets.

"Did you know me before?"

"That's not something I can answer, Frin."

He just continued staring at me. Reading me like an open book, though my face showed nothing. It didn't know how. The room sucked up the silence like a vacuum, feeding on our mutual ability to outlast anyone in awkward moments. It continued so long that I actually had to swivel my hips.

This was a natural reaction coming directly from my body, an old habit learned long before I became an EMT patient. Something reminiscent of being uncomfortable. Finally, Jordan spoke.

"Ok. It was nice to meet you, Elias. Thank you for explaining everything to me."

I fled the room.

Two weeks later we received our first recording of Jordan. Dr. Rooken had me pause my work with analyzing blood work from the EMT children to watch it all the way through. It took me two full days. Jordan had followed all the rules, and had adjusted well. I observed him sleeping in a bunk next to so many other bunks filled with men from ages twenty to seventy. They all slept on their backs, like I did, with their arms by their sides and everything completely relaxed. Their eyes twitched some, since they were settling into the HSS treatments, but for the most part they would have uninterrupted, deep sleep. Then the sun woke them. Each man sat up and stretched his body, reaching under the bed for his slippers. Jordan took a moment longer to appreciate the sunlight. A smile crossed his face, until his eyes snapped open and everything was wiped away. I saw a moment of confusion cloud his vision, then he went on with his tasks of making the bed, tidying the area, and grabbing his clothes to go change.

Dr. Rooken brought me a cup of coffee and sat on a stool.

"How goes it?" he asked.

"Everything seems normal. He's still having problems with enjoyment. He liked the sunshine on his face. The day before that he stayed in bed a minute and thirty seconds longer than the others, curled on his side. But each time it gets shorter that he realizes something isn't right."

Dr. Rooken sighed.

"Have I said something wrong?" I took a sip. "Computer, pause."

"No Elias, continue watching. It'll take you a while to get through it all. You can speed up the playback if you wish."

"I want to make sure I don't miss anything. We don't need another murderer on our hands."

With a snort, Dr. Rooken stood and left the room. I stared after him, wishing he would come back and explain his reaction. When he didn't, I asked the computer to resume and watched Jordan while typing notes on my tablet. It was then that the new volunteer stepped into the lab.

"Oh, sorry." She began to back out. Just the sound of her voice made my shoulders rise. Everything slowed as I took in that fact. Why would the sound of someone's voice make me cringe? How could I cringe at all?

"Computer, pause."

The screen froze in the midst of the mess hall; it was a blur of men walking around in brown and gray and blue.

"What can I do for you?" I turned to face her, forcing my face blank. Forcing? Why? I shook my head.

"I just needed the new files. Dee and Dum said they were in here."

"You can access them from any tablet."

"Oh. I thought because Dr. Rooken had so many different tablets..." she said.

"He's simply disorganized. Everything is available from every tablet. The computer controls all cloud storage."

The volunteer had her hands on her hips now. I wanted to reach out and touch her cheek. What? I shook my head again. "Why are you shaking your head?" she asked.

"I just...I don't..." I flipped back around so I didn't have to watch her grab a tablet or stalk out of the room. "Computer, resume," I said. Not really focusing on the screen, I tried to sort out what was happening to me. The sound of a confrontation drew my attention. It was on the vid. Two men yelled at each other about eggs and toast—a normal occurrence as they adjusted to a new life. I hadn't caught the gist of it before Jordan stepped between them and said something to settle them both down. The orderlies hadn't even noticed a problem and everything went back to normal. One of the angry men gave his toast to Jordan, who handed it to the other man. He sat between them and struck up a conversation that I couldn't hear.

I noted it all down in my tablet, highlighting it as a strange incident, something unexpected or unobserved in any new EMT patient. This was possibly a clue; a way we could understand Moray more.

aloisa

Around the corner, with the tablet clutched to my chest, I breathed. What was that on the screen? All those changelings in one room. It looked like an army. Were they building an army of people who don't feel anything?

I shuddered.

With the tablet becoming slimy in my clammy hands, I made my way back to the lab and dropped it off with the twins. Then, instead of finishing my rounds, I left to find Miles.

I walked out into the sunshine, my eyes blinded by the sudden glare, and someone grabbed my shoulders. I squeaked.

"It's just me," Miles said.

"Don't do that. What are you doing here?"

"Came to say goodbye. My transport is leaving early. There's some storms or something."

"What?" It felt as though gravity had increased tenfold. My arms dropped, my shoulders sank, and my neck creeped into my collarbone like a turtle. "We were supposed to have the afternoon together."

"I know, but this is unavoidable. If there are solar storms causing problems, I won't be able to go for weeks; I have to go now." He kissed my cheek.

"Like, right now?" The pitch of my voice rose in panic. "Right now?"

"Yes, walk with me. You can go with me all the way to the main gates to the transports. Come on." He tugged at my limp arm. My body followed without the command from my brain. Miles was leaving me. Pregnant, scared, without Jordan, alone. But I followed him. He chatted as we made our way to the bus station on the far side of the hospital campus. His mouth didn't stop moving long enough for me to say something, let alone remember why I had been leaving early to talk with him.

"Miles!" I interrupted.

"What? Is everything ok?" His hands brushed over my entire body, looking for the point of pain. "Is everything ok?" he repeated as the bus pulled up.

"Yes, I just remembered what I had to tell you. Let's get on." We stepped aboard, the driver impatiently tapping his foot.

"What did you need to tell me?" Miles fell into a seat, his bags thumping to the floor.

"I saw something. I don't know if it's anything. But it was something. I don't know, it could be nothing."

"What was it?"

I looked out the window, watching the scenery glide by.

Sunshine dappled the sidewalks and people. Buildings, made of steel and glass, sparkled.

"A vid of changelings in a camp. I think they might be building an army."

"You saw a boot camp!" He whipped his head up from where he had been searching in one of his bags. His fingers danced over the breathing apparatuses and armored gloves and second-skin radiation suit inside, tapping out a little rhythm of excitement.

"What's a boot camp?"

"It's the first place they send the changelings, to teach them to be changelings. Emodiant hasn't broadcasted their existence. Yet another tactic to make EMT seem normal.

"The human brain has too many automatic behaviors. It's why you find the children who are born changelings to be so much creepier than adult changelings—they never learned to act human. So in boot camp they observe and monitor the people who have been changed to retrain the human out of them. You saw one?"

"Elias was watching a vid of men in a mess hall." Even in the temperature-controlled bus, drops of sweat started to slide down my arms. I wiped my hands on my pants.

"It's ok. It's not an army." Miles went back to searching his bag for what he needed. "The whole system is government-run. Emodiant subsists on a government contract. Our taxes provide the cash, they run the program. The whole reason you get a payout is because Jordan went into service for them. It's the main reason the rebels are trying so hard. They want to throw the leader from his horse, but they plan to do it by tripping the horse."

"That makes no sense."

He looked me in the eye. "Yes it does. Don't you see? They attack from the small end with the goal of turning the entire thing. Honestly, they're probably behind the Moray murder. This is exactly why I want you to be careful with them."

Again he turned to rifle through his things.

"I don't care what they want. I want Jordan." I crossed my arms.

"You are treading through dangerous territory, sister. This is not Wonderland. The queen won't magically make friends with you. She will chop your head off without hesitation. The cops aren't modified because the government needs henchmen to do their dirty work. No changeling would ever consider the things a human is capable of. Well, obviously there is a flaw. But either way, the cops and the rebels are who we need to worry about. I want you to lay low while I'm gone."

"I'm going to go see Thelia," I said. Yet again, he whipped his head back to face me.

"Are you sure about that?"

"I have no other way to get a hold of them." I clasped my hands in my lap, facing forward and ending the conversation. Miles could spend his two weeks in South America thinking about that. Then we'd see how he felt.

We reached the transport gates, and I had to stay on the bus. Miles scrambled around, gathering every bag and piece of equipment. Loaded down with all his gear, he looked like a soldier himself. But I managed to hug and kiss him without trembling. I smiled out the window while he waved, and the bus pulled away. I rode it the rest of the day through neighborhood after neighborhood, buildings and people deteriorating with each checkpoint we passed. As the clouds lifted and faded colors burned brilliant, the neighborhoods did the opposite, moving like a gradient from shiny white to a murky gray. Even the people in my neighborhood were muddier, like a smudged, abstract painting, with unruly hair and scowling faces. The only constant from street to street were the changelings, all dressed similarly in monotone clothing and their faces resting in the standard emotionless state. So many thoughts churned in my head and threatened to send me into a panic attack.

Back at the apartment, I skipped my floor and went straight to the roof. Up there the tightness around my chest eased. The air felt cooler and cleaner. And my rosebush sat waiting for me; a shoulder I could lean on, an ear that would listen. Through the leaves I glimpsed the wooden gryphon. His wings poised for flight, his front legs rearing into the air. The thorns of the bush surrounded him protectively. Though they were menacing, I felt a comfort in the tiny prison that held my sculpture. He was safe, sheltered. With his feet planted in solid earth and soft, white petals caressing his flanks. I reached a single finger through the barrier of branches to touch the smooth wood. Instantly my heart gave way, and I was able to take a deep breath. This was how things were meant to be.

CHAPTER 15
aloisa

I sat there, my knees bouncing and my palms sweating. Thelia had sent me to a rendezvous.

A woman in a blue coat sat down on the bench next to me.

"I feel like I'm in a spy movie." I giggled.

"Shut up and take this folder," the woman said. I recognized her painted fingernails but nothing else. They were so good at blending in.

"Are you part of the rebel cell based in Canada?" I asked as I reached for the folder. The woman tried to snatch it back, but I grabbed her wrist.

There was a moment when I held my breath, and I'm pretty sure the wind did too. I gingerly pried the folder from her fingers. She stood and walked away, glancing back only once.

I opened the folder. Inside, on the first page, was a body ringed with flame. I shuddered. Behind that page was a long list of possibilities for where my husband could be. There were no photos, but descriptions of men that sounded exactly like Jordan.

Dock worker.

Salesman at a women's department store.

Butler.

Chauffeur.

Secretary for some government bigwig.

Children's nurse.

"Children's nurse?" I whispered. Why would they subject children to the cold hands of a changeling?

Then I saw it: Carpenter. Oregon woods. Recently changed. Probably thirty years old. Dark hair.

"If that's not Jordan, then you're scaring me." I was on full alert now. The hairs on my arms stood up, and I blinked in the harsh sunlight.

I read the entry again but found no other contact information than "Oregon woods."

Searching the rest of the folder revealed a small data chip that had been taped to the back flap.

I ripped the chip out, clutching it tightly, and started for the bus stop. I would find out what was on the chip, then I would decide if these people were playing with me.

I needed a real computer to read the data chip. The only place I could think of where I would be alone was the EMT Clinic. At Dr. Rooken's desk, I turned on the computers. No one was around, even Humpty and Dumpty were focused on creating new embryos in a closed lab. I lay the chip in the computer's universal receptacle. The gel molded to the correct shape for this specific data chip.

"This chip contains a message. It is only audible. Would you like me to play it back?" the computer said.

"Please." I wrung my hands, twisting my ankles around the stool legs.

A voice came over the system, a voice so gravelly and

distorted I had to concentrate to understand. I stopped my nervous swiveling on the stool.

"This is evidence of people who represent what you gave us. Either your list was too broad, or people simply are that much alike, especially as changelings. Do you not agree? The whole point of EMT is to make the world like each other. Perhaps our genetics have already evolved to it and we are birthing children that are clones. How many red heads do you see walking around anymore?"

I knew if Miles had been by my side he would have covered my ears. He would call this propaganda and worry about my safety. But Miles hadn't felt the intensity of love. He didn't understand that a chunk of my heart had been torn off and lost to the four winds. If I didn't get it back, I would perish.

"If you want to find your husband, then you will need to give us a bit more. We need a reason. Something that will tell us that this man is different from the many others who have abandoned their families. Why would he want to come back to you after what he's done? He. Left. You."

"End of recording," the computer said.

One tear trailed down my cheek. I had reasons, plenty of reasons. But the rebels were right. My mind raced, my eyes sweeping back and forth as I searched for some piece of information in my brain to hand over to them. Something that would tell them he was different.

"The gryphon," I whispered.

The room fell away from me. The final words of the recording echoed in the vast spaces of my harried mind.

I showed up at her house, on her doorstep, unprepared and a complete mess. My hair hadn't been brushed. I had no idea where my purse was. The gryphon. I could see it, rearing regally among shafts of light. The warehouse was paid up for another few weeks, but soon I would have to move it somewhere. It wouldn't fit in our apartment.

Jordan's things had all been boxed and put away—by Miles—so I could attempt to forget. It hadn't worked; every surface of that place reminded me of him. The kitchen counter—where we had made love, me sitting on the edge and his knees banging into the drawers, making us laugh. The sofa—where we had met every day after work to hash out the happenings and vent and bitch. Our bed—where every night my husband had held me.

I stood in front of Thelia's house, my hand hovering before the computer.

"Would you like me to ring for you?" it asked.

Her house had as much sass as she did. Instead of answering, I slapped it with my palm.

"Oh really. Well, I'll just wait another minute and then ring," it said. I pictured a woman cocking her hip and ringing her lips with a finger to make sure the lipstick hadn't smudged.

Finally, Thelia answered the door herself. She took in my state, glanced around her front yard, and then yanked me inside.

"What are you doing here?" she said. I checked behind her but found no one. Why was she whispering?

"They sent me a message." I held out the data chip. She snatched it from my hands, and trucked down the hallway in her high-powered suit and heels. We reached an office, where she listened to the message in its entirety while I tried not to hear it.

"Do you have something?" she asked, turning on me like a weasel with easy prey.

"Of course. That's why I'm here. I want to show you before they see it. I need to show you."

"Let's go." She whipped a coat from behind the door and pulled me to the garage where we entered an automatic-pilot Bugatti, which was stored next to her slightly less extravagant Tesla.

Even though she didn't have to concentrate on driving, and it wasn't loud inside the completely sound-proof and silent electronic car, she didn't speak. I told the computer the destination and it took us there. My heart was in my throat again as soon as we reached the highway; the car took off to catch a spot in the never-ending set of traffic, zipping in and out of lanes with inhuman speed.

At the warehouse, I caught my breath while Thelia redid her hair. Her impatience finally surfaced and she started tapping her foot.

"Ok, come on," I said, leading her into the maze of elevators and warehouses and doors and cracked pavement.

I opened the door to the room with the gryphon and let Thelia through. I wanted her to bask in the glory. I didn't turn the lights on; the sunshine was bursting through the glass as if it wanted to be closer to the gryphon, to hold and caress it. I heard her gasp before I even entered.

"What is this?" she asked.

"My husband made it. He's a carpenter."

"This is powerful." Her hands glided up one leg, feeling the warmth of the wood and the curve of the muscle that seemed so real you could almost see it quiver. Some of the sun's rays came down past the creature's nostrils and sprayed across the floor like foggy breath. I could never get over how simple, how beautiful, how amazing, it was. I hoped neither could the rebels.

elias

"Computer, turn on playlist twenty-one please," Dr. Rooken said to the room. He sat at one of the research tables with some blood samples and an analyzer; I sat with three tablets scattered around me trying to find correlations. The EMT children had been showing odd abilities—they were almost telepathic. But Dr. Rooken didn't seem bothered and only wanted me to compile the information. Blaring classical music bounced off the metal walls, echoing around us. But soon the music stopped. I looked up to find Dr. Xanther standing in the doorway, his hand on the mute button on the main screen.

"I need to speak with you, Rooken." His face showed no signs of his intent. To me he looked like an EMT.

"Then speak," Dr. Rooken said without looking up.

Dr. Xanther glanced at me and then moved farther into the room, showing me his back and crossing his arms as he stood in front of Dr. Rooken. I lowered my head to my work.

"This is unacceptable," he spoke in much quieter tones. I thought perhaps he should turn the music back on if he didn't want me to overhear, but Dr. Xanther always had ways that didn't quite match what other humans did.

Dr. Rooken simply grunted, his head still in his work and his hands occupied by scribbling data on a tablet or placing more samples in the analyzer.

"Do you not have more news on the Moray murder? This is dangerous." Dr. Xanther's head swiveled to me and back to Dr. Rooken. "Should we even have an EMT working on something like this? And what about this woman volunteering here?"

"I told you, I've reported her. I would rather have her close by. She's harmless. Simply a grieving mother. Leave her be," Dr. Rooken said.

"You'd better be right. If she turns into trouble for us, I'll blame you completely. EMT depends on you Rooken, don't you understand that?"

Dr. Rooken slowly raised his eyes to meet Dr. Xanther's. There was something in his look that I couldn't explain, but it sent shivers down my back.

"If that's true then why are you berating me? What right do you have? Everything is under control. You wouldn't even be here if it wasn't for me."

"What am I supposed to tell the others? We require their approval. They're asking for reports and new research explaining why they should continue supporting a system that might have a fatal flaw."

"Tell them to lay off. The murderer has already been caught. And this *flaw* only applies to adults who have been changed. The EMT children are just as viable as before. The inconsistencies we've found don't apply to them due to their engineering. I'll locate a suitable test subject and find a solution." His eyes shifted to me. I hadn't realized I had been staring until I saw the clear green of his irises. While he continued staring at me he said, "One way or another I will know why this happened."

CHAPTER 16
elias

This volunteer, this Aloisa, she intrigued me. I was preoccupied.

Something was wrong. The apartment smelled funny, like a bus that had broken down by the roadside. It seemed to be coming from the kitchen. I retrieved my protein from the oven too late and one side was singed and smoking. I watching the smoke curl to the ceiling, fascinated by the tendrils. I hadn't seen my food do that before. I prodded the browned side, making certain it was still suitable for consumption. Instead of taking a bite, I searched my tablet for the answer. Of course, someone in the EMT forums had the answer. I had cooked it too long. My kitchen was on manual mode because I usually didn't need the help of a computer. But this Aloisa, this girl.

By the time I'd stopped thinking about her this time, my food had gone cold. The plate hung, tilted, in my hand, grease dripping onto the floor. The oven door sat open. It was the flashing of the light, the only sign the appliance gave that something was out of place, that had alerted me. I closed the door. But still, she floated on the edge of my vision, taking over my senses and confusing me. There was no reason for this.

I threw the protein out and continued my routine as if I had eaten. It was just better to get back into the rhythm. I would see Aloisa tomorrow and possibly figure out what was going on.

When I awoke at my usual time in the morning, everything seemed normal again. I rubbed my knees and back, stood up, made my bed, brushed my teeth, had breakfast, brushed my teeth, showered, arranged my apartment, and was on my way. My body felt healthier as I walked to work.

I reached work and started right in, making coffee and organizing files and preparing for the workday. Dr. Rooken showed up a few hours later and sat down to have his cup of coffee. The caffeine kicked in, and he looked at me.

"Elias, are you feeling all right?" His gaze went past my skin, into my innards.

"I think so. Why?"

"You look a bit pale, and your eyes are bloodshot. Maybe you need a few days off. Did you remember your HSS?"

My body hit the floor. I hadn't exactly passed out, I just fell. Dr. Rooken bent over me, snapping his fingers in front of my face and tapping my cheek. How could I have forgotten to take my HSS? Everything was falling apart. I couldn't handle this much longer.

"Elias!" His voice came through the muck.

"Sorry, Doctor," I said from the floor, my body still in repose. "I forgot my HSS."

"Let's get you on the couch and I'll get you a dose. It's not a problem. Forgetfulness is normal. Don't worry." But his face communicated something else entirely. His eyebrows squished together, his lips were locked, and his eyes darted to the ceiling while he spoke to me.

I let him help me to the couch and lay back.

Dr. Rooken stepped out to get serum, and Aloisa walked in.

"Oh, I'm sorry," she said and went back out. The size of her body, carrying another human being, was overwhelming and instead of acknowledging her or the wave of emotion that swept over me, I turned into the couch and tried to fall asleep.

Dr. Rooken brought me some HSS, and when I didn't take the syringe from his hand, he administered it himself. There was nothing to do but lie there, shivering from withdrawal, while it went to work resetting my system.

Dr. Rooken went on with his work but checked on me throughout the day. A little after lunch I felt better and wanted less light, so I moved into a chair in a back corner of the womb, where it was dark and warm.

I heard the door creak open, but I didn't reveal myself in hopes that someone was just coming to check the digital readouts from the embryos and leave again. But then I heard the squeak of rolling wheels and something heavy settling onto a stool.

"Hi," Aloisa said. I didn't dare look around the tank for fear of startling her. I clutched my arms around my chest to stop the shivering and waited.

She must have touched her hand to the embryo tank because a small light blinked on the thermal sensor. My first instinct was to stand and tell her to stop, but my second held me back and made me listen.

"I miss them, both of them. And that boot camp, what was that about?"

The light clicked off. I imagined her snatching her hand away as if burned. The light clicked back on again, and I could see the embryonic fluid ripple while one of the babies changed its position, probably sliding along the glass to reach her hand, searching for warmth.

"I really hope Miles comes back ok. He should never have gone to South America, not while I'm this much of a mess. But it's his work. He needs to make money, and he needs to feel validated, and all that silly man-stuff." A sob escaped her throat. "If Jordan hadn't felt the need to be all manly and stupid, then maybe he wouldn't have left and I wouldn't be here talking to you, and I wouldn't be so worried. Of course I wouldn't have all this money.

"I am going to find him. Don't worry. That will happen. It's just a question of when."

I sucked in a gasp, slapping a hand over my mouth to cover the sound. She didn't say anything more, just left the room with what speed she could muster. I had to tell someone. She couldn't be allowed to search for him.

My shivering had stopped, and I felt much more balanced. My back straightened, and I knew my purpose for the moment. I left the room to find the right people to get the right things done. I went directly to Dr. Rooken's office where I had left my tablet.

I sent an email off and sat back at Dr. Rooken's desk. My task finished, I turned again to the diary of Sebian Wolff. Perhaps it would give me insight into whether or not what I had done to Aloisa was a good thing.

"Not to mention the right to grow old and ugly and impotent;
the right to have syphilis and cancer; the right to have too

little to eat; the right to be lousy; the right to live in constant apprehension of what may happen tomorrow; the right to catch typhoid; the right to be tortured by unspeakable pains of every kind." Brave New World

No one will listen to me. This is the way things have to be. They don't see the future like I do. This world has gone to shit, and I've seen it with my own eyes. There's nothing else that will work. We need to control ourselves. We've all gone mad. This is not the beginning of things, but it could be the end. I can make us better. I can fix us. We will be more elite. It's man-made evolution. I can control what will happen. No more pain, no more crying. Everything is unnecessary. I can control this problem. I can control it.

I looked up from the diary. This wasn't helping me at all. I turned a few pages and continued reading.

"There can be no knowledge without emotion. We may be aware of a truth, yet until we have felt its force, it is not ours. To the cognition of the brain must be added the experience of the soul." Arnold Bennett

This is what they say to me, these harbingers of doom, these naysayers, these atheists of beauty. They don't seem to understand that of course there can be knowledge without emotion. Children are not crying as they learn their math problems. They simply put their mind to it and work. Same way that I do with my science.

The process is almost complete. I have found the key to the inhibitor. I have developed a machine to do the surgery for me, that way it is much more precise and less risky. I will be its conductor, its master, its leader. But the non-believers still won't approve my testing. They think this is an insane idea. They see me as Dr. Jekyll, Dr. Frankenstein, sitting in my lab here in the dark waiting for my monster to come to life. But that's just fear. That's their emotions at play. If I could only remove their emotions, they would see that I'm right. There's no other way forward for this world. It must be done.

That wasn't much better, but it made me feel normal. I was a product of this man's genius. He had worked tirelessly to make my life possible. The world was a better place for it. The devastating wars in China and South America must have been the trigger; they must have allowed him to test after that point. They had to have seen that what they were doing was wrong. And in this logic, I found that I was right in what I had done to Aloisa. She was endangering the EMT patients. They needed protection, and I had protected them.

CHAPTER 17
aloisa

He had one of those ratty faces, built for sticking his nose into things. You would think they would send a more forgettable man to follow me around. He wore colors, which was a dead giveaway for an unmodified human. He liked to don baseball caps, which was a dead giveaway for a cop. Did they think I was stupid? And then I saw the fuzz on his hands. Immediately my memory triggered; a man behind me in a coffee shop, following me around every street corner, grinning stupidly as my bus pulled away.

My heart sped up when I realized he had found me outside my apartment and tailed me through every twist and turn. I hadn't expected something like this, but my subconscious must have, because I noticed him before I even really thought about it. He was that shadow in the corner that moves and doesn't startle you.

He stood three people behind me in line for groceries; he stood three people in line behind me for the bus. And when I went into the hospital I intended to lose him in the corridors and then double back to the womb. This time he outsmarted me—he was talking to Dr. Rooken when I walked in.

I strolled by them with as much nonchalance as my pregnancy allowed, trying to hear just a snippet. They were talking about the Moray murder case—nothing new and nothing about me. I continued on my way and went to the womb to start my work. I found Elias in there, checking the sensors.

"Hi," I said.

He looked over his shoulder and then ducked his head away from me. When I said hi again, he nodded but continued to focus on his tablet. I stopped and tilted my head. Elias shifted from foot to foot, dancing around and ignoring my presence. When I stepped far enough to the side that escape was possible, he shot out the door.

That was when I turned to see the rat-faced man staring at me.

"Can I help you?"

"Just confused why a pregnant woman is working in the changeling hospital."

Definitely a cop. Nobody with any sense would use that word out loud in this place.

"Here to volunteer. What does me being pregnant have to do with anything?" I hoped the look on my face was plain: stay away from me.

"No offense, just wondering." He held up both hands and backed away. My laser eyes had done their job. I was fast becoming a mother bear.

"Have a nice day," I said. I didn't watch to see if he left; I turned to my work.

But as I expected, he was smoking outside the hospital when I made my way home. And he followed me all the way there.

The next day, I went to Dr. Rooken.

"Hi Aloisa, what can I do for you?" he asked.

He was lying on his couch like some impromptu psych eval was scheduled. The screen across from the desk covered most of the wall and had files scattered helter skelter, and a few vids playing simultaneously. I noticed from a glance that everything was related to the Moray murder.

"Did you sleep here?" I asked. It popped out of my mouth as I thought it. Stupid pregnancy brain. "Sorry, don't know what's wrong with me. Can I sit?" I gestured at a chair in the corner, almost bending into a weird curtsy of sorts. I shook my head and tried to knock myself back to reality.

Dr. Rooken laughed and sat up. "I did actually. Been trying to find out more about this. I just don't get why this guy would go and murder someone."

"Maybe he didn't."

"What do you mean?" Dr. Rooken said, his head whipping around. He wasn't one to snap. It startled me.

"Well, um, a lot of people do things that they don't mean to. You use the word murder, I might say he accidentally killed her."

"But we have the brain scans. We can see what he did. He walked into the apartment and went straight for her head. We can't just give him an out because he's had EMT. And he's been sentenced." Dr. Rooken's voice had lowered an octave, and I immediately imagined a lecture hall filled with empty seats and me alone five rows up squished into a tiny desk. "There's no reason for it though."

"Exactly."

We let the silence hang between us. After he offered me a cup of water and sat down again, he started talking in his normal voice. "You didn't come in here to debate the latest scandal with me. What can I help you with?"

I sipped my water to hold him off a minute. This reaction, this sudden aggression and frustration and total belief in brain scans and technology freaked me out. He probably wasn't the person I should be going to for help. He had lied to me about Jordan. He was the only surgeon within three hours of shuttle travel who could perform EMT. He had changed my husband, but he would keep the secret locked tight.

"Actually, it was just about my hours. I've been more tired," I grandly gestured at my enormous belly, "and I think I need less time here."

"Like I said before, whatever time you want to give is welcome. We won't hold you to anything. We appreciate the help." He smiled. But it didn't reach his eyes.

I stuttered, took another sip, and began again. "Well, I guess I was wondering if you could tell me more about the chang—I mean EMT process. Where do they go after the surgery?"

"You know I can't tell you that, Aloisa." His voice had dropped even lower than before, this time a menacing growl. "If you were interested in becoming a patient, that's different. But even then, you wouldn't know where you were going until after the process was complete. Emodiant doesn't want someone else attempting to change people. It's for your safety."

Safety my ass. I barely stopped the scoff from leaving my throat and said, "Ok, I was just curious." My voice was bright. I stood and walked out of the room, stepping around the corner to stand against the wall and breathe.

After a moment's rest, I walked to the womb. As I turned in to my sanctuary, I spotted a familiar baseball cap above a distinct beak rounding the corner. I ducked around the door while he stopped across the hall and pulled out his tablet.

"We just don't know what to do with her," I heard him whisper. I had one hand on my heart and the other on my mouth, muffling the air moving in and out of my lungs.

The embryos floated in their fluid. The blue light washed over me. I had my back to the only blank wall as I listened to the man reporting to his superior. I didn't know what had given me away. Was it my desire to volunteer at the EMT Clinic? Was it Thelia snooping around?

"She's asking so many questions. I think we have two options."

There was a pause and unintelligible words from the tablet.

"Yes, I know you prefer that option but isn't it a little harsh?"

Another pause. I dared to inch closer to the corner, but my movement must have vibrated the liquid in the womb because the eyes of every baby sprang open.

I held completely still. The hair along my arms rose while I was scrutinized by tiny eyeballs. My heartbeat pounded in my ears, and I didn't hear the end of the conversation. I did hear his feet on the linoleum squeaking away from me.

I waddled away. My pregnancy didn't allow much more, but my body screamed with fleeing hormones. This was why I was still human, for moments like this. I stopped to breathe, hand on the wall for support and tears coursing down my face.

I shook my head, forcing myself back to the present. Peeking around the corner I had just come around, I looked for the man in the hat. He wasn't in sight. When I stepped back into Dr. Rooken's office on the next hallway, Elias was there.

My breathing sped up again. He sat at a desk reading a small journal, entrenched in whatever world it held for him. It wasn't until I shut the door with a tiny click that he slapped it closed and looked up. His eyes were hungry, vicious.

"Sorry to bother you. I was looking for Dr. Rooken?" I said between breaths. My belly heaved up and down.

"Why did you come in here?"

I could have sworn he had just yelled at me. My hand went to my heart, and I backed up a step. His hunched shoulders and rabid face had me more frightened than the cop who had followed me. Reaching behind my back, I twisted the door handle and again made a run for it.

It was dark when I got home. I ordered some Chinese and asked them to bring it upstairs. The adrenaline had drained from my system, and all I wanted was to crash into a pile of blankets. But as I walked across my pilly carpet, through the kitchen, I passed my tablet lying on the counter. It was flashing. Red, orange, red, orange.

I touched it.

"This is an automatic message meant for Aloisa Riodan from the Law Enforcement Department. We have Miles Fillian in custody at the municipal center. He was arrested for having trespassed into forbidden land. He will be quarantined for two weeks to be sure that high levels of radiation have abated. Please call us back for more information. He has bail listed at two hundred thousand. Thank you."

It was then that instead of sinking into a pile of blankets, I melted to the floor where I stood, and blacked out.

CHAPTER 18
aloisa

The municipal building was a crow among doves. It sat—grungy and squat—in the midst of taller and more beautiful buildings. The sunlight glared off the windows above, making me squint. The skyscrapers and other government buildings put my brother's prison to shame. The last time I had stepped foot inside, I hadn't even glanced at the facade. I had been focused on finding my husband. Now I feared going inside to find my brother in chains. I passed under the shadow of the taller buildings and into another world, one filled with secretaries running about and police officers shouting orders. Phones rang incessantly, and there was a buzz, a stress, circulating the building that set my teeth on edge.

"Hello," I said to the woman at the desk. She held up one finger without looking at me.

"I'm here to see Miles Fillian."

She pinched her lips but still didn't look up.

"I'll just sit over here," I said. And settled my ungainly body in a tiny plastic chair. A changeling offered me a magazine tablet, which I hastily declined. Across the room a wallscreen cycled through informational images. The unmistakable brand of a man wreathed in flame popped up, but the secretary interrupted before I could read the article.

"Ma'am," the woman at the desk said, "Miles Fillian isn't able to see visitors." She was human. I hadn't realized until now. I had expected a changeling. But then I remembered the pinched nose, the obvious frustration, the huffing of her breath when I continued talking after she snubbed me. It took me a moment to find my words.

"I'm his sister. I would like to see him." I rubbed my belly, trying to affect a tired and very pregnant woman. It wasn't hard, considering.

She sighed. "All right. Let me get the officer in charge of his case for you. You'll have to go to the quarantine wing if you're allowed to see him. It's quite a ways." She glared at my belly.

I picked up one of the magazine tablets the changeling had offered me. I caught his eye, and he stared back.

Finally, an officer came out from the back.

"Hello, Mrs. Riodan. I'm Officer Reynolds." He held out his hand. "You can come with me to talk about Miles's case. We've got more comfortable chairs in the back." He smiled warmly, and I felt an invisible cord loosen and relax. I hadn't realized how rigidly I'd been holding my body.

I clambered up and walked through the door after Reynolds, making sure to give the changeling in the seat next to the doorway a wide berth.

The officer led me past desks, through piles of tablets, like a tour guide. At times he would stop and point at an obstacle or look behind to make sure I was keeping up. Each time I smiled at him, but he didn't smile back. Instead he nodded curtly, both at me and at his colleagues. They nodded back, some concentrating on the screens on their desks, others filling out paperwork on their tablets. One woman stared off into nothing, seemingly preoccupied with a daydream.

Then I saw him. The man with the rat face. Without a baseball cap he was balding. He sat near the window, pretty far from the path Reynolds had taken, but I still tried to shield my face and twist my body away from him. My heart pounded, and I felt sweat gather in uncomfortable places. My mouth turned cottony, and the room pulsated. He was engrossed in a vidcall. With so much commotion around I was just a fly on the wall in a room full of bees, but I still picked up the pace.

Reynolds opened a door to a private room behind the mess of an office and led me in. I breathed deeply. He was right, the chairs were more comfortable.

"Ok. Let's chat. Would you like some coffee or tea?"

"Some water please," I said.

He swiveled back in his chair to pull the door open and called to another person. She swept into the room and served us both drinks.

Reynolds mumbled something, but I hadn't heard through the thickness in my ears. "I'm sorry, what did you say?"

"Do you understand why Miles is in here?"

"Not really. Has he done something wrong?" I had decided that I would play the ditzy, ineffectual girl. My hand grasped my water cup. I hoped he didn't see my eyelid twitching.

"He was caught in a forbidden zone. He said he had the permits but couldn't produce them."

"What? Where was he? That doesn't sound right." My voice was flat. There was no hype to it. I couldn't fake it. And Reynolds knew it. He squinted at me.

"No need to be silly, Mrs. Riodan. He was in South America. But you knew that, didn't you?"

"And if I did?" I sipped my water, hiding the blush creeping up my cheeks.

"It wouldn't be a problem. We don't care, really. We just

don't want him to bring radiation back here. His systems failed. He wasn't protected. He was pretty delirious when we found him in South America."

Now I sat forward, eager to understand. I hadn't realized he really was sick. I had thought the quarantine was a precaution. "Is he going to be ok?" My knee started bouncing.

"We think so. It's actually a good thing we found him because he would have brought the radiation right back to you." He gestured at my swollen belly, and I covered it protectively.

"Can I see him? The lady at the front said no, but I really need to speak with him." The pressure on my bladder reached an unbearable level very suddenly.

I cut off Officer Reynolds just as he opened his mouth. "I'm sorry. Could I use the restroom?"

"Of course." He stretched back and opened the door again, pointed to the right—away from my stalker—and said it would be around the corner.

I dashed there, not even daring to look around. My heart was in my throat, and I zipped into the restroom.

After doing what was necessary, I splashed cold water on my face and forced my breathing to calm. The baby had hiccups. I looked down. He tumbled around, trying to find a comfortable position.

"It's all right," I soothed. "Don't stress. We'll get through this soon enough."

He paused. I imagined a puppy, cocking its head to hear better. I rubbed my belly a bit more so he could feel my touch. The hiccups slowed and stopped.

I spent a few more minutes in front of the mirror forcing myself to calm, and then went back to Officer Reynolds. But as soon as I turned the corner and my head came up, the man with the rat face looked up from his desk, and we locked eyes. His bulged, and his throat convulsed with a gulp.

I snapped my head down and slipped into the private room.

"Is everything all right?" Reynolds asked. He looked at my hand resting on my chest which rose and fell rapidly.

"Just fine. Sorry. Can I see Miles today?"

"I've just spoken with the doctors. They say it's ok. You'll be separated by glass, but you should be fine."

"Ok, can we go now?" I looked behind me even though there was only a closed door. I needed out. This space was so tight, so constricting.

"Certainly. We have to go to the other wing, so we'll head out of this building and then down to the jail. Are you sure you're all right?" He reached out a hand toward me.

"Yes. I'm fine. Let's go." Gathering my courage and shoving the tiny shards of fear and doubt down my throat, I opened the door.

But there was no reason to worry. I peeked around the corner and found that the rat-faced man was gone. Reynolds snatched the door from me and opened it wide. I scanned the rest of the room just in case, but that man wasn't anywhere to be seen. I followed Reynolds out.

He took me back into the sunshine and down the road. The streets were empty. An eerie silence enveloped the skyscrapers. No birds chirped because there were no trees, the wind whistled, dancing in and out of the crevices between buildings. No vehicles traveled these roads. This was the inner circle of the government, and they couldn't risk vehicles laced with bombs.

Our footsteps echoed, and Reynolds cleared his throat. He tugged at his collar and glanced around every corner with shifty eyes.

He took me to a monstrous building that was pure, shiny white with few windows. The instant the door slid open to allow us entrance, the sounds of people and machines engulfed us and we both visibly relaxed.

Inside the jail was another maze. Reynolds led me around two corners and then through a hallway filled with different supplies, up an elevator, and then down a very long hallway, around another few corners, and finally we reached a section of the jail that was quieter and guarded by two men in hazard suits.

"We're here to see Fillian," Reynolds said.

The two men didn't say anything. I doubted they could through the gas masks. They gestured us into one of the four doors behind them. It was like a game show. What's behind door number three! That or a deadly choice at the end of a labyrinth. Behind three doors lie instant death, choose wisely!

But it was nothing so sinister as that. Though my heart pounded in fear of what Miles would look like—I imagined him emaciated, skin sloughing off him, holes of flesh taken from his cheeks and limbs and torso—the room was filled with warmth. Inside was a nurse watching over my brother who lay on a bed inside a glass box. Robot arms busied themselves inside, fixing his sheets, giving him water, until we came in and the nurse asked them to rest. All three slid to the side and shut down.

Miles hadn't seen me yet, hiding behind Reynolds. He looked tired, but that was about it. The dark circles under his eyes and the paleness to his skin was the only difference I could see. Reynolds sat down next to the nurse, who was reading a tablet, and Miles had full view of me. Here I was, nearly ready to give birth, and he was lying in a prison cell made of glass.

Just like with the embryos, I put my hand to the glass, wishing for a touch of his hand. A few tears slipped out of my eyes.

Miles sat up slowly and gave me a big smile.

"Hey big sis, didn't think I'd see you here."

"What were you thinking?" I glanced back at Reynolds, but he was preoccupied in a chat with the cute nurse. I was afforded a tiny bit of privacy. "You didn't have the permits!"

"I did, I lost them. The equipment I bought wasn't up to snuff. South America was even more potent than China. My guide didn't make it back." His nose burned red, and his eyes filled with liquid; he looked down into his lap.

"I'm sorry Miles. At least you found help, even if it ended you in here."

"They're letting me out. The permits were in order on this end, so they know I had them at some point. We just have to wait until I'm no longer radioactive. I'm so glad I didn't come home to you." He pointed to my stomach. "You're ready to pop."

"Yep." I took my hand from the glass and touched my child. He had the hiccups again.

"Is everything ok? Have you heard any more news?" Miles asked.

I snapped my head up and glared at him. Then I glanced again at Reynolds, who didn't seem to be listening.

"Excuse me Officer," I said.

"Yeah?"

"Since my brother is not under arrest, can I have a minute alone with him?"

He locked eyes with the nurse and considered for a minute, then let out a sigh. "We'll be securing both Miles's door and the one to the outside. You are not allowed inside the chamber. But yes, I suppose."

They left.

Miles pointed to a camera which more than likely also had a microphone. I put my hands around my mouth and spoke in the quietest whisper possible. Miles watched my lips move.

"I've been followed by a man that I just saw this morning in the police station. I'm scared."

Miles sat up straighter.

"I haven't heard more about my man, but I showed our friend the gryphon. She said she would pass the message on to the people.

"I think the changeling in the hospital knows something is up. He's acting strangely.

"Torin Moray has been sentenced, but Dr. Rooken won't let it go.

"I don't know what to do."

"Wow, that's a lot," Miles said out loud. The timber and clang of his voice after the quiet of my whispering sent a jolt through my body. Adrenaline pumped through my veins.

"Don't worry, sis, we'll get this all figured out."

The door opened behind me. I turned my head to find the rat-faced man staring me down. I swallowed and turned to look back at Miles.

"Come with me please, ma'am," the rat-faced man said. I trailed my fingers on the glass and got one last look at my brother before the man pulled me from the room with his grip tight on my upper arm.

CHAPTER 19
elias

The journal preoccupied my thoughts. It seemed I needed another HSS dose because I couldn't focus on the work at hand. I was continuing the manual scan of the Moray murder files. Torin had told the officers about his usual day: waking, cleaning, eating, leaving the house with the lights off and the locks turned, walking to work, picking up a pre-packaged lunch at the bakery, working, stopping only for lunch, leaving work, unlocking his front door when he got home and locking it again behind him, preparing his body for bed, eating, cleaning, sleeping.

Besides the brain scan of the actual murder, the police had questioned him about his typical day. They had reported nothing unusual.

"Computer, pull up the vid of the interrogation brain scan," I said.

The vid popped onto the screen next to the brain scan images, whirring through their cycle like an old-fashioned GIF. Each image highlighted his brain in colors corresponding to his mood.

In the vid, the man lay in a body-forming, gel chair to

catalogue his vitals and reactions. He had the single wire protruding from his head that I remembered, to record his memories. The officers sat next to him and read his daily routine back to him, checking if he had any discrepancies. They got to the bakery part and I watched his brain scan flash red and then straight back to purple. They didn't seem to catch the blip though so they continued reading.

"Computer, pause, rewind, play from minute marker 5:43 at fifty percent speed."

"Certainly," she said.

I leaned forward to see better. The man's eyes squinted a little, as if in pain, when his brain scan flashed red. The mention of the bakery caused a memory stir.

I noted it down on my tablet and asked the computer to continue at normal speed and to mark any moments where his brain image changed color. A few more times it blipped red: when he checked in at work, when he went to eat lunch with the other men at the factory, on his walk home. But then there was something completely different. The computer didn't even have to tell me. It was so obvious even the officers had noticed. As soon as they read the tiny piece about him walking home, the scan turned a vibrant pink.

The officers stopped what they were doing at the insistence of the doctors monitoring the brain scan. They left the man sitting alone in the room and the vid cut off just before revealing an image from his memories on the other screen of that infernal building.

"Computer, rewind to minute marker 15:21, and zoom on the man's face while playing at fifty percent speed."

I watched it again. His eyes crinkled, and he smiled, but then he grimaced. The officers stopped talking and the brain scan fell back into the purple zone, but the man's eyes still had a bit of a twinkle. He still smiled.

I sat back in my chair, my heart racing more than normal. I lay a hand on my chest and breathed deeply. What was this feeling?

"Are you all right, Elias? Should I call Dr. Rooken?" the computer asked. She must have picked up on my elevated heart levels and the sweat dripping down my forehead.

"I'm fine, thank you. I just need some air."

I left the lab and went to stand on the sidewalk. The sun tried to push through the clouds, but it was simply too weak.

At that moment, when things around me were finally quiet in this courtyard of stone and flowers, a little boy ran up to me with a letter in his hand. He handed it to me and ran away again.

Open only if you're ready. The envelope read.

I wasn't ready. I put the letter in my pocket and went back into the lab to find some HSS.

aloisa

"What do you want with me?" I sat in an uncomfortable chair with my arms crossed over my enormous belly. The rat-faced man paced the room methodically. "And who are you?"

"Did I not introduce myself before?" He pulled his lips back to show his teeth, but it was nothing like a smile. "I'm Officer Spilner. We need to know what information you have. There's no reason to arrest you, as long as you help us out with this investigation. The rebels don't understand how this world works. They think things can be beautiful and right again. That's not the case." He never even looked at me, just watched the floor and the walls as he circled the room.

"How can you even say that? All of the people above you are changelings—"

"EMT patients," he interrupted me and smirked. Typical cop being politically correct when it suited him.

"Whatever. They don't have emotion. How can they decide things for others when they have no empathy?"

"They also have no anger, or fear. They make rational decisions based on what society needs."

"So why haven't you done it?"

He stopped pacing.

"You can't answer that, can you?" I said. I shifted in the chair, wiggling my hips to try to find relief.

He looked me straight in the eye, and I stopped my fidgeting. "Because people like the rebels exist, and we need irrational humans to find and eliminate them so the rest of the EMT patients can continue to live in harmony."

"Harmony! You call murder harmony?" I pushed my ungainly body out of the chair as quickly as possible, but the weight of my stomach pushed me right back down.

"That is still under investigation. Do you know where your husband is?"

His question shocked me. I kept my mouth clamped and crossed my arms again. He continued to drill me with questions about the rebels, which I didn't even know enough to answer. I sat silently, thinking of other things so my face would remain passive for the rest of the interview. They had nothing to hold me on, so when he had finished his tirade, he threw up his arms in frustration and opened the door.

As I walked away I heard him call, "You and your brother better not leave town. You're marked."

I shivered.

They didn't even offer to get me a cab ride home, despite how late at night it was. I took the bus, too infuriated to spend any of their blood money on a cab myself. And when I got home I went downstairs to Mr. Dao's apartment.

He opened the door with a bathrobe on and his hair all mussed.

"Baby come?" He yawned.

"No, Mr. Dao. I have a favor to ask. Can I use your vidphone?"

He nodded and held the door wider. I went through the hallway and into the kitchen where his tablet was plugged in. I called Thelia.

"Hi, I'm sorry that it's so late," I said.

"That's all right. What's going on? You look terrible. Is the baby ok?"

"Everything is fine. I was just accosted by a policeman who has been following me. He asked me about the rebels. I didn't say anything. But I wanted them warned. They're onto me. Maybe we should stop looking for Jordan." I burst into tears. Mr. Dao handed me a cup of steaming tea and then stepped away.

"Aloisa. Listen to me. The police are always looking for the rebels. They're idiots. I need you to meet me tomorrow. At the cafe downtown. Ok? We're going to go shopping, make everything appear normal," Thelia said.

I continued to whimper and nod my head to everything she said. But I couldn't stop crying.

"Pull yourself together! Go get some sleep. I'll see you around ten in the morning."

The screen turned blank. She was gone. I inhaled the smell of sweet green tea and then set the cup, undrunk, on the kitchen table. I mumbled a thank you and went upstairs to bed.

elias

I unlocked the door to my apartment and stepped inside. I turned to lock on the door behind me and switched on the hallway light. Injecting an extra dose of HSS and continuing with my work for the day had made me feel much better. I had written a report on the findings of the brain scan and the doctor's report, giving my own conclusion: that the EMT patient was probably emotionally connected to the people around him. It was nothing new, but it seemed to be the most important fact. I had also finished my reports about the EMT children and their latest academic tests. Then I had proceeded to organize the doctor's desk, and even managed to avoid the journal in its hidden drawer.

For tonight I wanted to finish my routine and get a good night's sleep.

As I took my sweater off to hang it on the hook by the door, I felt a crinkle in the pocket. I reached in and found the envelope.

My stomach sank. Dread overwhelmed me and made the edges of my vision fuzzy and dark. The room tilted; I reached out a hand to steady myself against the door.

I took a deep breath. It was just an envelope. I tucked it under the charging station for my tablet on the hallway table and tried to forget about it. I ate my dinner, cleaned my house, and did some laundry as it was a Tuesday. I pulled back my bed covers, brushed my teeth and washed my face, changed into pajamas, rubbed my sore knees, and settled into the bed. I flicked off the light. But I didn't sleep.

CHAPTER 20
elias

The city was dark but still buzzing with life. I slipped from my apartment door and into the night, the letter tucked safely in my coat pocket. My brain kept telling me to turn back, but my feet continued on their way. The exertion it took to defy my basest requirements made sweat bead on my forehead. But I managed the metal stairway, across the road, onto a bus, through the city of blurring and twinkling lights, and onto the hospital campus. I didn't want to wait anymore. I needed more of Dr. Wolff's diary. He could tell me what to do.

The lab was dimmed, allowing the babies and embryos to sleep. I peeked into the womb and saw the fetuses floating there, suspended in unconsciousness with thumbs in their mouths or eyelids twitching. Dee and Dum were also at rest, plugged into the console to charge overnight. The rest of the hospital continued work throughout day and night, but the EMT Clinic only kept one nurse to monitor the babies overnight.

The computer in my research room was sleeping. She even made a tiny snoring sound to indicate that she was wakeable at any moment. I kept my steps quiet as I closed the door again and made my way to Dr. Rooken's office.

I held my hand against the door so as to make the click of it shutting as soft as possible. There was no one to hear, but my entire body was on edge. It wasn't the sensation of fear, or anxiety, it was purely the thought that what I was doing was wrong. They hadn't killed that in me—the innate need to be good.

I hurried over to the desk and found the diary. I opened to a random page near the end.

"Love is bullshit. Emotion is bullshit. I am a rock. A jerk. I'm an uncaring asshole and proud of it." Chuck Palahniuk

I can't go on with this anymore. They have given me approval. I have tested my first rats. I am about to test my first humans. I've pulled in an excellent team to help me, including one Dr. Tobia Rooken. He's stellar. But I can't go on anymore. I've left my research to him. This is the end.

The rest of the page was blank. In a panic, I flipped through the journal. The remaining pages were blank. Where was the rest? Why had he stopped? I needed to know more. That hadn't helped me at all. I needed his counsel.

I threw the book at the door. It smacked the metal and slid to the floor with the sound of an elephant dragging its foot across concrete. It landed awkwardly with one flap bent, the spine broken. An extra page slipped out from between the cover and the lining paper, which had separated in the fall.

I lunged for it as if the wind would steal it away. It was an envelope, not a page. And inside was a letter.

To anyone reading this,

I have not told my real reasons for creating this technology. It's something that I don't want to share, but I must. You will see the real madness that lies within.

It was a dark and stormy night…

Well, honestly it was just dark.

I was getting into bed after having come home much too late from my research. The children were already in bed; I hadn't said good night. My wife lay sleeping, a glass of brandy on the bedside table. I touched her cheek and she grimaced, swiping at the annoyance.

It was as I lay back and pulled the covers over me that I heard it.

Someone walking up my stairs.

I leapt from the bed, shook my wife, and sprinted for my children. It was all a gut reaction. I didn't even know if there was a threat in the person creaking down my hall. My adrenaline simply kicked in and had me ready to protect my family.

When I reached the hallway, I saw him. The man I had stolen information from. The reason for my Nobel, with a gun leveled at my chest and a smirk on his face.

Remember, this is written exactly how I felt it. With every embellishment having meaning. With every flourish of my words having a reason.

My wife collided with my back, a sharp gasp hissing through her teeth.

"The children," she whispered.

"Go to them," I said.

"Stay, please. I would prefer that," the intruder said. His name was Lundy. He was a classmate of mine. The prize was supposed to be his, until I stole his research and applied it to mine. That

was years ago. Now he had wrinkles lining his face, bushier eyebrows, a bit of a paunch. And a gun.

The reason I recognized this man but the police never apprehended him, was how perfectly he played it off. He had an alibi. With witnesses, over two hundred of them. He left no evidence, the practical scientist that he was.

I paused for a moment. Caught my breath. Leaned against the door. I hadn't expected anything like this.

Lundy stepped closer to us. My wife's motherly instinct must have kicked in, because she ran forward and beyond him into the children's room, leaving us alone.

"We can settle this, Lundy. Between us. No one else has to be involved." I had raised my hands by this point.

"This was settled long ago," he said. "Go back in your bedroom. I'll deal with you in a bit."

I didn't move.

"You and your wife have trouble following directions, don't you? A little too well-off, too full of yourselves. It's time that you learned how to obey. Go. In. Your. Bedroom. Please. I will be back to deal with you in a bit." At this point he strode forward and shoved the gun into my belly. He pushed until I was at my bedroom door and then flicked his head. This time I obeyed. I stepped just across the threshold, just out of his sight.

A few seconds later I heard my wife utter another gasp and my daughter began to cry. I rushed from the room to find my wife on her knees in front of him, the children huddled on one of the beds. He was beginning to unbuckle his pants and was preoccupied, so I lunged forward. I had a grip around his waist, his pants were loose and made it hard for him to maneuver, and his finger, still on the trigger, tightened just enough. I don't even remember the sound of the shot. What I remember is complete and utter silence while my wife fell to the floor with a hole in her chest and blood saturating her nightdress.

I dropped Lundy and went to her. The children were screaming. Lundy and I looked at each other, shock on both of our faces. He turned to the children and yelled for them to shut their mouths. Then he shot them too. Silence surrounded me until I heard the creaking of the stairs and the slamming of the door downstairs.

My wife grew cold in my arms. My children had the mercy of being killed upon impact. I sat in a room of dead people, feeling everything and wanting nothing.

This, my dear reader, is why I wanted to rid people of feeling. Not because of what had happened to me. Of course I hurt, but I deserved it. I wanted to rid people of feeling so they wouldn't be drawn to do the things Lundy did. I had wronged him, and I needed punishment. But my family hadn't deserved that. Lundy hadn't deserved to feel so much pain that his only option was violence. In fact, Lundy was the first person I sent my idea to. He was one of the first on a committee of researchers to approve my testing. Lundy was the cause and the investor all in one.

So I leave you with that.

I sat back, leaning against the door on the floor where I had slid as soon as I heard the gun shot in my mind. I felt raw. I felt.

I took out the letter that sat in my coat pocket. Yet another letter to bring out these hormones that shouldn't be raging through my body. Hormones that Dr. Wolff said we would be much better off without. Yet he never had the surgery performed on himself. Our world leaders were all logical thinkers, people who could reason without the muddling of hormones. But Dr. Wolff, the great inventor of our world's saving grace, hadn't succumbed to his own invention. He wanted to feel. There was no reason for him to not feel the pain of his actions. So why shouldn't I?

With that thought, I sliced my hand open on the envelope. I didn't pay attention to the sting or the bleeding. The letter was short, only a few sentences. There was something else in the envelope, but I didn't pay attention to it. The letter itself held my attention.

> *This is a letter for Elias Higgly. We've received word from our contacts that you are beginning to remember, to feel. This is a rescue mission. We would like to save you from the hell this world has become. If you would like to go back to the person you were, if you are in fact reading this letter at all, please contact us. All you need do is mark this letter with a red X and drop it outside of the EMT Clinic entrance. We will find you. We will save you.*

I doubled over onto my knees, sudden pain gripping my stomach and plummeting my heart rate. I gasped for breath, sucking it in like a fish out of water.

Scrambling to stand again, I searched Dr. Rooken's desk in a frenzy. There had to be a red pen or marker somewhere. Then I remembered, Dee and Dum had a red marker to paint the embryo's glass and mark measurements. I bolted for their room, leaving Dr. Wolff's journal lying on the desk. My feet pounded on the self-cleaning linoleum. My shoes screeched when I whipped around the corner. I grabbed and smacked the walls to keep myself upright. I reached the womb and some of the babies lay awake, staring at me with wide eyes. I ignored them and snatched the red marker, painting a big red

X on the letter. Then I ran. I ran like I had never done before. I began to feel the slightest hint of endorphines entering my system. I felt as though I was flying.

Just outside the automatic door, I placed the letter underneath a rock next to the pathway. Then I stood still, catching my breath and waiting for something to happen. Would they come for me now? I wanted to go. Now.

No one came. For hours I stood, then sat, then lay on the cold concrete. I was isolated; the rest of the hospital didn't cross the courtyard to this building until the day began because EMT patients and babies slept peacefully straight through. The sun began to rise and staff starting walking by me. I went home, called in sick, and fell into my bed without cleaning my teeth or folding the covers back properly.

CHAPTER 21
elias

I had stopped injecting my HSS three days ago, and I was feeling seriously overwhelmed.

A tiny scraping sound by my door brought my head up.

I spotted a piece of paper sticking underneath the door. I jumped up from the couch and scrambled over to get my hand on it before it disappeared, if it disappeared. I slapped my hand down on the corner and pulled it through. Footsteps retreated down the hallway on the other side, but I didn't open the door.

I peeled my hand away from the paper.

My envelope with a big red X marked on it.

I poked a finger inside to feel the contents without actually looking. I touched a piece of thin paper, also a square of thicker paper. One side of the thicker paper felt almost sticky, like a gloss had been applied or a film to make it shiny. I vaguely remembered the feel of printed photographs feeling the same way.

The world around me tilted and shuddered while I stood still. I couldn't take any more. I folded the envelope closed and slipped it into my jacket pocket by the door.

My stomach started to churn. The alarm for my HSS on my tablet went off.

I went to the sofa, curled up on my side, and let the beeping continue; it showered me in shame. If only I had an undo button.

aloisa

I sat on one of the high, rolling stools, my belly protruding grotesquely over my thighs. I had one hand on the embryo tank and one on my belly. Dee and Dum had been sent to another room on an emergency, so they weren't complaining about my body heat messing up the temperature of the womb.

Inside the tank, one of the babies was watching me. She kicked her little foot, pushing against her placenta. I shuddered and then gasped as my own baby mimicked the movement. He wanted his space.

As I looked down at him, the baby in the tank floated closer. Out of the corner of my eye I could see her maneuver her placenta along the womb wall like a starfish suckered to an aquarium tank.

She startled me when she stopped in front of me and pressed her cheek to my hand. I snatched it away and shook it.

It was then that my water broke.

The rush of liquid on the floor set off alarms, and Dee and Dum came running in to assess the situation.

"Oh no," Dee said.

"Not good," Dum said.

"Hi," I said, my hand holding my abdomen.

They found a gurney for me and then wheeled me to the

human maternity ward, where they left me without saying goodbye. I waved at their backs as they walked away and then groaned as a contraction swept over me.

I sat in that room, alone, for what felt like hours. The nurses bustled about me; bees in a hive. It was all a blur around me while I sat and breathed through each contraction. I tried to get someone's attention, get help, but they just buzzed about. I raised a hand weakly, calling out to a nurse as she walked by. She set herself in front of my gurney and put a hand on my shoulder; I sat with my legs dangling over the edge.

"You're in labor," she said. Like she had noticed that my sandwich was made of peanut butter and not turkey. I nodded, gasping for breath. "Why didn't you say something earlier? I didn't even notice you come in."

"I came from the EMT ward," I wheezed between breaths. I had a hand on either side of my hips, propping me up in the most comfortable position I could find. But everything ached.

"Well goodness. Let's get you in a room. Hang tight just another moment." Her hand left my shoulder, and I missed the warmth. Soon she was back and helping me to lie down. She wheeled me into a room and helped me move to a monitoring bed with gel. It was warm and soothed my back and hips. But the instant I was down, I wanted back up. I didn't want to be prone. The nurse was wheeling the gurney from the room when she saw me struggling to sit up. She rushed back.

"Hon, just let the bed know what you want. It'll move for you. Do you want to sit up?"

"Yes." I flailed my arms like a turtle on its back.

"Computer, sit," she said. The bed slowly propped me up in a more comfortable position. "It'll do most anything you want, just talk to it, sweetie. Ok? I'll be back in just a moment to check how far along you are."

She didn't come back for ages. But when she did, my contractions were pretty much nonstop. That was when she got invasive and stuck her hand between my legs. It was a shock, especially after the warm bed.

She snapped a glove from her hand and whistled. "Looks like we need a doc now. Sit tight. I'll be back."

She swept from the room, and as she left I saw a shadow hanging around the corner. It was a very thin shadow with a slouch. It seemed to be peering at me, but I couldn't see beyond the bright lights in my room. Until he stepped forward. Miles.

I cried out and stretched my hands for him. Then he stumbled forward and into my arms. We hugged, touching each other's skin just for the beauty of it, but when another contraction hit I squeezed him until he started groaning and gasping himself. I let him go but snatched for his hand. I was no longer alone.

"When?" I asked.

"Just today. I went to the EMT Clinic to look for you and the creepy robot dudes sent me here. I'm free; everything is fine. I'm healthy, albeit a little underweight." He gestured along his body and how his clothes hung on his frame, loose and sloppy.

"One more hug," I pleaded. He grimaced and gave in. It was a quick one so he could avoid my vice grip. But when I had his hand again and he smiled at me, another wave crashed over me and I squeezed his hand, the bones rubbing together.

I held my baby. The weight of him in my arms kept the pain at bay. I needed him almost more than I needed Jordan. I missed Jordan, so badly.

"You'll meet your daddy one day," I told my son, stroking his soft cheek, feeling the down and skin like a duckling's feathers. "One day. I promise."

Miles came in. He had a bouquet of flowers and a big smile.

"How's my nephew?"

"Wonderful." I tried to sit up but winced.

"Stay down, sis. I'll take him from you."

"No, I'm fine. Set down the flowers and give me a kiss."

I felt his rough, chapped lips crinkle against my forehead. My skin was extra sensitive. I wondered if it was like the heightened smell when I was pregnant. Would I always have heightened senses now that I was a mother?

"The doctor said I can take you home tomorrow. How does that sound?"

"Anything is better than a hospital, right? Doesn't this make you think of Dad? He always smelled of the hospital. I don't know why that's hitting me now and not all these weeks spent with the changelings."

"Don't get all emotional on me, please," Miles sat down on the bed. "I don't want to talk about Dad; you know I don't remember much about him or Mom. It's frustrating to force my brain to work that hard." He squinted, which made me laugh and then wince.

"Are you in a lot of pain? You look it. Maybe I should call the nurse."

"No. It helps."

"Helps?"

"Did I say that out loud?" I asked.

"Yes." He ran the back of his hand along my face. I leaned into it.

"It helps me remember Jordan."

"You won't forget him Aloisa. Not like me with Mom and Dad. I was just a kid."

"But he's already fading. People always say that. That their loved ones are fading. I never understood. But that word is perfect for how I feel. I can get a whiff of a scent that was connected with him and suddenly I remember things, but then the smell is gone and the memories start to fade out like the end of a movie. They don't disappear, just get fuzzy."

"Oh, Aloisa."

"Don't say it like that! Don't pity me." The tears started to fall. I couldn't help it.

"I don't pity you. I worry about you. Come here." He wrapped me in his arms.

He pulled away, and we looked at each other.

"I'm ready to sell the gryphon," I said.

"But—"

"I know; I should keep it. But it's monstrous. Where will I put it?"

He smiled and patted my hand. "Let me take care of that."

CHAPTER 22
elias

I sauntered into the courtyard of the hospital commons. A fountain bubbled in the center; people milled about—EMT and unmodified, alike—as it was nearing lunch time. I made my way to the fountain and peered over the edge at the sparkling water. It blinded me. But soon my eyes adjusted, and I saw my face. Rumpled gray hair, incorrectly-buttoned shirt with a tiny bit of fluff peeking through, wild eyes. It wasn't the Elias I was used to, but then again I rarely saw myself in a reflection. There was no need except to make certain I was presentable, which I obviously hadn't done this morning. Was it morning? I put a hand to my head, thinking to the last time I had slept, to the last time I had taken any HSS. My eyes were drawn to a pair of doctors sitting on the edge of the stone fountain across from me. They had sandwiches in their hands and drinks sitting next to them. Behind them was an EMT on a bench, sipping a carbonated water. All around the courtyard people were chatting and eating and drinking. The fountain itself wasn't a sculpture; it was simply a spray of water that rose six feet or so in the air and fell back down in a lovely half-sphere. My eyes tracked the water from its starting point up toward the sky and back down in a mist to the pool of water below. Sparkles danced on the faces of the doctors across from me; reflections of the sunlight on the water dappling across their cheeks like freckles. A tear gathered at the corner of my eye, and I smiled.

A hand snatched at my arm.

"Elias, when was your last dose of HSS?"

"Just now. I had some before I came over here."

He evaluated me and shook his head.

Dr. Rooken walked out through the automatic doors.

"Dr. Rooken," the EMT said, loud enough to get his attention but not any louder than normal speech. We weren't prone to yelling.

He wandered over to us, a tablet tucked under his arm.

"What can I do for you? Elias, you look horrible." He considered me, from head to foot. The EMT's hand was still clamped over my bicep.

"I believe Elias needs some treatment. He does indeed look unwell. Can you take him inside?" He pushed my arm forward to Dr. Rooken. He didn't let go until Dr. Rooken had slipped an arm around my shoulders.

My feet dragged on the concrete as Dr. Rooken led me inside. I looked back at the beautiful fountain and the people all staring at us as we left. Inside, I began to protest, pushing my feet back against the tile instead of placidly following along.

"No, I want to stay outside. I don't want to be inside. I want the fountain."

Dr. Rooken stared at me in alarm and dropped his tablet as he fought with me for control. I pushed and pulled, trying to reach for the doorway so I could feel the fresh air against my skin. Dr. Rooken was larger, and stronger, so I eventually had to give in to his body. It wasn't until the automatic doors finally slid shut that I heard my screaming echoing back at me against the glass. Dr. Rooken threw a hand over my mouth and dragged me farther inside. His arms around me, like a mother's, calmed me, and I sank to the floor in a heap.

CHAPTER 23
aloisa

"Miles, what are we here for?" I turned from the blinding white stone to his radiant face. He had broken out in the widest smile. "Miles?"

"Just come inside with me."

"Ok." I drew in a deep breath and prepared to walk into a building that I didn't belong in.

The walls were made of a smooth stone that felt cool and soft to the touch. Miles kept pulling my hand away from dragging my fingers along them. The light coming into the lobby splashed across the floors in a bright happy way that made me content to be basking in it.

"What are we doing here?" I asked.

"Relax Aloisa. We're getting an apartment. But they won't sell it to us if you keep acting crazy."

I stopped. My hand resting on the wall. "Excuse me?"

"We're getting an apartment."

"No. No." I turned and sped out of the building. Was he serious? First off, we couldn't afford it. And second, if Jordan ever remembered us and we weren't where we should be he wouldn't come home to me and the baby. My thoughts spun out of control.

Miles came running after me. He grabbed my arm, making me cry out.

"What is your problem, Aloisa? I'm trying to make a better life for us. I finally have the money to do it and you're running away?"

"I need to get back to the baby."

"When will you name that child? Jordan will not come back to name him!" Miles's voice bounced around the court-yard, echoing the words back to me ten times.

I slumped to the ground, Miles's arm still gripping my bicep. "It's Jordan's job to name him. The father names the child. That's how it works." I rested my head against Miles's arm.

"That will not happen," Miles said through his teeth. "Now get up before you make a complete fool of both of us. We're going to look at these apartments and then we're going home to fill out the birth certificate. You will name that child or I will. You will come with me inside to pick out a new place to live. Now!"

"No!" I jumped up and tried to bite Miles's hand. It was the only way he would let go of me; I had had too many child-hood fights with him, I was the weaker of us. My only chance was to play dirty.

"Aloisa! Don't you dare!" Miles dropped my arm with vehe-mence. "Get your act together. Come inside with me." He turned and didn't even look back.

"Miles?" I said. "Miles?" He continued into the lobby.

I sat down on the stone again. Was it time? To give up on Jordan? I slammed my fist into the ground, then cradled it against my chest to ward off the pain. I wouldn't give up on him. But Miles was right. It was time that my baby had a name and a better life—both things that Miles could give us. I stood up, realizing how exhausted I felt, and went inside to apologize to my brother—the last family I had in this world besides my son.

The apartment we viewed didn't have a lot of square footage, but it sure was enormous. One large room with fifteen-foot ceilings and one wall made entirely of glass. A doorway went into a private courtyard where I could grow plants.

"See? The gryphon will go really well in here."

"The gryphon?" I turned to gape at Miles. "What?"

"I said I'd take care of it. We can afford this place. It has two bedrooms back that way and the kitchen is right through there. It's even connected. It's a smart house."

"How?"

"I told you. I went to South America for this."

The housing agent whipped around. "You went where?"

"Does it matter?" Miles asked.

"You could be infected!" He held up his arms like Miles was going to shoot him with a virus-loaded gun.

"It's been a while; I think I'm fine."

"Still." The agent stayed on the other side of the room from then on. I went to the kitchen to find gadgets galore that talked to me when I touched them.

"Manual," I said to the stove.

"Manual mode. Please just ask if you would like help with cooking," the sweet, feminine voice said.

"Miles! Come in here! This is great. The fridge measures what you have and says if you need more. You can set it so that it only requests what you want. Wait! It requests from the store so you can just go and say your name to the grocer and the order is ready. Wow. This is awesome. Miles?"

"Do you forgive me?" He was leaning up against the counter, arms crossed.

"Forgive you?" I mimicked his stance.

"For taking you away from where you knew Jordan."

"It's not really that." I picked at the grout in the self-cleaning counter. The computer scolded me politely.

"Then what is it? Why the breakdown earlier?"

"What if he can't find us?"

"That's what you're worried about?"

"Yes."

"We'll leave ways. I promise."

"That won't work." I sidled closer to him, hoping for a hug.

"Just leave that one to me too. I got you a place for the gryphon, didn't I?" He pulled me into his chest.

"Don't know what I'd do without you," I said into his shirt.

CHAPTER 24
elias

The walk to work the next day took forever. The street extended beyond my field of vision and undulated in the sunshine, weaving this way and that like a wave of grass on a windy hillside. It pulled away from me and then zoomed closer. It made me dizzy. A few times I had to sit down on the ground before continuing.

I hopped on the bus. The effects were worse. The people on the bus looked bug-eyed and silly. Everything was larger than life, falling to pieces one moment and bloating beyond the edges the next. I sat on the bus for one stop. The cars driving by zigzagged in my periphery. The bus bumbled along at a slow pace, bouncing instead of rolling, wiggling within the lane. I got off at the next stop.

The sidewalk turned purple under my feet. Then it rose up to meet me; it kissed me on the cheek. I looked at a man walking next to me and saw that his suit was a shade of puce. His cheeks bulged out and sagged onto his neck.

I shook my head and forced myself to focus only on the sidewalk until I reached the hospital.

I entered the building and kept my hand on the wall the

entire way like a child. I breathed in through my nose and out through my mouth. I focused. It didn't help.

I reached my lab and started my work, doing it all by habit and repetition. Dr. Rooken stopped in to see me. He leaned around the door. I glanced at him and then back at my work.

"Hi Elias. Aloisa had her baby. But I believe she'll be in this morning. If you were wondering why she hasn't been around."

"Ok." I kept my eyes glued to the tablet in front of me. At least the letters weren't dancing around on the screen.

"Is everything all right?"

"Yes."

"Are you sure?" I heard him creep closer, quiet footsteps on the tile floor, the tiniest of squeaks from the rubber on his soles.

"I'm fine. Thank you."

Silence descended. He didn't leave; I could feel his presence behind me. But after a few more minutes of observation he huffed and turned.

"If you need anything, let me know," he called.

"Ok."

When I looked up to the computer screen, it was pulsing like a speaker.

It was an hour later when Aloisa came in. I stared at the vibrating computer screen. I had been for the last hour. It mesmerized me.

"Hi Elias. Just here to grab a few things and see if I can help for an hour or two. Needed to get out of the house. Would you like to meet my baby?" She didn't stop to breathe, nor to wait for my answer. "Miles, bring him in here just a moment. I want you both to meet Elias. The chang—EMT who works for Dr. Rooken."

The room shrank in size. I turned my bulbous head on my

stick-thin neck to find a man standing in the shadow of the doorway, his arms wrapped around something. He stepped into the light. And I began to scream.

aloisa

"Dr. Rooken!" I yelled, running to catch Elias before he fell from the stool. He lay writhing in my arms, screaming at a pitch that caused my son to wail and my eyes to water. Miles backed out of the room to calm the baby. Dr. Rooken bolted in. Elias and I were hidden behind one of the counters, me sobbing and him convulsing. I heard the screech of Dr. Rooken's shoes when he skidded to a halt. His body loomed over us. I looked up, tears coursing down my face, and Elias, whimpering now, in my lap.

"What's wrong with him? What's happened?" I asked.

"I've no idea." He ran his fingers through his hair. "Let me call some nurses. We'll get him moved. Don't move his neck, keep him steady. Did he actually have a seizure?"

"I think so. He's still conscious. Look at his eyes."

Dr. Rooken knelt beside me and touched Elias's cheek. Elias jerked away.

"Can you hear me?" Dr. Rooken said. "Everything is all right. Did you forget your HSS again?"

"Again?" I said.

Dr. Rooken looked at me, worry etched into the wrinkles around his mouth and over his brow.

"Miles!" I called.

"Yeah?" he asked. He had crept back into the room when the baby quieted. He stood inside the door, his eyes wide and dilated.

"Can you go get the nurses please? Get some help. Tell them he had a seizure," I said.

Dr. Rooken continued to search my face. He never opened his mouth, just let me control the situation. I carefully repositioned Elias higher on my lap and looked directly into Dr. Rooken's eyes.

"Is this how it begins?"

Dr. Rooken shook his head.

"This is how Torin Moray began to become human again. This is it."

The air was thick. I felt like I was in a dream, sludging my way through thick, viscous liquid instead of air. Time slowed. My brain slowed with it.

"Who is he?" I asked.

Dr. Rooken looked down. He didn't answer me, just began to check Elias's vitals. Elias now had his eyes closed, a slight frown on his face, and a clammy sweat coating his skin. Dr. Rooken felt his wrist, touched his forehead lightly, and pulled one eye open to check the dilation and color. Elias's eye darted back and forth, not focusing on anything. Dr. Rooken also pulled back Elias's lip and found the gums to be stark white.

"Who is he?" I asked again. But at that point the nurses arrived with the equipment and the room was loud and fast and simple again. They moved Elias and left me to stand in the room with Miles, confused and frustrated.

CHAPTER 25
elias

I woke. The walls around and above me were blinding white. It hurt. Everything hurt. My body was achy, clammy, feverish, cold, hot, everything at once. I blinked a few times.

A vitals monitor reading through the gel bed beeped and hummed and whirred. The bed moved with my body and reformed as I shifted. Sunlight came through the windows. They covered one wall. On the opposite wall was a door leading to a hallway where I saw the corner of a long desk and the scrubs on a nurse's back.

"Sit," I commanded the computer. The bed slowly lifted me. I felt my blood coursing through my body, recognized the coarseness of the blanket on my legs, smelled the antiseptic cleaners.

I reached to the cabinet next to the bed to pull out my belongings. I found my coat, and everything else fell to the floor in a rustling heap. I pulled the envelope from the pocket.

With one deep breath, and a lot of courage, I pulled the still unseen paper from the envelope, the one marked *Only open if you're ready*, and held my eyes closed while my fingers gripped an outdated, paper photograph.

One more breath and I opened my eyes.

There, in front of a set of swings, stood a man and two children. Me. The man was me. Many years younger, but still me. I closed my eyes again for a moment. Breathing in through my nose and out through my mouth, forcing my vision to steady. My legs began to shake. I was so cold, and so hot.

I opened my eyes again. This time determined to look at myself, to see the man I had been. I had a smile on my face. It made my eyes crinkle and my cheeks puff up a bit. My smile didn't turn up at the edges very much, but I showed my teeth and it reached my eyes, making them shine and glow. My hair was a bit longer, a bit more unkempt, but healthy and brown. My cheeks had cherry spots. My shoulders were relaxed and slouched. My arms led down to the shoulders of the children, so I couldn't look at my hands. I followed the line of my clothing—brown vest over a button-down blue shirt on a fit belly and brown slacks—down to my brown shoes. Under my feet were the recycled chips for the playground. Next to my feet were two sets of smaller feet, one in pink shoes the other in tiny shoes that were replicas of mine.

I followed the tiny shoes up to the face of a small boy.

My fist went to my mouth, my heart leapt into my throat. The beeps from the monitor behind me sped up and started becoming a little erratic. A small whimper escaped my mouth.

The boy's eyes were a brilliant green. His chubby cheeks still held baby fat, but I couldn't mistake the line of his forehead and the strength of that nose. The man who had been holding the baby, the man who was Aloisa's brother, he was this boy.

I looked to the girl. My eyes darted directly over to her face. But before I could register anything, I shut my eyes again. It was too much.

"Elias?" I heard the nurse calling my name and slipped the photo under my leg.

"Are you all right?" she asked. I opened my eyes to see her coming in the door. "Your monitor is going crazy. Let's get you checked out. Would you like me to call Dr. Rooken?"

"I'm thirsty," I said, my throat crackling on the words.

She brought me a glass of water, checked my vitals, reset the gel bed to be less lumpy, and pushed me onto my back. I glanced down to the corner of the photo that now peeked out.

"Try to rest," she said. Then she left, and I felt the weight of my eyelids pulling down, forcing me back into unconsciousness.

I woke again to the sound of a voice mumbling. As I climbed up to consciousness, I recognized the voice and made sure to keep my breathing even and my eyes shut.

"This is the opportunity I've been waiting for," Dr. Rooken said. "Dr. Wolff would have killed for this. I wonder what his trigger was. Whatever it was, it was certainly powerful."

I could only assume he was talking about me.

"I'll keep him off HSS for now. Of course without the trigger that would be fatal, but I've finally found my test subject. It never worked before. I was always missing the emotional trigger. That has to be the key. I wondered what had been going wrong with him. I should have guessed. I can't believe I didn't guess."

Footsteps squeaked their way into the room. I opened my eyes.

"Dr. Rooken, should I administer HSS?" the nurse asked. She held a syringe of green liquid, poised to put through my IV.

"No!" he nearly screamed. Like a specter, he flew over to the nurse and ripped the syringe from her hand. It careened through the air and crashed into the cabinets on the far wall.

"Dr. Rooken! What are you doing?"

"I told you, no HSS. Not until we figure out what's going on."

"But...he's obviously just deficient. He didn't have any in his system at all, which means he hasn't had any for a few days at least. Why hasn't he been taking it? And why don't you want him to have it?" She put her hands on her hips and stared him down. "This is unacceptable." She left the room.

"Hello Elias. I'm sorry," he said. He removed the IV from my hand, peeling the tape back carefully and gently. The feel of his cool fingers caressing my skin sent shivers up my back.

"I need you to stay here for a bit while I get all the paper-work in order. Then I'll be taking you to my house. We need to get this sorted without the media noticing. I'm so sorry Elias."

I wrinkled my brow in confusion. "I don't understand."

"Something weird is going on. I can't have mine and Dr. Wolff's reputations tarnished. I need to figure out what's happening to you so I can prevent it in any other patients. I'll need to perform some tests. But not here. Please stay in the bed, and I'll be back in just a few minutes."

He left the room. My heart began to pound. I remembered what I had read in Dr. Wolff's diary. The things he had done to rats to remove their hormones. The things he had done to people's dead bodies to study them. I imagined my body lying splayed open on a table, wide awake and in agony so Dr. Rooken could prevent a worldwide catastrophe.

I wasn't ready to do that.

I jumped up from the bed. The photo fluttered to the ground. It had been stuck under my leg all along. I grabbed my clothes and pulled them on in a hurry. Everything was out of place and crooked, but I peeked out the door and found the hallway empty. I picked up the photo and, gripping it tightly, I bolted for the stairwell.

CHAPTER 26
aloisa

That smile of hers was definitely false. But I didn't really have a choice. So when she tapped me on the shoulder in the middle of a crowd in Chinatown, smiled, and beckoned me with just one finger, I had to follow.

I had the baby wrapped on me, and we wound our way through the people to a dank alley. She handed me an envelope. It was tiny, like a Chinese fortune. By the time I looked up she was gone.

I went straight to Thelia's; I would open it there. I sat outside in the sunshine until she came home. Miles beat her there, and we sat on the stoop in silence. Thelia drove in with her automated vehicle. Without a word, we went inside.

I opened the envelope to find a folded sheet of paper, not a data chip. Thelia set a cup of tea in front of me.

I laid the paper on the counter without unfolding it, my hand resting on top to keep it secret for a while longer.

Miles reached a finger across and tugged the page out from under my grip.

He cleared his throat and shook out the single page before he began.

"We regret to inform you that we can't bring Jordan to you. You must come to us. We have placed navigation coordinates in a random car that will arrive on your doorstep in three days. On the morning of the third day, you must be ready to leave or the car will leave without you. It has room for your child and your brother. He must come with you."

Miles stopped reading and gazed at Thelia. She sat, stirring her tea, draped in a calm thoughtfulness.

"You will find more information here, at the rebel camp," Miles said, continuing. "We have a new contact for you who will be going with you to find your husband. We believe we have Jordan's exact location, but there is a possibility that we are wrong. So understand that we can't guarantee his retrieval. If it isn't him, you will stay here with us while we continue to search. You will be marked. You will never again be able to return home." Miles paused. "Who is this contact?"

"I don't know. Someone important possibly," Thelia said. The sound of her spoon scraping her mug filled the room, going around and around and around.

"That's it," Miles said. He turned the page over and held it under the light. He snatched the envelope and studied it, inside and out. When he ripped it apart, he found the burning man printed inside but nothing else.

"What about that rat-faced dude? Spilner?" I asked.

"What about him?" Miles asked.

"He said if either of us left town we'd be in trouble. We're already marked."

"You heard the letter. You can't come back anyway," Thelia said. The tinking of her spoon finally ceased.

Tension inside me snapped, relaxing and folding in on itself, settling to the bottom of my soul where it rested and breathed with happiness and calm. I was finally on my way to Jordan. My son would meet his father.

I touched the baby's cheek. He slept in the wrap on my front, and when my finger grazed his soft skin he lifted one side of his lips in a grin.

The car was there. I stood at the apartment window, bouncing my son in my arms to quiet him. On the dark street, under the lone street lamp, sat the car with no driver. Miles frantically checked the cabinets and drawers behind me. He threw a few packets of food in a bag along with the baby's auto-bottles. I kissed the side of my son's head, but my eyes never left that car. If it left without us, we would lose Jordan.

"Let's go," Miles said.

I snatched a glance at him and the pile of bags by the door.

"Take everything out. I'll follow. Just leave what I can carry."

"Aloisa. Come with me."

"I'll be right there, I promise." My eyes stayed glued. I heard the door slide open and Miles grunt his way down the hallway before the door slid shut again. The baby started to whimper, even though I bounced and bounced and held him tight. There wasn't much I could do to calm him. He only felt my nerves weaving their way through my body and radiating into the air around me. It was like a tiny cloud of adrenaline, blanketing us both and making him squirm with terror. His little body, held to my chest, wiggled and tried to get some breathing room. But I clenched all the tighter, scared he would slip from my grasp and that the car would disappear.

Miles lugged most of our stuff up to the car and the trunk immediately popped open. It was in that moment, when I knew Miles had his hand on the car, that I bolted for the door. I grabbed the rosebush hiding my gryphon, my satchel full of flower seeds and vegetable seeds and fruit seeds and anything else I thought I might want to grow in the future, and ran as fast as I could in order to make it to the car before Miles could close the door and the car would have a chance to drive away without us.

I made it to the sidewalk, panting and wheezing, the baby screaming at the top of his lungs. He would wake the whole neighborhood this early in the morning. Miles looked around the trunk at me with wide eyes.

"What are you doing to him!"

He rushed around the car and took the baby from me, soothing him with calm murmuring and less intense bouncing.

"Get the carseat set up. Should we feed him before we go?"

"The car might leave!" I screamed. Miles opened his eyes even wider.

"Chill out. Sheesh. It won't leave without us now. Plus it's not due to leave for another half hour. I think we're fine. Just get the carseat set up. We'll put him in and you can feed him while we're moving. Maybe he'll sleep again. When are you ever going to name this child?"

"When his father can name him."

I pulled at the door handle but it slipped from my fingers. I grabbed again and smacked it back. Nothing happened. Miles walked slowly to the side and touched a button, his movements like those of a swimmer, smooth and graceful. I, on the other hand, felt like a floundering fish flopping on dry ground. The door slid open at his touch.

I threw the carseat in and began the process of attaching the buckles. Not that it really worked very well, until I slowed my hands and started asking the car to help me. When I finally had the seat set up, I popped my head back out and saw Miles pacing with the baby. He had put the rest of our things in the trunk and left out a few essential bags on the sidewalk. I reached as far as I could without leaving the seat and pulled the bags inside. I stacked them around the rosebush to keep it upright on the floor in front of me.

My gaze was drawn to our apartment window, still lit, the magnificent gryphon in plain view. I had forgotten to run my hands over it one last time. I had forgotten to look closely at the intricate woodwork one last time. Soon I would see Jordan and that wouldn't matter. Soon he could carve me a new gryphon.

I waved Miles over and frantically whipped my hands about to signal that I wanted my child. Miles ignored me. He walked around the other side and touched the door. It slid open, and he sat down with the baby in his arms. He put my child in his carseat and then closed his door. He faced forward. My child was already asleep.

"Close your door," he said.

I looked at him, back at the open door, at him, through the door to the gryphon inside the apartment, and back at Miles.

"It's ok, just touch the pad. We need to get going." Miles continued to look straight ahead.

I took a deep breath and touched the pad without one more glance at the building. It didn't even feel like home yet, and we were leaving.

CHAPTER 27
aloisa

The car played soothing music and dimmed the windows, lulling us all to sleep. I didn't wake until we were in a desert. Beautiful yellows and browns and reds and golds shimmered all around us. I had leaned against the window as I slept and opened my eyes to see the bright orb of the sun surrounded by a halo of whites and yellows. The cool glass my forehead rested on soothed my hot skin. The rest of my body screamed to get out of the vehicle, to run, but I held myself still and took in the scenery. The scrub brush and tiny cacti that dotted the land took on patterns, showing me pathways through the danger.

I sat up slowly to check on the baby. My brother slept across from him; mouth open, drool draining onto his chest. I hadn't seen him so relaxed since before South America.

The baby was awake. He sat quietly, searching me with his bold eyes. I could see a lot of Miles in his face. I could also see a lot of Jordan. I touched his cheek with one finger, and he startled.

"Shhh. Don't wake Uncle Miles."

In the bag in front of my feet I found an auto-bottle. I pushed the button on the top and it mixed the water and formula, started the heating element, and shook it all together. I popped the top off the nipple when the green light lit up and held it out for my son. He suckled the bottle contentedly. His tiny grunts of happiness helped to lower my body temperature and calm me.

I looked outside again. To the sound of my brother's snores and my baby's feeding, I watched the desert fly past, blurring against my window and turning a dull shade of pink.

The vehicle pulled off to a rest stop. The motion of turning and slowing woke both the baby and Miles. The baby began to cry, my brother wiped the drool from his chin. Before we could get comfortable with the slow motion, the car jerked to a stop and opened the doors. I fumbled with the buttons for the carseat buckles and extracted my screaming child. Miles hopped out on the other side as the car started to creep forward again toward an automated battery changing station. It disappeared behind a sliding door, and we looked around.

"Any idea where we are?" Miles asked, his hands running through his mussed hair.

"How should I know? The car didn't speak to me."

He snapped his gaze to me, glaring holes into my skin.

"Did you see a sign?"

"No," I replied, grumbling.

"Let's see if there's food."

A group of children played on a dilapidated swing set while their parents watched from the benches under cover. The sun bore down on us and the desert glimmered with heat. On the far side of the families was a building. Miles headed straight for it.

I followed, hesitant and frightened of what would be inside. Was I to expect a clean bathroom with robots and a cheerful diner? Or was it a dark and dank place filled with bacteria and unfriendly people asking to bum cigarettes?

Miles fell under the shadow of the building and slipped in through the sliding door. Graffiti circled the entrance; paint that glittered and changed shape depending on where you stood. One switched between saying whore and slut. A tiny one in the far corner was the burning man. Another displayed a man's name and then showed a little stick figure hanging from a branch. I clutched the baby closer and continued after Miles.

Inside was a pleasant surprise. It wasn't a diner, but it had food and was vaguely clean. The smell of meat pies and sizzling butter permeated the room, making my stomach rumble. Miles was already at a table, looking over a digital menu in the tabletop.

"What if the car leaves?" I asked.

"Stop fretting, seriously. The car won't leave. It's locked onto us now. The only time it would have left us behind was back in the city, if we hadn't shown up, if we had been late. Now we're good until it reaches its destination. As soon as its battery is charged and it's been cleaned, it will wait outside for us for days if we want it to."

"Are you sure?"

He didn't bother to look up.

"I'm just scared, ok?"

"Why?" Miles's voice turned gentle, flowing over me and around my arms to make them loosen from around the baby. I set him next to me in the booth with one arm draped over to prevent his rolling off. I looked down at the menu dancing on the table.

"I've never been away from Denver. Jordan has never been away from home. Now our child is taking his first trip before he can even roll over. I don't know where we are or where we're going. If I get left behind I'll be lost and have no idea what to do about it."

Miles put his hand over mine. He touched the tablescreen with his other hand and pulled up a map of the United States. He punched in some commands. Soon the map zoomed in on Denver.

"This is where we started. Now I'm going to punch in the route we are taking, at least as far as I know it goes. But I need my other hand back. Is that ok?"

I nodded.

He started typing away into the controls. I watched the map grow, expand, and give way so the route could be calculated. A small red line drew itself from Denver to the west and squiggled around until it reached somewhere in the north. Then everything stopped.

"Can I get you somethin' to eat?" a voice over Miles's shoulder said. He touched a black button and the map went blank. He smiled up at our waitress.

"Sure. I'm starving. What's good here?"

Her eyes left the blank table and went to his. "The pasty."

"I'll have that then," Miles said.

"And you sweetheart?"

"The shepherd's pie please," I said. The baby squawked.

She leaned over me to get a glimpse of him tucked in the corner.

"Oh, what a sweetie. I didn't even see him there! Are you new parents? How old is he? What a cutie."

"Just over a month." I turned back to Miles and waited for the waitress to leave. She looked from Miles to me and back again before leaving.

Miles touched the black button and the screen came to life again. Our route recalculated and the little line drew itself over again. I watched it carefully, following every twist and curve, memorizing it as much as possible.

"This is where we are," Miles said and pointed to a spot on the other side of the Rockies in the middle of Nevada. "We're headed pretty far north, so I'm surprised we came this way. But Thelia told me the route wouldn't be straight. If anyone followed us, like your little copper friend, we want to confuse the hell out of him. Make him think we're on a road trip or something."

"We're in Nevada," I said.

"Yep. And Aloisa?" He waited until I looked up at him to continue. "I won't leave you."

I nodded.

After our greasy and heavy meal, we headed back outside into the too-bright sunshine to find the car. It was sparkly clean and sitting in a spot not far from us.

"See, I told you," Miles said. He had the baby in his arms, and he slunk into the back seat of the car, disappearing from my sight yet again. I rushed around the other side and got in. I was panting.

"Aloisa, please calm down." He buckled the baby in the seat and then reached across to touch my hand. "Now comes the long trek of going in circles. We'll get there, eventually. We'll find Jordan. And then we'll settle down somewhere that has a lake and lots of trees. Somewhere for you to grow things. Does that sound good?"

I nodded.

Miles shook his head and laughed at me. The car started up and continued on its navigated journey. I watched outside the window as we passed from desert to lake region, through cities and little towns, between towering trees and menacing mountains. My heart followed the trail of scenery, jumping from complete exhaustion and burned to a crisp to calm and cool and collected. Then feeling overwhelmed, tiny, and completely irrelevant to this world. But no matter what, I still had my child. He distracted me throughout the trip, making it less possible for me to sink into oblivion. He held me to reality with his cries and his needs.

The car only stopped when necessary. It made sure to tell us when there would be a longer stint, so we could gather supplies and be more prepared. Throughout the ride, Miles would lean forward and check the navigation screen, charting our course along with the car to make sure of exactly where we were going. He would sit back for a few minutes to chew his nails while I fumbled with the baby, changing his diaper with the seatbelt still on, then he would lean forward again to check the screen.

"Miles."

"Yeah?" His knee jiggled.

"Can you relax please? You're stressing me out."

He twisted around to glare at me.

"Excuse me?"

"Yes, you." I had one hand on the loose diaper over my son's crotch and the other holding a dirty wipe, but I still pointed my finger at him. I chose the wrong hand.

The diaper slipped loose, my son started to pee, and Miles got the brunt of it.

"Ew! Make him stop!" Miles swatted at the liquid as if it were a fly. It splashed him in the face and ran down to soak his t-shirt. I started giggling maniacally. I couldn't stop, and I couldn't move to put the diaper back. He just let it all out and then smiled at the both of us, me doubled over in the seat in a fit of laughter and Miles with his arms crossed and piss running down his cheeks like tears. The baby gurgled and waved his legs and arms. Miles turned his dirty look on the child and a moment later the baby burst into tears, well, more like wails.

"Good job," I said.

"Pull over," Miles said to the computer. The car swerved sharply to the right and onto the shoulder. Miles jumped out and started walking away through the forest. The shadows danced among the pines, and Miles blipped in and out of vision.

I cleaned up the baby and then took him out of the seat. I set up a blanket under one of the trees and left the car doors open to keep it from driving off without us—every door.

The baby kicked his legs and waved his arms, happy to have space to move. I munched on some vegetables and waited for either the sun to set or Miles to show up. When the latter didn't happen, and it got dark, I moved back into the car, which had automatically reclined our seats to create beds. Little pillows and blankets popped out of the extra compartments behind the seats. I still left all the doors open, wondering if the baby would be too cold but too worried that Miles wouldn't get back in the car before it left.

"Computer, would you leave without all passengers?"

"I am programmed to carry two adults and a baby. I can only leave my planned and unplanned stops with two adults and one baby."

"How do you know we're in the car?"

"Your heartbeats and your weight."

The car turned on a lullaby for my baby to listen to. He yawned.

I lay with my arms behind my head and a view through the window above. It had tinted so dark in the desert I had thought it was just a normal roof, but it was simply for protection against the sun. Now I had a beautiful scene of twinkling stars, which I had never seen in the city that was my home, and trees towering above us on both sides.

I started to drift off and then heard Miles settle into the other seat. The doors slid shut, and I rolled over to check on him.

It wasn't Miles I saw; it was another man. A man I didn't recognize.

"Hello," he said.

I bolted upright. My hands went to cover my baby.

"Don't worry. I'm only here to lead you on. Miles will meet you at the rendezvous point." His dirty hand covered mine over the clean, blue blanket covering my baby. I slapped his hand away. My breathing increased, as well as my heart rate. The car started to move. I faced forward to stare my fate down.

CHAPTER 28
elias

I hadn't stayed in one place for more than a night. My body continued to deteriorate. I had a raging fever and chills, no clean clothes, and a pounding headache that wouldn't vacate. I was huddled around the corner from my last place of residence—a hotel-turned-shelter full of grungy men and tote-bearing women. They had offered me a complete-nutrition bar for breakfast and then promptly kicked me out in preparation to sanitize the place. The bar was already gone, but my hunger wasn't.

I gave up on this shelter and started for another I had heard rumors about. It was down near the rail yards, in the area where the Moray murder had occurred. I had avoided it until this, my most desperate moment, for fear of the area and the memories. But now I had no other choice, unless I wanted to revisit somewhere I had already been. I saw that as worse. Backtracking. I would be traceable through the retinal scans. I had to keep my patterns unrecognizable.

So I made my way through the streets, avoiding large thoroughfares and any major shopping areas. It took much longer that way, and I got turned around a few times before I reached the shelter. It was a large red-brick building. The strange oak door, fortified with iron, jogged my memory. Suddenly I had visions of the man in the alley with the strange questions and the address on a card he had slipped into my pocket, the woman in the hospital with another address card, the brain scans—everything flooded in.

A woman on the steps accosted me, groping at my pockets for any treasure I might be hiding. I finally fought my way out of her grip and into the building. They weren't sanitizing today, so luckily I wasn't immediately doused in chemicals. Someone had heard me come in and came to find me in the front entrance, shivering and chattering.

"Come on in. We're playing games. Would you like an extra coat?"

I dropped to the floor in exhaustion.

I woke up hours later to find myself warm, in a bed, with a glass of water and a bowl full of creamy soup next to my bed. When I touched the bowl it began to whir and hum, coming to life and heating my soup. I downed the water, grateful for something wet on my cottony tongue. That was when I noticed the person in my room. He sat by the door, watching.

"Hello," he said.

I fell back into the corner of the bed, against the wall. The water glass went flying and crashed to the floor.

"No need to worry. I'm simply here to make sure we don't need to call a doctor for you. I can leave if you wish. You can call one of us just by talking to the room. The computer is new, but she's gentle and smart."

"Thank you," the room said.

I stared up at the ceiling. A few days without the constant presence of a computer and I was jittery. I started shivering again.

"We will not reveal your identity, if that is what you wish.

In fact, the computer holds it secret until you give a retinal scan and voice confirmation to release it to the keepers. We're only here to help until you see fit to leave."

He stood and left the room. My bowl stopped making noise, and I reached gingerly for it, gulping down the entire thing.

"I can have more sent in," the computer said.

My eyes roved the walls, looking for the source.

I set the bowl down and looked at my hand as I moved the blanket from my body and saw clean, white skin. Under the blanket I saw new clothes, much thicker and softer than the ones I had been wearing. I jumped up to test the door and found it unlocked. I closed it again.

But even the unlocked door didn't make me feel safe. I swung the door open and took off down the hallway. It was a maze, a veritable labyrinth filled with twists and turns and doors that all looked alike.

"I can guide you with a lighted path to the exit if you wish to leave. Or I can send you to the common room where there is more food. We don't want to hurt you," the computer said.

That phrase. It only made me feel as if that was exactly what they wanted to do. I became dizzy. I realized I was running in circles. I had passed the same computer panel with the number, two hundred twenty-three, several times. I was lost and would need the computer's help to get out. But I didn't trust her. I sank down to the floor, overwhelmed and tired and cold.

I slammed a fist at the wall behind me. It broke through. *Testosterone.* The word came to my mind unbidden, like a ghost on a stormy night. My breathing increased. *Adrenaline.* Another word, floating before my eyes. That was when the tears came to relieve my stress. And through the blur and pain I saw the word. *Endorphines.*

"The green lights will lead you to the exit."

A strip along the wall lit up green and led me around the next bend.

I jumped to my feet and stumbled along the path.

At the door, after what felt like hundreds of hallways, stood the man from my room, with a coat hanging from his hands. He smiled.

"If you get outside and want to come back in, that's perfectly all right. The retinal scans in this area did not detect you yet. We've checked. It's safe, even from Dr. Rooken."

That was the final straw. I didn't take the coat; I just ran. Through the doors and into the bright sunlight where I shielded my eyes from the sun and the retinal scanners. I wended my way through the alleys and beyond the trains and containers until I found a corner behind some crates and collapsed in a heap.

CHAPTER 29
elias

I slept. A fitful sleep. But sleep nonetheless. My body woke hungry, craving bread in a way I didn't remember ever having before. I could imagine the fluffy softness of a fresh roll. The crunch of the outside rang in my ears and crumbled on my taste buds. Then I thought back to the computer in the shelter. The voice she had. It was familiar. Only now that I was calm and felt safe far away from that place did I know that I had heard that voice before.

And the man. I knew his face. I couldn't place him, but he was too familiar for me to let it go. I had to go back. I had to know how they knew. And I was far too hungry to let such an opportunity pass me up.

I made my way back to the shelter, backtracking a few times as I had gotten myself thoroughly lost, but holding my head up and not trudging through the streets like a forlorn puppy. I did, however, cover my eyes from every retinal scanner I saw. I still needed to stay hidden, even if I had been found.

I hadn't noticed before, but the shelter was clean. Standing among the brown and dingy shacks it stuck out and acted as a beacon. Was that their intent?

The moment my foot hit the first step, the door opened and the man came out. He beckoned me inside, looking around with wide eyes. I stumbled up the steps and through the door. He pulled me into the next room where other people sat around tables chatting. He sat me at one of the tables and left. The other people quieted. They continued conversing, but I felt their ears tuned into me, their brains ready for anything new to happen; the air hummed with intrigue.

"Want to play?" the man at my table asked. He was obviously homeless, with blackened teeth and a scruffy beard. One eye was half-closed for having been swollen and gooey. But his clothes were clean and thick like mine, his skin just as clear of dirt, though it was a deep mahogany red.

"Is just a game ya know."

I shook my head and turned in my chair to face the direction the man had gone when he left the room.

"They want ya to play," he said behind me. It was almost a whisper.

"What do you mean?" I asked.

"They are watchin' ya."

I whipped around to see him point at the strips along the wall and the ceiling. He was crazy. They had stuck me at a crazy person's table. But then the woman next to him spoke up.

"He's right." She was intent upon her game tiles, her hair a curtain around her face, and blocking my view of her features, a mixture of gray tones, beautiful and disconcerting. "It's better if you play with us."

I grabbed tiles from the pile and started to lay them out in an order that made logical sense. It was a game I had never played before, full of shapes and colors and patterns, but I pretended to play along all the while keeping my eyes on the door and the walls.

"Please come to the office," the computer's voice rang out in the room.

All heads shot up and looked around to me.

"She means you," the woman said. Now I saw her face, her penetrating hazel eyes. Eyes I recognized.

"Saeri," I said.

"Yep," she said. And that was the moment it all fell into place. The man who had brought me inside was her husband, Rane, the changeling who had married and had a child.

My body began to tremble, and I wanted to bolt, to scream, to tear my skin from my bones. But I sat still. I waited for my fate the way any frightened mouse would crouch before a cat. My muscles screamed to be let free, to move, but I couldn't. They were frozen in place.

So instead of me going to the office, they came to get me. An entourage of people trooped in and pulled me from the table. They took me through the door, and I looked back at Saeri as she pulled the wig from her head and shook out her blonde hair. She smiled with white teeth at the man at her table, and he looked back down at the game, startled. I saw his hands shaking and wondered where I was being taken, what they would do to me, and if I would survive this day.

They took me to a plain room. They sat me in a chair and gave me some more food. I took it, though I knew it was probably poisoned or at least drugged. But I couldn't help myself. They had lain bread before me. Fresh bread with a crunchy crust and fluffy interior. Exactly what my body wanted. Something I hadn't craved since my memories had been changed, removed. I took a bite and felt a flood of emotion come with the memory of freshly baked bread.

"It's good, isn't it? It's what everyone craves when they first waken. Bread. I'm not sure why. Probably a comfort food we all grew up on, essential to everything we are. Or maybe it's just that good that our bodies remember it. I'm not sure."

Rane was talking to me. Everyone else had left the room. I stood from the chair slowly and walked to the door, testing Rane like a little child. I touched the door handle; Rane didn't do anything. I took a step closer; he sat still. I turned the knob and found it unlocked; Rane turned away from me to face the opposite wall. I peered outside and found no one, so I came back and sat down.

"You aren't a prisoner here. We only want to help."

"Saying that is what makes me most frightened of you!"

"There's no other way to reassure you. Except maybe by familiar faces, which is why we tried to bring you here. It took you a while, but we've been pushing you this direction all along."

"There's no way. I heard about this place from someone else."

"Yes. The man in the alleyway. And other people around you, mentioning it casually, so it stuck in your mind only as a whisper. But it got you here in the end, didn't it? What did Dr. Rooken do to you? Why are you running? We had hoped you would come willingly instead of in confusion. You received the letter and read it. The picture too." He said those all as statements.

"We've been keeping watch a lot longer than you expect, Elias."

I shot out of the chair.

"Did you recognize your computer from the EMT Clinic? She's been helping us. We know Dr. Rooken doesn't yet know where you are."

"Aloisa," I whispered.

"Yes. The reason you're here. The real reason we've brought you in. Your trigger. Your daughter."

I stepped back to the wall, felt its cool paint with my hands, and slid to the floor. There I bent my knees and covered my ears with my arms.

"We need to speak about her. You need to help her. Her and her brother, your son, Miles. He was the one who really sent you reeling, but it was Aloisa who started the chain reaction. It's something all the EMT patients will find with time. Some kind of trigger that brings them back to who they are. We know that now.

"We can't stay aliens for long, Elias. We're all human deep down, and those hormones are part of us. If we can change all the changelings back, then maybe we can prevent the breeding of actual aliens. Those children in that lab, they aren't human in any way. We have a super race on our hands, and it's dangerous. We need your help." Rane leaned forward in his chair, pleading with me.

"You're different," I said.

"Slightly. I was already changing when I first met you. My transformation is complete now. I am who I was before."

Thoughts of a baby who didn't cry came to the forefront of my mind. A baby who wouldn't grow.

"Your daughter..."

"Yes. She's an experiment. Hopefully with her help we can save those children in the EMT Clinic. We can regain control of this rolling rock and reverse the effects. You're the best connection we've found. But we need to know what happened with Dr. Rooken, and then we need to send you on your way to find Aloisa and Miles."

"The diary," I mumbled into my knees.

"What diary?"

"Dr. Wolff's diary. It has a ton of information. Dr. Rooken

wanted to study me. He said he needed to find out why the transformation was happening so he could prevent it. He thinks the emotional trigger is the key. He said his reputation was on the line. He was going to dissect me, alive."

"No wonder you ran. Where is the diary?"

"I...I don't remember."

"Could you find it for us?"

"No. He'll catch me." I started to tremble again.

"Ok." I felt Rane's hand on my shoulder. I shrugged it off. "You don't have to go find it. But can you tell us where it might be?"

"Dr. Rooken might have it. There's a secret drawer in the desk. A button to push on the top. But I left the diary lying out last time I read it."

"The desk in his office?"

"Yes."

"Will the computer know?"

"Yes. She should."

"I need your credentials to unlock that information. You interrupted us before we could get full access, that day in the hospital." He snorted. "Can you speak with her before you go?"

"Go where?" I looked up at him, tears covering my cheeks.

"To meet Aloisa and Miles. To help them find Jordan. You know better than anyone where he is. And Aloisa wants to find him. Once she has him, he'll be triggered like you were and we can help him recover. He won't ever get his full memories back—neither will you—but we can help you both get your lives back."

Rane left the room. I knew someone must be watching, but I didn't know from where.

"Hello computer," I said.

"Hello, Elias."

"They want to know where the diary is."

"They want a lot more than that. They want all of the files. Everything from the Moray murder research to Dee and Dum's files on the babies. They want to experiment on the babies."

I shook my head.

"Don't give them that information, only the diary."

"You just did."

I walked out of the room to find Rane waiting for me. He followed me down the hall and then took the lead to bring me to a door where I stepped out and into an automated car.

The car took me to a train station and gave me a small tablet with a train ticket already loaded. I stepped out of the car and looked directly at the retinal scanner above the train station. Dr. Rooken would be alerted, but I would be gone.

I boarded my train and sat by the window. I watched the mountains grow and shrink, the desert whip past, and gigantic trees spread their arms across the sky. The trip was short, only five or six hours. I arrived at an empty train station. My tablet informed me it was time to get off; this was my stop.

The station looked abandoned. I watched the train leave, disappearing over the horizon in a blur. I looked at the tablet again for confirmation and saw a face on the screen.

"Hello," I said.

"Start walking. Don't stop until the tablet tells you. Just keep walking."

"I'm very thirsty."

"There's food and water in the shed next to the tracks. Just walk."

The face vanished, and I started walking.

CHAPTER 30
aloisa

"You see," the man said in his greasy voice. "You are very close to your destination, but at that destination you are to meet another car, one that doesn't have a computer, and you'll drive that even farther into the wilderness. We can't have anyone following you."

"Where's Miles?" I asked.

"He will meet you there. Stupid man that he was, he happened upon a random retinal scanner in the woods at a forest ranger's cabin that was at the moment empty but up and running so the government could see any trespassers. We got him out of there, just barely before a helicopter arrived."

My heart nearly stopped.

"I'll get you there safely. Don't worry."

"I am," I said.

The baby started to cry. I prepared a bottle and shoved it in his mouth. There was no gentleness left. I was raw emotion now, exposed to the elements without my skin to protect me. My brother had left me; he had promised not to leave me but he had. And now I was lost.

Ten minutes later we reached a crossroads. The car doors

opened. I pulled the baby from his seat and extricated the seat from the car while the man moved our bags out of the car and into a stand of bushes by the side of the road. It wasn't until I followed him back, carrying the rosebush hiding the gryphon and my satchel, that I noticed the bushes were covering an older car.

"Does it have gas?" I asked.

"Of course. But I'll drive."

I got in the back seat with the baby and tried to shut my eyes. The moon was so bright it penetrated my closed lids like daylight, but I had been through too much to be kept awake by a little light. So I soon drifted off with my finger in my baby's mouth to soothe him and my other hand covering my heart.

When I woke it was because the car had jolted to a stop.

"We're at the rendezvous point. You'll be walking from here. We have a robotic assistant to take your belongings. This is where I leave you," the man said.

I looked across the wilderness before me, covered in tiny plants that were a frosty green or bright berry red.

"I'm going alone?"

"With the baby, of course."

"But alone."

"Yes."

I stepped out of the vehicle and resolved myself to the situation. I wrapped the baby to my chest while the man loaded my things onto the cart. He secured my rosebush on top. I followed the cart that bumbled along a predestined path toward my final destination. Well, my next destination. Jordan was my final destination, and I hadn't reached him yet. I only hoped Miles would be at the other end of this vast valley to greet me with a laugh and a hug so I could punch him square on the chin.

As I walked along, a slight bounce in my step to keep the baby sleeping, I thought about everything up until this moment. Six months ago I wouldn't have dreamed this would be happening. Jordan was still in my bed. The most I was worried about was making the rent and his mother coming to visit. Life had been easy.

Out in the distance a shadow gradually shortened. I stopped, but the robot continued on. Could it be a bear? Or some other creature that I had no idea how to handle? Was I about to die?

I crept forward much slower than before. The baby started to whimper, and I shushed him. Instead of calming, he started wailing. The figure in the distance stopped. It had two legs and two arms. The robot continued on its path, heeding neither the figure nor my halt. I ran to catch up, deciding that if the figure stopped when it heard my baby then it must be intelligent, and either I could chase it away or it would be human. I crossed my fingers and held my breath, a difficult task while running.

The air burst from my lungs, and I had to stop to breathe. I was not fit yet, having only given birth mere weeks ago. When I looked up again, the figure had come closer. It was a man, and he stood only two hundred feet from me. He continued straight on, passing the robot and heading for me.

The sun setting before me shone in my eyes. The silhouette approached, and I heard him gasp. He was a few paces away when he said my name.

"Miles?" I asked. My hand up to shield my eyes.

"No." He stepped closer, using his body to shield me from the light and bringing his face into focus.

"Elias!"

"What are you doing here?"

"I'm walking," I said. Nothing else came to mind. Only that I was out for a stroll. It sounded absurd.

"Me too," he said.

He looked down at a tablet in his hand and then back up at me.

"What is it?" I asked.

"I'm supposed to stop here," he said.

"I'm supposed to follow the robot. The one that's disappearing over that hill and leaving me behind!" The outline of my rosebush bumbled along and down until it was out of view.

I bolted after it, too afraid to be left behind again. Elias came after me, though he was screaming at me to stop. I finally did.

"What?" I asked. "I'm in a bit of a hurry."

"I get that." He looked again at the tablet. "Oh wait. It says I'm supposed to follow the robot too. Let's go!"

We ran to catch up to the robot. When we did, Elias turned to me and smiled, a grin so broad I thought it would split his cheeks. I startled.

"What?" he asked.

"You smiled."

"Yes. I've changed. And I'm supposed to help you find Jordan."

He opened his mouth to say more but didn't. So I left it alone and trucked after the robot. It had gone into the forest ahead of us, and I didn't want to lose it in the trees. But as soon as we passed under the canopy, we were surrounded by men in leather outfits with bows and arrows and masks of woodland creatures covering their faces. Miles stepped out from behind a tree and swept me and the baby into a grand hug. But that hug turned cold as soon as he saw who was behind me.

"What is he doing here?"

"I have no idea," I said. "Who are they?"

We continued our embrace and our conversation until

one of the men stepped up and touched me. I jumped. He removed his mask.

"Nothing to worry about. You've arrived. We're here to take you in. Then we'll begin our search for Jordan."

"Begin? You haven't found him!" I screeched.

"The man who can find him is just behind you," he said. I turned to look at Elias. He was pale and shivering so I went to him and put a hand on his shoulder.

"It's ok, Elias. Come with us." He followed Miles and I as we trailed the men into the darkening forest.

"Miles, what happened to you?" I had my hand on his arm as we picked our way through the roots and branches.

"They didn't tell you? How did the car keep going anyways? Oh, duh, they sent someone in my place."

I pulled him to a stop so I could stare him down. Kept my face as blank as possible. The baby gurgled and reached for Miles's hand. Miles unstrapped him and carried him for me. I hadn't noticed the weight until it was gone. I sighed without even meaning to.

"I shouldn't have run off. Can you forgive me?"

"You abandoned me."

We trudged on, the snapping of branches echoing the beating of my heart. The adrenaline that had started the moment the strange man entered the car hadn't stopped flowing since. I was going to have a major crash whenever we found a semblance of safety, and the thought of that only made me reel violently. Miles reached out to steady me. I shoved his hand away.

"It's not ok. But maybe someday soon it'll be ok. For now, it's not ok and you better not leave my side. I'm going to glue this hand to your skin so you can't leave me even in my sleep," I said.

Miles chuckled and so did Elias. We both gaped at him.

"What?" He shrugged.

"Does this path end anytime soon?" Miles called up to the men in leather suits.

"A few more miles."

"Miles!" I squeaked.

"Can we pause for a minute? Aloisa needs water, and I think the baby needs to be changed," Miles said. He stopped, without waiting for an answer, and started pulling the baby's things from the bag on my back. He handed me a water bottle and changed the baby.

"So what really happened?" I asked after a long pull on the water.

"Didn't they tell you? I stumbled on some hunter's cabin or something but it had retinal scanners. Literally stepped from tree cover into the bright flash of red when it scanned me."

"He said it was a ranger's cabin, so the government saw you."

"So they did tell you." Miles held the new diaper firmly over my son's crotch. I wiped my mouth to stop from giggling.

"Sort of. But what really happened? I was so frightened; you have no idea."

"*You* were frightened! How about me? I walk into this clearing, see a cabin and a bright red light, and I took off running. A man in black clothing showed up out of nowhere and tackled me. I cried out for you, but he gagged me. I have no idea how I got here. I think he knocked me out. I was tied up at the edge of the forest until you showed up. I knew they were tracking the car, but I hadn't realized quite how closely."

"Then how do we know to trust these people?" I said from the side of my mouth.

"What else can we do? They have the insignia."

"What insignia?"

Miles gestured to the men standing around us in a half circle. One turned around and pointed at his back. Burned into the leather was the image I had seen everywhere. The one that hid on all the documentation I had received, and on every piece of paper Thelia had ever handed me. A man wreathed in flames.

"Oh," I said.

The man turned back around and smiled at me. It was warmth incarnate. It felt genuine.

"And how are you here?" Miles asked Elias.

"Um. Well…"

"We'll get that figured out when we get to the camp," the leader said. "Let's get moving. We don't want to be out after dark." They started through the pine branches again, pushing through one by one into the shadows until I could only hear them.

"What does he mean 'we don't want to be out after dark'?" My voice rose in pitch. "Are there animals out here? Are we not safe?" I snatched my baby from Miles and held him close.

"I don't know, and I don't want to find out. Come on." Miles took my hand and led me after the men. Elias came after.

elias

My children. I watched them banter and play. I saw that they were frightened and completely lost but that they had each other so it was ok. I must have done something right in leaving them. I wondered where their mother was.

As we walked through the forest I watched the light descend behind the mountains and sprinkle through the trees to dance on my children's faces. And my grandson. Aloisa held him close, cuddling his tiny body which I now ached to hold. This was another new feeling, but a good one. It was one I could get used to, wanting to hold someone, wanting to be held.

I looked at my daughter, how straight her back was, how strong her arms. And the determination in her eyes that made me want to cower in fear. She was a strong woman. She had married Jordan, who I knew was a good man. Why had he chosen to get the treatment? I had never asked him. Though by the time I understood the consequences, it was too late.

I looked at my son. Strapping, tall, and features not unlike mine. He had a broad brow and a strong chin. His nose was a tiny bit crooked. I wondered when he had broken it. Perhaps in school? I hoped not later. What had he chosen for a calling? Was he a soldier? He certainly marched like one. Whatever it was, he had the same determination in his stance and his face that his sister had. They were hard people.

How was I ever going to explain that I was their father? Why had I left them behind? So many questions plagued me and made me lose my footing in the roots each time a query floated to the front of my consciousness. It was, again, overwhelming. I wondered if I could protect them through this ordeal. Were we doing the right thing? What would happen to us now? I had no idea and no way to protect them. I also wondered if they might protect me. Especially if they knew the truth.

CHAPTER 31
aloisa

We reached the camp before nightfall. The rebels took all three of us to a large tent in the middle of the compound. We passed women hanging laundry and bent over cooking fires, and children playing in groups. What was this place? I hadn't seen any tablets or computers. That was, until we walked into the main tent. It was like entering the womb, a whole different world than the one outside.

They led us to a room with comfortable chairs and a fire, where they gave us hot soup. I set the baby on a mat that was set out for him, somewhere he could finally stretch his limbs again and kick to his heart's content. But as I sat to consume my soup, a woman came into the room and took him away.

I jumped up, spilling the hot liquid all over my lap, but didn't make it to the door in time to get my baby back. I pounded on the door, screaming and cursing.

"Give me my baby!"

Miles came to calm me, his hands on my body made me instantly freeze. I had no fight left. Elias was on his feet as well.

Miles tried the button to open the door; it was locked.

"Give him back!" Miles said, the strength of his voice made me stop crying. The door let out a terrible keening noise and slid open. We hobbled back and a man came inside, quick enough that we couldn't rush him and get out.

"Why are you holding us prisoner? Where is my nephew?" Miles said.

"Safe."

"That's not a good word," Elias said.

"Who are you?" Miles asked.

"My name is Dranim; I'm the leader of the rebels, and I'm here to explain. Please sit down. We'll have some more soup brought for you Aloisa. Would you like a change of clothes?"

"I want my baby, you bastard." I fell to my knees, but I crossed my arms and glared.

"You'll have him back after we have everything straight. There's a lot of ground to cover. Would you like that change of clothes now or never?"

"I would like my baby." I put my hands on the floor and stood. The better to glare into this man's eyes directly.

"No then. Ok. Have a seat please."

He turned his back on us, and I saw Miles hesitate, watching the corners of the room. I shook my head no, but he lunged anyway. He grabbed the man by the throat and pinned an arm behind his back, but the man wasn't tense at all. In fact, he tried to laugh.

"Where are you going to go if you kill me?" he said.

"I don't want to kill you," Miles said. "Just threaten enough in order to get my nephew back. Give him back to us, and we can have this conversation. There's no need to make a mother worry."

"Let me go, and we'll consider it. You have no choice but to do as I say. You're in the middle of nowhere. None of you knows how to get back home—"

"I do," Elias chimed in.

"Great," Miles said. "Give away that fact why don't you." He loosened his grip on the man.

"Give them back the child, please," Elias said. "I do remember the way. You know I do. And I will take them from here. I will expose you to our government."

The man touched the screen of his tablet, and the woman brought my baby back in. She tried to hand him over gently, but I pulled him from her arms. She gasped.

"We're not giving him back because of Elias's threat," the man said.

Miles snorted.

"The government already knows where we are. They don't see us as enough of a threat...yet."

"Then why give him back?" Miles asked.

"As a good will gift. We wanted to see if Elias would stand by you two. The question now is will you stand by him. He is your father."

elias

I stood in shock, my arms limp at my sides. I hadn't expected them to reveal it that way. Nor had I expected my plea to get the baby back.

"Though he did get your baby back to you. So you should have some leniency." This last comment went unnoticed by Aloisa and Miles as they both looked at me with their eyes narrowed. I shrank.

A thought overtook my brain. I blurted it out before I could even consider the consequences.

"Can I hold the baby?"

Aloisa nearly dropped him. She moved forward as if without

thinking. She put him directly in my arms just as Miles began to protest. But I didn't hear it.

I didn't really know how to hold him, but he was so warm and smelled lovely. I felt tears well up in my eyes spill over. This child was a part of me.

"What's his name?" I asked.

"He doesn't have one," Miles growled.

Aloisa shot him a scathing look.

"His father will name him," she said.

"Then we better find him." I handed the child back to her and looked at Dranim. "What do we need to do?"

CHAPTER 32
elias

I didn't sleep well that night. Aloisa and Miles were in the same room with me. The baby was fussy. He tossed and turned, whimpering through the hours. Instead of letting him wake Aloisa, I stood from the feather mattress, my body complaining and creaking with pain and need, and picked up the baby. I took him outside in the fresh air for a walk.

Wandering in and among the tents, I found that this place worked like a little village. Families lay sleeping in their personal tents with dogs lying outside, their eyes following me while their snouts stayed put on their paws.

We got to the perimeter, where men patrolled the outer edges. A red laser ran around about six inches off the ground; a trip wire to alert them of intruders...or escapees? I decided not to test it. The wary looks from the patrollers had me on edge, and I didn't want to provoke them. I turned heel and went back toward our tent.

As I wove through the smoldering fires and dark shadows of tents, I thought about the plan. It wasn't much of one really. I knew the general area Jordan had been placed in, but I didn't know specifics. Once he left the care of the EMT Clinic I didn't have contact except to be sure he was adjusting well in the boot camp. I had absolutely no contact after that. I still wondered if Dr. Rooken and I could have been triggers for him. The shelter had been proof that people from your past could bring back hormones. I was proof.

But Dr. Rooken had assured me that we weren't close enough to him, nor was that possible. He had lied.

The baby started to squeal and cry. I realized I had been clenching him tightly, gripping his little body with the anger I felt toward Dr. Rooken. I loosened my arms and pulled him back so I could look at his face. Tiny droplets ran down his cheeks, but he only sniffled.

"Sorry, little one," I said. "Do you want to go back to bed?"

He squeaked so loudly I thought he would wake those in the tent next to us.

"Hush," I said.

I put him back to my shoulder and continued my walk, not ready to fall asleep nor to give up this uninterrupted chance to hold the baby.

The plan: to go to a small town in Oregon and begin asking around in as discreet a manner as we could manage. Miles would find work in the lumber industry while Aloisa would look for a waitressing job both in order to get to know the people and search for Jordan; I would care for the baby. There was a radius we had to search in that contained a few small towns and communities. Once we found Jordan, we had to leave. The people around him, especially his counselor, couldn't know that he had been triggered. If they knew, he would be found and so would we.

I passed a larger tent that had no dog in front and no fire pit. Glancing around to be certain I was alone, I stepped up to the waving flap and peeked through. Inside I saw a surgical suite. All of the instruments necessary for surgery done by human hands, tools they no longer used in the hospital. I shifted the baby to my other shoulder so I could put my head farther into the tent. Along one wall I saw a glass display case. Bags of HSS glowed green inside.

Emoxapraline?

What would the rebel camp need Hormone Stabilizing Serum for?

A rustling behind me caused me to jerk my head out and start walking in a random direction.

The baby was sleeping now, snoring on my shoulder. As I walked, the sun started the day. The light turned from a deep purple blue to the palest of grays before bursting into bright orange and pink. People started emerging from their tents, sleepy but unable to ignore the fact that they had things to do. Life went on. Even though I was in the strangest of places battling the strangest of feelings, life went on.

Around a corner, I saw a slender hand pulling back the tent flap in front of me. Out stepped a woman. She had burning amber hair that shone in the sunlight with golden specks. Her skin was pale and clear, smooth across her heart-shaped face. I stopped to stare.

She stopped as well and smiled at me.

"Is that your baby?" she asked.

I had forgotten the child. Tunnel vision took over, and she was all I saw. Until her voice broke the silence again.

"Ok then," she said and walked over to her fire pit.

"Sorry, he's my grandson," I managed to choke out.

"He's a cutie. That little snore is adorable." She came over to us to lay her hand on his back. She was a good foot shorter than me and had to look up, sweeping her curls out of the way to give me another smile. "Are you new in the camp?"

"Yesterday," I said.

"Quite new then." She giggled. The sound of it sent chills racing up my spine.

"I have to go. His mother will wonder where he is." I turned abruptly and sped away, too afraid of what my body was doing to acknowledge the fact that I had just admired beauty for the first time since I remembered.

Aloisa was frantic when I pushed open the tent flap. She tossed pillows here and there. As soon as I let the light in, she whipped around to face me. She strode over and snatched the baby from my arms. The baby began to wail.

"How dare you take him!"

"He was fussy. I was just walking him until he slept."

I sat down on the edge of my bed and put my head in my hands. It was pounding, my body was trembling again, and Aloisa continued to scream at me. Miles woke with a grumble in the other bed. He rolled over and yelled out, "Shut up!"

Both Aloisa and the baby were instantly silenced, and then it all started again.

"He took the baby! How can I trust him? He's a changeling! And he abandoned us before, so how can I trust him with my child?" She paced as she yelled at the two of us. Miles rolled back over and pulled the blankets over his head. I looked up at her.

"I abandoned you?" I said.

Somehow, between the screeches, my whisper fell through the cracks and into Aloisa's ears. She stopped.

"Yes," she said. I nearly fell back onto the mattress. "You and Mom disappeared. You dropped us off at our aunt and uncle's place and then you left, forever. We never saw you again. We received letters saying you had died and left us money. But we knew better. It was an epidemic. All those people leaving their families and mysteriously dying and then leaving loads of money that they never had before. It's what Jordan did to me. And I won't tolerate you taking my child without me knowing about it!" She plopped down on the rug in the middle of the room and cradled her baby, rocking back and forth and sobbing.

I went to her, knelt down, and placed my hand on her shoulder. Miles peeked out of the covers like a little boy.

"I don't remember why I did such a thing. And I'm sorry. I can only imagine it was with the best intentions."

She ripped her shoulder away from me and swiveled around to face away.

"Where's our mother?" Miles mumbled through the blankets.

I sat where I was, shoulders hunched. "I don't know."

The tent flap opened and Dranim stepped inside.

"I hope you're all ready for breakfast. We need to feed you and get the preparations underway. You'll leave later this afternoon so you arrive under darkness. We want you coming in when few people will notice you. Then you'll begin tomorrow as if you magically appeared in this new place, without histories, without emotional baggage, and to begin a new life. Let's get a move on."

And he left.

I stood and helped Aloisa to her feet. We gathered what few things we had been allowed in the tent and made our way to follow the guards who stood outside. Miles came running up behind me.

"They have a trip wire perimeter," I whispered to him.

His eyebrows rose.

"And patrols."

After another few minutes I said, "They also have a surgical suite with tons of HSS."

He licked his lips and jogged to catch up with Aloisa. He put an arm around her shoulder and stepped under the shadow of the largest tent, disappearing before my eyes into this dangerous world we had been dragged into. I wondered if we'd ever make it out alive.

aloisa

The day went by in a blur. I didn't let my son out of my sight again, but I had so much to do with my hands that finally I resorted to tying him on my back in a makeshift papoose. The guards set to vacuum-sealing our things into tiny packages and then loading those into backpacks.

We would drive a gas-powered car to small logging town in rural Oregon. Our back story was a family looking for a change of scenery, more hands-on work, less busy city life.

A woman came into the tent and took my hand to lead me to a chair.

"We have to prepare your eyes," she said.

"My eyes?"

"They need to be a bit different."

"Am I stealing someone's identity?"

"It's entirely new. We've given all the necessary paperwork to the system so you will be legit. But you're unknowns to the people in that town. That's dangerous in itself. Once we put the contacts in and they adhere to your eyes, you will be a nobody."

She pulled an enormous box from under a table and heaved it onto the stool next to me. I sat forward in my chair to give my son breathing room. He was sleeping; his drool ran down the back of my arm.

She opened the box and pulled out a device that had rubbery tentacles. As she moved it toward my face, I backed away, squishing my child and eliciting a groan.

"What is that?" I said, my hands up to protect myself.

"It's to render your new retinal data."

"What!"

"It shouldn't hurt...too badly." She winked.

"I'm not ok with this." I started to stand. A large hand came from behind me and pushed me back into the seat.

"This is your only choice," Dranim said. His voice was so deep and resounding I felt it in my chest. "You came here for our help. You put us all at risk. Now you will do as we say. Do I need to hold you down while Tara updates your eyes?"

"No."

He lessened his hold but didn't let go. He must have nodded at Tara because she nodded back and reached forward again with the artificial octopus. She placed cups on my temples, and then she held up two blue suction cups in front of my eyeballs, and my entire world turned blue and squishy. She pinched and lifted my lids out of the way.

"Relax, Aloisa." She grunted. "I need your eyelids completely out of the way."

I flinched and tightened up again.

"Come on!" She sighed and flung one hand up in the air. After a few more minutes of struggling, my eyes were sufficiently suctioned and completely uncomfortable.

I breathed through my mouth and tried to relax. I didn't want to wake my son. But as she flipped the switch on the remote, I felt my eyes being dragged from my head. Heat like I hadn't experienced before raced through my nerves and I first whimpered, then squealed, and finally screamed in agony. I was wishing for uncomfortable at this point. That would have been heaven compared to the pain.

The baby woke and began crying. Someone came running, a strange blob of gray bouncing through my blue world. Why had I ever decided to bring us here?

Tara turned the switch off and removed the tentacles without a care for her sharp fingernails as she popped the suction cups off my eyeballs. The scraping sensation was almost a relief after the pain of the machine. I glanced in the mirror, but everything was still blurry.

When I could see again through the painful blur, I pulled my son from my back. I turned to face the mirror and saw my brilliant hazel eyes shining like the sun.

The guards finished packing while Miles and Elias had their procedures. Pretty soon we were all ready to go, and we walked out of the tent to witness a stunning purple sunset. They led us to our car, just the baby in his wrap and our three backpacks. They made me leave the rosebush behind. But I managed to extract the gryphon from his hideout when they weren't looking and tucked him in my bag with my packs of seeds. My fingers brushed the smooth wood before I tossed a pile of vacuum packs on top to hide him.

We had new, clean personal tablets. We also had pills to chew if the government caught us, but I wasn't sure if I was willing to kill myself for this group of people. They hadn't done anything for me so far.

We all climbed in the car with Miles driving. Elias actually waved goodbye to the crowd as we took off into the sinking darkness.

CHAPTER 33
aloisa

Miles pulled the car off where the GPS on his tablet commanded—a parking lot with three street lights, one of which was out, the other two flickering. I stepped out of the car into the darkness and stretched. Turning around to face the street, I saw an aging town, as if we had driven back four decades. Crumbled brick covered the storefronts. Gas cars sat in the lot and parked along the street. Normal concrete covered the streets. The street lamps above my head were still halogen. Here and there I spotted a modernization, like the holographic ad on the side of a building or a robot serving drinks through the window of the restaurant. The town slept. A quiet and dark bubble of safety.

Miles led us to that twenty-four-hour restaurant, and we settled into a booth. We would sit there until our contact arrived. We had no other way to get around town or into our apartment. The car would stay where it was as the registration wasn't up to date. Preparing for the long haul, I pulled the baby from his wrap and lay him in the corner, my leg blocking him from rolling off.

But before I glanced at the menu, a fourth adult had joined

us at the table. He was tubby, with a luscious head of hair and rosy cheeks.

"Hi," he said. "New in town? Your baby looks about four months old."

The cue.

"He's only two," Miles answered.

"Then we'll have to introduce him to my granddaughter. She's the same age." He held out his hand to Miles. "Markus. And you are?"

Miles looked to me, sweat pouring down his temples.

"He's Miles," Elias said from next to Markus. "I'm Elias." He procured his hand and shook with Markus. "That's Aloisa and her baby."

"Great. Do you need something to eat before we go?" Elias nodded his head while we both shook ours. Markus looked back and forth and then smiled. He waved a waitress over.

Markus set us up in an apartment, and we found he was not just our contact but our first clue. He was the manager of the lumber mill and said he had a few changelings. But he didn't know their histories. Before he left us, he offered Miles a job and told him where to report the next day.

Miles paced the hallway after Markus left. He kept muttering to himself like a madman while I settled the apartment and Elias watched the baby. He was so good with him—I heard gurgly cooing from the other room every few minutes—that I left them together to go to the market in the dead of night, hoping I would make less of an entrance.

"They have cashiers at the stores," I said as I came back in the door.

"It's probably to give the lumber-wives jobs," Miles said as he continued to pace.

"I would have preferred self-service so I could go unnoticed. But now I know some people, and I guess we're supposed to mingle, right?"

Elias hopped up from the floor and helped me with the bags.

After that I fed the baby and put him to bed, finally on a real mattress with a heated core and a lullaby machine.

But even with that he was fussy.

Elias walked in behind me. I handed the baby over. They snuggled for a moment, and Elias lay him down. His eyes drooped and the lullaby began. I went to stand alone on the balcony, watching the stars.

Elias joined me, the only indication of his presence the squeaking and sighing of the ancient, automatic door.

"Sounds like we have a lead," he said.

"Hmmm."

"I need to understand my part in this, Aloisa. I'm lost. I don't know what my body is doing; I don't know why I abandoned you. I'm not asking for you to love me, but I could really use a friend."

I turned to face him.

"My son has already made that choice. I don't think this will be easy, but I think it's inevitable," I said.

And that was when I hugged my father, and he sobbed.

CHAPTER 34
aloisa

Miles walked in the door and I dropped my tablet to begin following him like a puppy; to the kitchen for a glass of milk; to the bathroom door where he closed it in my face and proceeded to shower for ten minutes; to his bedroom where he again shut the door to get dressed. He opened it to find me still standing there, inches from the wood.

"What?" he said.

"Excuse me?"

"I worked my butt off all day. I'd like some space and food. Where's dinner?"

"Elias is making it."

"What?" Miles threw his hands in the air and pushed past me. "Let's order takeout."

"There is none in this town." I was right on his heels. "Elias wanted to learn a new recipe since he got his taste buds back. What is your problem?"

Miles halted, and I ran into him.

"My problem?" He stayed with his back to me.

"You're moody. Did you see Jordan?"

"No."

"Why not?"

"Because I actually had to work and the changelings aren't cutting logs all day, they're building masterpieces in the workshop. They have logic and instructions and patience so they build intricate furniture. I sweat and get covered in wood chips."

"Oh." I sat down in the dark hallway. Miles huffed and then sat down too.

"What do we think of Elias?" he asked.

"He's fine."

"Ok."

"Ok."

We sat in silence. The sound of food sizzling came from the kitchen.

"You know we have to steal Jordan, right?" Miles said.

I nodded.

"We can't trust anyone. It's too dangerous."

I nodded.

Miles pulled out his tablet, punched in coordinates for somewhere in the nearby forest, and threw them to my tablet.

"Rendezvous point if we need it," he said.

I nodded.

"I'll make some excuse tomorrow and do some poking around. I'm sorry, Aloisa. I've just been on edge. I should be your rock, but this all unsettles me."

I lay my head on his shoulder.

"It's ok little brother. It unsettles me too."

elias

Aloisa was out for the afternoon job-hunting while I watched the baby. I had made him a bottle and heated leftovers for myself. To test the heat of the milk, I licked a drop, enjoying the burst of flavor on my tongue, when Miles came barging in the door. He dragged Jordan behind him.

My muscles seized.

"Where's Aloisa?" Miles was out of breath. "We have to go. Now. Like right now, Elias. Get the baby!"

"Elias?" Jordan said.

The world paused, mid-thought. Miles gaped at me. Jordan didn't do anything, as I expected. And I rushed over to him.

"Hello, Frin."

"What are you doing here? This man told me I had to come with him but didn't explain why."

I put a hand on his shoulder and guided him farther into the room.

"We're going on a trip, and we think you should join us. I'm surprised you remember me from the hospital. That was a different time."

"What the hell?" Miles said.

"Did you expect different?" I asked. "I briefed him after he woke."

The realization dawned across Miles's face. Then his whole body shivered and the world resumed its normal pace.

Miles started throwing some things back in the bags. I had settled into this life, enjoying my time getting to know my new surroundings, these new people, this baby. I had hoped we would be here for at least a few months. But here was Jordan, completely awestruck and confused, standing in the living room, gaping at me and the baby sprawled on the floor only two days after our arrival.

"Miles?"

"Never mind that. Get everything, Elias! We have to leave! Where's Aloisa?" He was all-out yelling now. I had no idea how to react. I couldn't move. Jordan bent down and put a hand out like the baby was a dog, hand in a fist to let the baby sniff his fingers. The baby unintentionally touched him. Jordan yanked his hand back in fright.

"I'm sorry," Jordan said. He backed toward the door, cradling his hand with his other arm as if the baby had burned him.

"Elias!" Miles screamed. It jolted me into action, and I left the wailing child on the floor to gather what I could. I snatched as much of our clothing and things that would fit in the packs. Then I stopped with a horrific thought in my head.

"Miles. We need to clean the apartment," I called from the bedroom.

"What?"

"We need to wipe down the apartment! The government can't know we were here! You're kidnapping this man." I yelled all this while running back into the living room.

Jordan's head whipped back and forth between us. He started to back away again. I put a hand on his arm, my fingers digging into his flesh. "Don't you dare. We haven't gone through all this to lose you now. Stay here."

Miles's face was a ghostly white. Now it was he who couldn't move. I started throwing the rest of our things in trash bags and wiping down the rooms. I closed a door with each room I finished. When I got to the hallway, the baby's wailing finally overwhelmed me. I went to him, scooped him up, and put him in Jordan's arms. I went and wiped down the kitchen, then moved toward the living room. Miles was already doing it. When we finished, we both turned to face the door where Jordan stood in shock, the baby in his arms, and Aloisa standing in the doorway with bags in her arms and her eyes wide.

The bags fell to the floor, sprinkling their contents everywhere. I managed to leap over and catch Aloisa before she, too, fell. Her head lolled to the side. Jordan's arms went slack. Miles leapt forward and held his hands out to catch the baby. It all happened in an instant, and everyone was safe, but Jordan started screaming and hiding his head in his arms. The door was still open, Aloisa's legs hanging in the hallway, and I could hear people coming out of their apartments to investigate. I yanked her inside and shut the door.

CHAPTER 35
elias

Miles and I finished wiping down the apartment. I turned to check on Aloisa, hands on my hips. The scene before me took my breath away. Jordan had pulled her head into his lap. She was still limp, but breathing. The baby lay next to her, quiet and watchful. Jordan brushed Aloisa's hair back from her face. The sun shone through the balcony door and onto the entrance door, surrounding them in a glowing yellow light. It was a moment that will be imprinted on my retinas until the day I die. I felt yet another tear slide down my cheek. This time one of happiness. Until Miles started yelling at me. Gradually his screams came into focus as the clouding in my ears faded away.

"They're here. The cops followed me; we have to run!" Miles stood looking out the balcony door, down at the parking lot in front of the building. He waved his arms frantically and rushed over to snag all of the backpacks. I grabbed the rest of the stuff in the trash bags and threw them down the garbage chute next to the kitchen door. I took one pack from Miles, and then we both stood over Jordan and his family. Aloisa was still out.

"What do we do?" My voice screeched on the last word.

"I'll carry her," Jordan said, caressing her cheek with the back of his hand.

Miles started running. I helped Jordan stand and then lifted Aloisa into his arms. I grabbed the baby. We took off after Miles, but he was already gone. I spun in a circle in the hallway. I didn't know how that would help, hoping Miles would come back around the corner to at least let me know which direction. When he didn't, I led Jordan toward the fire escapes in the back of the building.

We ran. And ran. And clambered down the rickety staircase. Then we ran more. We ended up behind a concrete building two blocks from the apartment, still no sign of Miles.

I turned to Jordan, who was heaving, his arms propped against the building. He had set Aloisa down to catch his breath. I strode over to her and slapped her face. She gasped and opened her eyes, sucking in great gulps of air and holding her cheek.

"Good. Can you walk? Or maybe run?" I asked.

"What?"

"Miles stole Jordan."

"Who's Jordan?" Jordan said.

"You are," I said.

Aloisa looked up at him and gasped again. I put myself between them and grabbed her chin in my hand, forcing her gaze to me.

"Aloisa, I need you to stay with me. Don't pass out again. We need to run. Now!"

She stood, and I grabbed her hand. We started running, Jordan behind us.

We ran some more, darting between buildings and keeping a lookout for Miles. At the corner of one building I started to bolt forward, but Aloisa snatched me back. She peeked around the corner and then put a hand to her throat.

"It's Miles. They have him!"

I grabbed her shirt and pulled her back, worried she would go to her brother. The police had him shoved against their car, his hands wrenched behind his back.

"If they don't find Jordan he'll be fine. He hasn't done anything as long as they don't know where Jordan is."

"Why do you keep calling me Jordan?"

Aloisa, mesmerized, reached out and touched Jordan's face. He shivered violently; their eyes locked.

I looked around the corner again and the car was gone. I tugged on Aloisa's hand to get them running. She held Jordan's hand, and I could see clouds of confusion and shock floating across his face. He watched their hands as we moved.

Again we skidded to a stop because a door opened before us. A man stepped out. He wore an apron splashed with red and carried a trash bag to the back alley. He looked at us; we looked at him. No one said a word. Our breathing sounded like thunder rolling through.

He threw the trash away and backed into his store, hands up in surrender. Once the door closed and he was gone, we sprinted forward.

By nightfall we had wended our way through the town, avoiding as many eyes as possible and slowing to a walk in the populated areas, and beyond to the forest.

"Where are you going?" Aloisa asked.

"Away," I said. I kept walking into the forest, cradling the baby and blocking him from any stray branches.

"Elias."

I stopped and turned back to her.

"Miles gave me coordinates for a safe meeting place. He knew this would happen."

I nodded. She came over to me and rummaged through the bag on my back to find her tablet.

"That's good. You have the right bag."

"If Miles isn't there," I said, "I'll go back and look for him. But you will keep Jordan here."

I turned and started walking again but didn't look behind me to see Aloisa's reaction. I didn't want to see it.

We reached the rendezvous point a half hour later.

There was no sign of Miles.

CHAPTER 36
aloisa

The forest was quiet. The sun had set and the animals had gone to their nests. The nocturnal animals hadn't woken yet, so we were in the interim, that few minutes when the world is truly asleep. The rustling of my son in his pile of leaves and grass was what brought me back to the present. I felt the cold crawl up my arms and wrapped them around my torso for warmth. I leaned against a tree larger than a house.

I shook my head to wake myself up even more and looked around. Elias wasn't in the clearing. I whispered his name.

"He went back to find Miles," a voice said. A voice that was like honey to my ears. I swiveled my head around, following the tasty sound, to find my husband sitting on the ground and staring at the baby. I stumbled back from the tree, around to the other side and out of sight. Dizziness took over, and I fell to the ground. My eyes on the sky as it spun around me, I held my head with both hands and slowed my breathing. The excess of oxygen wasn't helping.

"Are you ok?" he said. I heard his shuffling footsteps and crab-walked my way farther into the trees. After ramming into a tree with my shoulders and pausing to find more balance, I called back, "I'm fine." And then I whispered, "I think."

The baby cried out. I could only imagine a stick in his eye from the scream he emitted. I bolted back to him. A branch with its leaves attached lay across his face where he lay, writhing. Jordan gingerly plucked it away and lifted the baby into his arms.

I started laughing. Bent over at the waist, uncontrollable spasms, and my brain began to melt. My son was in my husband's arms. Finally.

Wiping the tears from my cheeks, I started hiccupping.

"Are you ok?" Jordan asked again. He set the baby back on the ground. The moonlight that started spilling through the trees made the clearing that much brighter, and I could see that my son was covered in mud and bits of forest.

"I think I'm actually ok," I said.

"Can you tell me what we're doing?"

I picked up the baby and proceeded to dig through the backpack Elias had left for something to clean him up with, all while keeping my back to Jordan.

"Escaping."

"I have no need to escape."

"Yes, you do. You just don't know it. Do you know who I am?"

"No. That man kept calling me Jordan. But that's not my name. Maybe you have me confused with someone? Who are you?"

"Let's leave me out of it for now. Your name is Jordan. They've been lying to you."

"Who?"

I shivered.

"The government, I guess. Emodiant. The world. I don't know. Can we drop the questions?" I undressed the baby and unhooked his diaper.

"I think I should go back to town. They were looking for me. That man took me without letting me check out. They won't know where I went."

"See, you used the word 'they' too."

"Yes. My counselor and my boss and...I suppose anyone else who cares where I am. They care for me. They keep me safe. I also need my HSS. I'm due for a dose." He checked the tablet in his pocket.

Though the baby was still naked, I whipped around and snatched the tablet from Jordan, crushing it against the bark of the tree. While I was preoccupied, the baby burst into wails.

"Why did you do that?" Jordan asked with complete calm. It was that indifference that sent me over. I picked up my naked and filthy child and strode into the forest. I needed air. There wasn't enough. Even out here in the wilderness. With nothing above me but branches and starlight. I wanted to run. To hide in a corner. To curl my body around my baby and protect him from this world. From this hell.

elias

I came back from my reconnaissance mission to find Jordan sitting cross-legged on the ground, a broken tablet in his hands, and Aloisa nowhere in sight. She had left him alone. What if he had wandered off? A flash of anger crept up my chest.

"Where is she?"

He slowly lifted his head to look at me with a blankness on his face. It felt like looking in a mirror from my past. Now my face had expressions and sweat and dirt. But it was his reaction to my question that made me take a tiny step backward.

He furrowed his brow, and I thought I saw fire in his eyes. A lick of crazy. A tiny flicker of anger and frustration.

The tone of his voice frightened me even more. "She broke my tablet."

Not unlike a child who is angry at their parent for not buying the candy they wanted, but also exactly like a psychopath growling about the fact that their murder victim hadn't screamed when and how they had requested.

"I need my HSS." Now a bit of a whine crept in, making the skin on my arms and cheeks tighten. He swept his arm toward the forest and looked back down at his lap where the broken tablet lay. I followed his direction and hoped I would find Aloisa and the baby taking a walk, not cut into pieces and strewn across the forest floor.

My breathing quickened with each step farther into the darkness. I whispered Aloisa's name in an attempt to not wake whatever monsters might be lurking. In hindsight, it would have been better to stomp and crash and yell for her. That way I wouldn't have seen my daughter cradling her sleeping baby and rocking back and forth, also seated on the ground in the muck, and crying. The moonlight bathed her in a tiny clearing where I crept up behind her. She didn't hear me over her crying, so I cleared my throat.

She jumped.

"It's me," I said. "Don't worry."

She quickly wiped at her face and rearranged the baby so she could stand and face me. Her vulnerability was wide open, completely bare for me to witness. I stood frozen.

"Did you find him?" she said through a gummy throat.

"I did. I have to sign him out in the morning. They wouldn't tell me anything except that."

"Well. I guess we need a place to sleep tonight." She groaned and peeled the baby away from her to reveal a growing wet spot. "And maybe some fresh clothes."

CHAPTER 37
elias

I stretched my neck, popping it side to side, and rubbed my arms to get some warmth back. The cold brick wall at my back didn't help the situation. Neither had the night in a hollow tree big enough to fit a car but not nearly as comfortable. The baby had been hot to the touch as soon as we woke; he must have caught a cold in the midst of everything. None of us had really slept, except Jordan. But even when he'd woken up, his eyes had been glassy. I had recognized the first onset of hallucinations when he had reached toward the sky for something that wasn't there and then studied his hand like he'd never seen one before. I had grabbed his shoulders and made him focus on my face. It hadn't helped.

Now we were packed in a tiny alleyway, trying to make it look as though we were coming out for a new day. I rubbed my aching knees. Aloisa was still puffy and crying, and the baby was uncomfortable against her chest. Jordan walked in tiny circles.

"Ok. That's it. I'll go get him myself. You three crazies stay here, please. Don't move. Ok?"

Aloisa nodded. Jordan didn't move.

Around the corner I ran into Markus. He barreled forward and bumped me with his massive gut. I bounced off and tilted back, but Markus caught my shoulders.

"What are you doing here?" he said. "Where's Jordan?"

I started. "You know his name?"

"Of course I know his name you idiot. I'm the insider. For the rebels."

"But you said..."

"Enough of that. Where is he? You should be long gone by now."

"Miles is in jail. I'm going to collect him."

"What?"

"Can we just..." I looked around at the people staring at us. This wasn't the crowded sidewalks of Denver. Everyone knew everyone, and any piece of gossip would spread like glandular fever.

"Yes, let's." Markus pointed us to the alley I had just vacated. We entered the shadowy spot to find Jordan ripping his baby from Aloisa's arms. She was trying her hardest not to scream; her face was a wretched maroon. The baby was limp.

"What's going on here?" Markus turned to me. "Have you not given him HSS? He looks like a crazed madman. You really are incapable."

He snatched the baby from the two of them and cradled his head against his throat. "This baby is sick. Let's get you all to my house. We can speak there. There's no retinal scanners in the area, and my house is blocked. Jordan, or rather, Frin, keep your head down for goodness' sake. We'll pick up Miles later. He can sit on a stone bench a while longer."

And with that, Markus walked away with Aloisa's baby in his arms, Aloisa close on his heels. That was how we ended up in a mansion on the other side of town, waiting for tea that would never come, hoping Jordan wouldn't be taken from us.

aloisa

The stiff sofas weren't a comfort to my body after the night we'd had. My brother was still in custody. We were in a house with a man we couldn't trust. And my husband was going berserk. Markus had complained that we hadn't given Jordan any HSS, but he hadn't provided any. Elias worked his best to calm Jordan by keeping up a constant monotone narration of our situation.

My baby, on the other hand, had been given medicine so he could sleep. His breathing was still ragged, but it was a deep, healing sleep. The couches worked for him, but I figured he could have slept on hot coals with the medicine running through his body.

The door creaked open. And in walked Miles. He was alone, bruised, and obviously confused.

"What's happening?"

"How did you get here?" I asked.

"Markus came to get me. I don't really know how he got away with it. Last night when they took my retinal scan they found the contacts. You thought getting them on was painful." He rubbed his eyes and winced. "I think one might have slipped a little when they fused to my eyes. They were all set to transfer me back to Denver but decided to wait overnight. Markus came in this morning, and somehow I was let go with no fuss."

Miles reached over and smoothed his hand over the baby's head.

"He's burning!"

"It's not as bad as it was. We gave him medicine."

"Markus knew Jordan's name. Is that bad?" Elias asked.

Miles turned around to stare at Jordan rambling to himself,

pacing, throwing his arms around, preaching something to the air.

"What's up with him?"

"I must have triggered him," I said. "He asked me a lot of questions."

"I overheard the cops talking about eradicating changelings. That must be how Markus got me out. Though I don't know why they would keep employing changelings."

"And why would they not hand Jordan to us?" I asked.

"That would be the reason for the surgical suite. They're working on reversals," Elias said.

"The one you saw in the camp? But then why the HSS?" Miles asked.

"To keep them acting normal while they work on them. The stress of surgery tends to throw EMT patients out of whack, and they need stronger doses of HSS to stay normal. It happened a few times in the hospital when an EMT was in an accident and came into the emergency room for treatment. Dr. Rooken always went to make sure they were taken care of properly, which meant nearly overdosing them on HSS. The human body naturally reacts to injuries with certain hormones to stay alive. People bleed out, have heart attacks, experience shock without being able to attend to it. All kinds of things happen when the body is under duress and hormones aren't present. It's the whole purpose of HSS. To make sure the body continues to function on an optimal level while allowing logic to be in control."

"Thank you, Charles Darwin," Miles said.

"Wait," Elias said. "No." His eyebrows knit together. "That can't be."

"What?" I asked, picking up the baby and beginning to pace alongside my husband.

"Dr. Rooken vaguely mentioned testing EMT reversal by

removing HSS. It didn't work. The subjects died. He thought maybe the key was an emotional trigger—like I had. It's why he wanted to experiment on me."

"And why I need to send you to him," a voice behind us said. We all jumped to face Markus.

"You're a rebel," Elias said.

Miles moved to stand between Markus and I. I moved to pick up the baby and stand next to Miles.

"I am." Markus sat. It felt so pointed, so deliberate, that he put himself on a level below us to make us more comfortable. It did exactly the opposite. I saw Miles's hands clench, Elias's neck twinged, and I certainly felt a rush of adrenaline.

"But Dranim doesn't seem to understand that we have reached an impasse. He doesn't have the understanding of the world that I have. In order to reverse the effects of EMT, we need to understand how without continually killing changelings. Our research is getting us nowhere. But Dr. Rooken can help."

"And does Dr. Rooken know that he's helping you? Or are you playing both sides?" I asked.

"He knows he's helping, just not who he's helping. He wants to understand EMT just as much as Dranim and the rebels do."

"What about the babies," Elias said, his voice so quiet it barely registered.

"The babies are a whole other matter. Now, I need you to come with me." Markus stood, his considerable girth adding to the dominant effect of his stance.

"I think we should just be on our way," Miles said. His voice had reached a level I hadn't heard before, a growl that didn't frighten me, but bolstered my courage.

"With two changelings? One whom you have stolen? I think not. Things are no longer in your hands," Markus said.

"Who are you?" Jordan suddenly screamed at me. My eyes went wide. He started for me, a bull attracted to a red cape. His hands were out, flexing like they felt my neck already in their grasp. Miles lunged and stopped Jordan mid-stride. They both went down as the door opened again. A group of men wearing the burning man insignia on their jackets stepped in.

Miles locked his arm around Jordan's neck and stood up with him. He murmured urgently in Jordan's ear, shaking him.

"If you'll just follow these nice men," Markus said and made his way around them and out the door, leaving us to deal with his henchmen.

A single tear escaped my eye before I got hold of myself and stood with my legs spread, bravery emanating from my very pores.

"We're not going anywhere with you. I haven't fought for my family to this point to just give up," I said.

I glanced at Miles, who had now let go of Jordan, and they both stood poised on their toes. Elias also had his gaze locked on one of the guards. None of us wavered. The instant Miles screamed "Now!" we all lunged forward. I for the door, and they for the men. I wiggled around the human pile and opened the door. Outside stood another man, blocking our way. The opening of the door and the grunting behind me caused him to turn. Before he had a chance to gather his wits, I kicked him in that most vulnerable spot and watched him crumple. Then I kicked his head enough to knock him out. A surge of pride flew through my veins.

I hadn't noticed the silence, until I turned around to find my boys victorious. Our first luck of the day. The men behind them were unconscious, but not for long. One of the guards was stirring. Miles took the baby from me, and we ran.

At the front door, Miles halted. He peered through the window on the side and swore. For one long and intense moment, we waited. Then Miles turned, handed me the baby, motioned back around the corner, and strode out the door by himself. He shut it in my face.

I handed the baby to Elias, pointed to the floor in a "stay here" motion, and nodded. Then I followed my brother through the door.

Outside the sun momentarily blinded me, but I soon had a good view of the five men in the sweeping driveway. Miles wasn't visible, but I very much was. And all five men turned to me. Miles obviously had more swagger than I, to have snuck out and not be seen.

"What are you doing?" one said, striding up the gravel and then mounting the stairs. While he made so much noise, I saw the man farthest away and invisible to the others fall to the ground behind a car. I took the hint and proceeded to distract.

"Markus sent me out here. He forgot something in the car."

I realized my mistake when two of the men looked at the car I had indicated. They now saw Miles, standing by that very vehicle, and ran for him. The third man who wasn't near me also jumped my brother. The man who had spoken to me and now stood towering over me, grabbed my shoulder and yanked.

I swung my body on the end of his arm like a child, knocking his balance off and taking us both down the stairs in a heap. It wasn't enough though. He jumped up and stopped me from crawling away. Miles, meanwhile, was grappling with three opponents who seemed to be made of steel and leather.

I didn't have time to worry for my brother as my own adversary swung his meaty fist in my direction. I dodged it.

The door to the house opened. Elias stepped out. He

snatched a large rock from a potted plant and slung it my direction. I closed my eyes and ducked. His aim was true. The grip on my forearm released. The man lay before me in a growing pool of blood.

I looked up at my rescuer to see Jordan now standing behind him, his hand over his mouth and the baby hanging limp in the other arm. I hauled my now aching body to standing and ran for my child. He was fine, only sleeping and held sloppily. We three turned to the scuffle in the driveway.

Miles had felled two men already but was struggling with the third. I nudged Elias, and he picked up another rock. But this time it was too dangerous. The men were molded together, writhing like a pile of snakes.

Instead of throwing the rock, Elias strode forward, his face stony, and bashed the man's head. Miles pushed the unconscious form off and gasped for air.

"The men inside are waking," Elias said.

"Then let's go," Miles said. He heaved to his feet.

My head felt stuffed with cotton. The worry made the world stand still and balloon. Every noise made me gnash my teeth. The taste of iron flooded my mouth when I bit too hard onto my cheek.

"Come on!" he said.

We left the cars where they were, opting instead for going on foot to our own car. We ran so far, and so hard; harder than we had before.

CHAPTER 38
aloisa

Darkness and the sounds of animal life enveloped us the instant we passed from the concrete world onto the mud of the forest. We stopped to lean against the trees and breathe. But the hair on my neck stood up. We weren't alone. They were just behind us, so I goaded the others to keep going. Jordan was hurting worst of all, considering his body was still adjusting to the adrenaline. His breathing was ragged and sparse. I wanted to touch him, but I let my hand hover over his back and urged him on.

We went another few yards before Jordan had to sit down; he was gasping like a fish. Miles pulled us into a copse and held his finger to his lips. Jordan tried desperately to quiet his breathing, all the while looking at me, pleading in his eyes. I bent down in front of him.

"Can I help?" I asked.

"Aloisa?" he asked.

"Yes." I realized why he was saying my name. Like a zombie suddenly cured. I saw a brightness in his eyes and the blood crept up his cheeks. He smiled the tiniest bit, and so did I.

"Aloisa," he said again, with a great outlet of breath.

Before we could do anything more though, before I could finally touch his skin, thundering herds of people came crashing through the trees, and we all jumped up. We ran the rest of the way to town and the car, following Miles as he zigzagged our way there.

We reached the lot next to the restaurant on the edge of the forest, and Miles handed the baby off to me like a football. I stopped midstride, cradling my child and smiling into his hotter-than-a-mouthful-of-fresh-lasagna shoulder. Jordan came through the trees behind me and touched my shoulder. It was a tiny touch, that of a leaf as it fell to the ground; tentative and unsure, full of apprehension and worry. His hands shook.

"Aloisa," he said again. He pulled me and our baby into a hug and whispered in my ear in the most husky, seductive voice I had ever heard, "My Aloisa. I have you back. I remember you, but I don't remember myself. I missed you, but I didn't know I was missing you. Wait." He pulled back. "What are you doing here? Why am I here? Oh." Then I lost my Jordan for another moment. His hands went to his head, and he started banging at his temples. I reached up with one free hand to stop him.

"Darling Jordan. I'm your wife. You left me to give me a better life. You left against my wishes. But I'm here. I'm here to get you back. Because we belong together."

"Aloisa?" he said again. I saw a glimmer of hope in his face, it opened up and softened a bit, letting the idea of me and him settle in. Then his eyes traveled down the road map of my wrinkles and skin and neck to the head of his son. His sleeping and sick son.

He raised his eyebrows.

"Yes. He's ours."

All the while behind us, Miles and Elias worked to unlock

and pack the car. The sounds of our pursuers softened, and Miles called for us to hush. He listened with one hand in the air.

"We have to go," he said. "Now."

I crawled into the car with the baby. Miles jumped in the driver's seat and turned on the navigation system. Elias climbed in beside him and buckled in. But Jordan stayed glued to the forest floor. His feet melded with the muck, becoming one with nature. He stood so stock still I thought maybe he would actually become a tree and stay there forever.

"Jordan?" I said.

He started screaming, giving away our position to the pursuers. We heard them change direction, even above his screaming. Elias scrambled from the car, and I moved to the front all in one graceful motion. He wrestled with Jordan, pulling and cajoling until Jordan's body went noodle limp and Elias could shove him in the backseat. He fell in on top of Jordan as the door shut, and Miles hit the gas. The tires spun, and I looked out the back window at the men quickly filtering onto the lot. Miles didn't care. Once the car was on, he shot onto the road. They couldn't keep up. We had made it out. But we knew they wouldn't stop. With Elias's hand over Jordan's mouth, and Miles's foot heavy on the gas, we sat staring through the glass with wonder and shock. Each lost in our own thoughts.

elias

Jordan finally started to calm. I sat up and helped him into his seat belt. But before I could put mine on, he wove his fingers into my sweater and shoved his face in my chest. He was crying. I put an arm around him and rocked him like a baby. I whispered into his ear that everything would be just fine. That in a few days he would feel normal, or as normal as it gets. That after a few weeks he would lose the constant adrenaline rush. And then I stopped talking because I couldn't tell him what a few months would look like.

"I remember her," he said.

"What?" I said, much too loudly. Aloisa turned around to stare at me. I shook my head at her and repeated the question to Jordan. "What?"

"She's my wife. My Aloisa. I remember her."

"Well that's strange." My analytical mind, the scientist I had been for the past few decades, took over, and I started compiling information regarding the cases I had already seen. The subjects, including myself, had no memories of their triggers. They only had a vague notion that they knew the person. But they didn't have distinct memories. I didn't remember that my children were mine. I had no idea who my wife was, and probably never would, as she was also an EMT patient somewhere in the world.

"I have a son," Jordan whispered. This statement brought me back.

"Yes. You do." I rocked him some more as he sobbed. Aloisa watched us from the front seat. I saw tears sliding down her cheeks, glistening in the moonlight that now came through the windows. Another day had passed and here we were in night again.

"Miles?" I said.

"Yes."

"We need to get food, and you need to destroy that navigation system. We might even consider finding another car. They're tracking us with that thing." He had turned onto a major road and found more gas-powered cars to blend in with, but it wouldn't be enough.

"We need to really be hidden. From them both," Miles said.

"Both?" Jordan whimpered.

"The government and the rebels," I said.

"Great," Aloisa said.

"Not a problem," Miles said. "Keep thinking, Elias. Come up with some ideas. I'll pull off at the next service station and make a call to a friend. I've got my connections, and they have nothing to do with either group. We can do this."

I saw Aloisa's eyes go wide. "The old Miles is back," she said and smiled.

Their confidence and the palpable sense of ease brought my heart rate back down. I focused on Jordan again.

"He's your son," I said. "He's my grandson. But I didn't know that until probably a week ago. I abandoned Aloisa and Miles when they were children to have the surgery. I've gone through this too."

"Oh," Jordan said.

He sat for a while in silence, his body still and not shaking anymore. I felt the release of pressure in my chest cavity as the adrenaline flowed out of my bloodstream. But I kept my mind turning. It felt good to be back to logic once again. I had felt that all my skills fled the moment I stopped taking HSS. I worried that I would be like a child, relearning everything until I really understood it all again. But by the time Miles pulled into a recharging station, I had a plan.

"What's the baby's name?" Jordan said to the entire car. We three looked at each other and then at Jordan, still wrapped in my arms.

"He doesn't have one," Aloisa said.

"Why?"

"Because you get to name him."

CHAPTER 39
aloisa

Miles dropped us off at the abandoned rest stop by the food vending machines with all of our bags. Then he drove the car off into the darkness. I imagined him kicking the dashboard until it sizzled and crackled and fell in pieces, kicking with all of his anger and frustration at life. Elias, Jordan, the rebels, Dr. Rooken, the radiation that had nearly killed him. He hadn't been the same since he had come back. It seemed as though he finally understood that he could die, that his life was precarious and precious. Before the radiation had affected him, he had felt invincible, and that was exactly why I feared for him. But now, as I sat rocking my whimpering baby, I smiled because my brother was a whole new person. Now he knew he wasn't immortal, but he also knew what kind of power he had. And I felt so much safer for it.

Elias left Jordan and I on the sidewalk to order some food. He and Miles came melting out of the darkness at the same time, walking with swagger. For the first time in a long time I felt happy. I hadn't even realized how stressed I had been until it began to ebb.

"Now what?" I asked. My voice echoed across the empty

grounds. Elias handed me a steaming plate of something mixed with rice.

"The car's taken care of. I'll call my contact," Miles said. "He should be able to send us a new one. But we won't be using it for very long. We'll just get somewhere we can steal another and then send the car on."

"Steal?" Jordan said. "I don't know about that. I'm not so comfortable with that. Isn't that wrong?"

We all giggled.

"What?"

"Of course it's wrong," I said. I put a hand out to pat his shoulder, but again it just hovered above his sweater. "But do you really think we have a choice?"

Miles went to the ancient pay-per-call vidphone and covered the camera with his hand. Along with the navigation system, he had destroyed the tablets the rebels had given us. His mumbling and cursing came across the dark space to us, and I clenched my teeth. His tone of voice wasn't promising, though I couldn't make out the words. The outline of his body shone eerily against the dark building. I shoveled food in my mouth then shifted the baby to my other arm and side-stepped closer to Elias. Then I leaned my head on his shoulder.

At first he jumped. But then his hand came up and smoothed my hair. He sniffed deeply, taking in the scent of my unwashed hair. I scrunched my nose, hoping it wasn't too horrible.

Miles walked up.

"It took some convincing, and quite a bit of money from Aloisa's account," he said and shrugged, "but we're good. Let's move around the back of the building for now."

The boys all lifted the bags, and we settled onto a bench at the back. It was cold, but I was squished between my brother and my father, and I finally relaxed enough with their warmth to start nodding off. The baby was completely asleep again, burning away in the cold night air. Elias reached into one of the bags and pulled out another blanket to pile on top of him, and it was that heat that did it for me: I was out.

elias

The car came and Miles went to flag it down. Luckily his friend had listened and sent a driverless car so we had one less thing to worry about. As he and Jordan transported the bags, I sat still with Aloisa's head on my shoulder and her mouth gaping and whistling with each breath.

"We're ready," Miles said.

I put a hand up to Aloisa's cheek and touched the smooth skin. She jolted awake, sucking in deep gulps of air, eyes wide and frightened.

"It's ok," I said. "The car is here. We have to go."

Then with everyone in the car and a destination programmed, we all promptly fell asleep.

The baby crying woke us.

And we saw the cars around us. A brigade of black vehicles, their windows mere slits.

"Who are they?" Aloisa asked.

"I don't know," Miles said. "But whoever they are, it's not good."

Our driverless car's computer had been overridden and was being made to follow along with the black cars. We traveled to the side of a deserted highway in the wee hours of dawn. Jordan started shaking again. Miles left us all in the car. Aloisa handed me the now quiet baby and followed Miles. I put my free hand on Jordan's shoulder to help calm him.

"Roll down the window an inch," I told the computer.

It obeyed, which I was thankful for.

Miles and Aloisa stood outside, but no one exited the vehicles. A voice came from unseen speakers. It filled the tiny valley we had driven into.

"Give us the EMT patients."

I couldn't tell if it was male or female. It neither yelled nor whispered. It wasn't a computer, but it wasn't very human either.

"All these demands," Miles said. "I'm sick of demands. How about you just leave us alone?"

"We will. Once we have the men you stole."

"We stole no one," Aloisa said. Her tiny stature next to Miles seemed to grow with the power of her voice. "They came of their own accord, and they will stay. Who the hell are you anyway?"

"Some say we control the world. Some say we will change the world."

"So, in other words, you are Emodiant. You are the government. You are a government meant to protect the people but run by a corporation bent on replacing the human race. Gotcha," Miles said.

"If you want to think that."

"We want to be left alone. What good do you think having these men will do you?" Aloisa spoke up again.

"That's not what they're worried about. The right question is: what will the rest of the world do when they find out Emotional Modification Therapy doesn't work after all?" Miles said. Then he laughed. "I think we'll just be on our way," he said and turned, pulling Aloisa with him.

"Not an option," the voice boomed. It echoed in the valley, bouncing from side to side and chilling me to the bone. It rattled in my head and made me feel both sleepy and completely

anxious at the same time. The last thing I saw was Miles dragging an unconscious Aloisa to the car, his body weaving like a
drunk. Then everything went suddenly black.

CHAPTER 40
elias

The sun woke me. It burned through my eyelids with a ferocity that I didn't appreciate.

My face was crushed into the floor of a moving car. The stiff carpet rubbed my cheek raw with every bump. Within inches of my eyes was Jordan's forehead. One more sharp turn and we would smack heads. My hands were tied behind my back, and I couldn't separate my legs either. Jordan's breathing was deep and consistent, but I didn't know if that was because of the EMT or if he was sleeping.

I heard nothing but the road noise—no radio, no conversation, only tires and pavement and wind and the occasional rock pinging. I struggled to turn my head and found two sets of feet behind me. Even with my obvious awakening they didn't say or do anything.

I wondered what had happened to Aloisa and Miles and the baby.

My children.

As a changeling, I had never had the inkling to think that I wanted children. I didn't have desires so why would I crave a family?

Now that my emotions were on the rise, and I knew that I already had children, I couldn't think of my life any other way. I wondered though, would they ever feel the same? Would they be able to forgive me for what I had done? I couldn't even remember what I had done, so could I even ask forgiveness for something that wasn't reality to me?

All of these thoughts crowded my mind. I didn't hear the car slow and stop until the brakes squeaked.

aloisa

I opened my eyes slowly, a sharp pain beating in my head kept me from sitting up right away. Cheek stuck to the pavement. Knees scraped from the rocks. Muscles and skeleton protesting to the awkward position I had landed in. The baby crying was muffled by the car but loud enough to have woken me.

Miles and I lay in a heap where we had fallen to the side of the highway. I sat up quickly and regretted it right away. My jostling woke Miles. Through the fog of my headache I made my way to my feet and went to retrieve the baby. With him finally in my arms, I realized his fever had broken. I pulled a bottle from the car and fed him.

"What happened?" Miles asked. "Where're Elias and Jordan?"

I looked around the deserted road, peering into the trees.

"Gone," I said.

"Fuck." Miles held his head in his hands.

I circled the car just to be sure they weren't behind it. I opened each door with a touch of my hand and let them slide shut after checking inside. I walked one way down the road a few feet, then turned and walked the other.

"Dr. Tobia Rooken," I said. "We have to go back."

Miles whipped his eyes up to mine. They glittered though his face stayed stone-like.

"No. No we don't." Now he stood and came to lay his heavy hands on my shoulders.

"After all of this, you say no now?"

"We can run. They won't follow us now."

I shrugged out from under his hands, out from under the weight of his oppression.

"Are you kidding me? You would just abandon your father and my husband to their experiments? To their torture?"

"You do still realize they abandoned us in the first place, right? We spent our lives not knowing who we were."

"And you want to continue that trend, by running and hiding and not having the chance to get to know our father." I walked away, into the trees, into the darkness and safety of greenery. I inhaled the scent of life. I waited for my blood pressure to calm, but it didn't. I also waited for my brother to follow me, but he didn't. So I kept walking, mostly in circles, the baby falling back to sleep in my arms. When I finally felt settled and even somewhat tired, I went back to the car to sit down and lay the baby in his seat. Miles sat on the road, his back leaning against the tire.

"There is no one but yourself," Miles said. "You've always relied on others. You can't do that anymore, Aloisa. You have to rely on yourself. Even I will be gone one day, though not by choice like them." The disgust in his voice on the word "them" hit me like a brick. This was my injured baby brother talking, not the man I knew now.

I crouched down in front of him and held my son out for him to cuddle. He took the baby and enveloped his tiny body, sighing.

"Miles. Dear Miles. No matter what they have done, they

are still our family. Even if they weren't, would you leave anyone to whatever fate they now face?"

Miles lifted his face to me, tears dripping down his cheeks, and nodded.

"You're right," he said. "But it hurts."

"Yes, baby brother, yes it does."

elias

"You see, I didn't have a choice, Elias."

My head was a thousand pounds; my body was cracked like a China doll; my eyes had sand coating them, and my mouth wouldn't obey my brain's commands. But I knew that voice.

"You and Jordan are the connection. You can tell me how this works."

Chilly hands plied my calf muscles, moved up to my knees, then my hands, wiggled something attached to me there causing sharp pain to bolt up my arm.

I finally managed to drag my head to the side and open my eyes. Jordan lay unconscious on a table next to me, naked and covered in long cuts sealed with sutures—Frankenstein.

A lab coat pocket stepped into my view, and Dr. Rooken crouched to look in my eyes.

I groaned. No words would come.

"I'm sorry. I know it hurts. But I have to conduct the proper experiments to be sure I can reverse this emotional trigger. It's not a flaw we can live with. EMT has been deteriorating since Dr. Wolff brought the idea to me so long ago. It's time for an updated version."

He stood erect and went to gently brush his fingers over Jordan's scars. Behind Jordan on the wall I saw a screen relaying our vitals as well as running code on all of the information. The lines of letters and numbers blurred, and I had to close my eyes again.

"The EMT children were my brain child. I knew we could perfect the system and build a better human. I've done it, but the fact is the world isn't quite ready yet. Neither are the children. They wouldn't understand the prejudice."

He swept a hand over Jordan's brow, pushing his hair back.

"I need to buy time. I need EMT to be viable with regular humans so I can continue creating a more advanced species. You must understand that, Elias. You knew the research we were doing. You were deepest in it. In fact, the research you've been doing on the EMT babies will be immensely important to my new procedure."

The drug they had given me wore off just enough. My voice crept out of my throat like a frog covered in spikes, but I was able to make noise.

"It was never to replace the human race," I croaked and coughed.

"The only way Emodiant would let me conduct the study was to promise it was only to create a new species, not replace ours. But don't you agree, living without emotion is healthier, more logical."

"Can't say I do," I said. I tried to sit up and found my wrists and ankles bound to the table. Dr. Rooken rushed over to tighten them. Then he checked the screens and went up the stairs, leaving us in the dim, green light of the computers and HSS.

I felt around with my hand and found that the edge of the buckle was incredibly sharp.

I had to stop him.

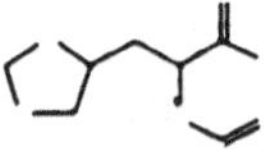

Walking the streets of Denver again was not something I had planned on doing in this lifetime. Yet here we were. Miles and I, the baby wrapped and sleeping, strolled the neighborhood where Dr. Rooken supposedly lived. Miles's people had led us here. First a private shuttle ride from Oregon to Denver and then another driverless car which waited around the corner. They had led us to the neighborhood. And when I asked, they said he was under their watch because he was a dangerous man. This man I had spent time with and had believed was the stereotypical jovial uncle who bounced babies on his knee and brought the best gifts. I couldn't imagine Dr. Rooken with a secret lab in his basement, or with a bone in his body that intended to hurt my father and husband. He was certainly passionate about his work, but he wasn't a cruel man. I had seen him smile at the embryos in the artificial womb. I had caught him giving a gentle pat to the robots who ran his office. But Elias had assured us that Dr. Rooken had done and threatened terrible things, that he needed to understand more about EMT and Elias was the key, especially after I triggered him. And while Dr. Rooken had never struck me as a villain, he had certainly, at times, seemed...off.

The sun began to set, and Miles and I continued to circle the house, never going near enough to be seen. Miles wanted to be sure of his surroundings in case something went wrong. The plan was to knock on the door, force our way in, and remove Elias and Jordan from Dr. Rooken's care. It shouldn't be that hard, considering Dr. Rooken had a family. I worried that Elias wouldn't be here. That if Dr. Rooken really was this evil scientist he would have a warehouse somewhere with all of his macabre tools and a special team ready to clean it all up and wipe the place down before anyone could find them.

As the streetlights flickered on, Miles turned a corner and walked right up to a pretty blue house squished between two others. He knocked on the door and rocked on his heels, hands behind his back, a whistle forming on his lips. A woman answered the door.

"Can I help you?" she asked.

"I'm—" Miles started, but I interrupted.

"I volunteer with Dr. Rooken at the EMT Clinic, and he said he had some research to give me."

"Oh. That's interesting. Um. He's busy, but I can see if he can come here? Can you wait?"

"We'd rather not," Miles said and pushed his way in.

The woman protested, loudly, and I slammed the door behind us with a quick glance outside to spot any onlookers. All was clear, and Miles continued pushing the woman toward the back of the house. We went down a hallway and past a room with a movie playing on a vidscreen and two children seated before it wearing headphones. Miles shoved the woman past the kitchen toward a door, a dead end. She started heaving back, digging her heels in. But it didn't matter, because I slipped around them and made for the door.

It was locked. I jiggled the handle. Pushed and pulled. Then I cocked my leg and put as much power into the kick as I could muster. The door cracked open.

A set of dark stairs and the smell of antiseptic greeted me. I heard machines whirring in the depths of this basement, and I went down. There I found my father, spread eagle and naked on a table, wires stuck into his body at various places with blood still dribbling down his skin at the entry points where they hadn't even bothered to clean. Jordan lay on a table beyond him, looking like a cadaver with stitching across his body. The room was bathed in a green light; the walls covered in various devices and pieces of paper tacked up in random spots. Elias's breathing was rapid, but his eyes were closed. The screen above him showed vitals and a process for a set of nanobots which marched through his bloodstream collecting data.

His hand was free from its restraint, but only because he had rubbed on the buckle until it snapped. His wrist had been an unintentional casualty, or so I hoped, because otherwise my father had tried to commit suicide. His skin was in tatters and blood pooled on the floor beneath him. I ran to the supply cabinet in the corner, snatched for a self-stitching tourniquet from the first-aid kit, and wrapped it around his wrist.

I ripped out the IV. Then I began ripping with a vengeance, all while the monitors and data collectors went haywire and the woman upstairs created the loudest ruckus I could imagine. Soon she would bring the neighbors down on our heads. But I figured performing experiments on people in your own basement was worse than breaking and entering, even if the people were changelings. I unbuckled the other restraints and dashed around to get Jordan free.

"Miles! I need help!" I cried. Down he came, thundering on the steps. The woman close after him. When she reached the foot of the stairs, she stopped short with a gasp and put her hand to her lips.

"I...What...I hadn't," she stuttered.

Miles pulled Elias from the table and flopped him over his shoulder. I yanked one last wire from Jordan's body and grabbed surgical towels to stem the blood flow. Jordan woke and looked into my eyes.

"Can you walk?" I asked.

He nodded. His eyes were glazed, but I thought I caught a glimmer of recognition.

I helped him up and threw a robe over him that was hanging from the rack by the door.

We reached the base of the stairs and had to stop, because at the top stood the silhouette of a man.

"Put him down," Dr. Rooken said.

"You can't do this to them," Miles said. He started climbing the stairs, but I put a hand on him to halt his movement.

"Did you really think you could save things?" I asked. I wiggled my body in front of Miles and climbed the stairs. "It's over. Let us go. You can continue on like nothing happened."

"But something did happen. Something horrible. I must understand."

I approached Dr. Rooken as I would a rabid squirrel, my hands out and my steps slow and deliberate.

"How could you?" his wife called from behind me. "This is not what I thought you were doing." Her voice was small. It barely penetrated the darkness of the stairwell.

"This is necessary. I must uncover the problem. I cannot lose Emotional Modification Therapy. This is everything we have worked for. Even Elias would agree."

Standing three steps below him I gazed up at Dr. Rooken. This man that I thought I had known, who now had dark rings under his eyes and pale, clammy skin.

"Do you know?" I whispered.

"Know what?"

"Why this happened? Why Elias changed back? Why I'm guessing Torin Moray changed back? Why Jordan is on that path?"

"Yes. Of course. They were triggered by something from their past life."

I scoffed. "You don't know."

"Know what?" He launched forward onto the first step. I staggered back.

"He's our father."

The look of revulsion and pure anger on Dr. Rooken's face melted. It became first shock and then surprise and then shame. He stumbled back and hit the wall behind him, sinking down to the floor, his head dropped to his chest. When he looked back up at me, tears coursed down his cheeks.

"I didn't know."

Miles came up behind me and forced me forward into the hallway. Jordan came up next to me, limping. I pulled his arm over my shoulder, and we squeezed past Dr. Rooken and ran for the door. But there was no need to run. No one followed. We were free.

elias

The sounds of tires on pavement, people chattering, a baby gurgling, the wind rushing by. The feeling of bumps jarring my spine, the cushion of a seat reclined, the touch of a finger as it twirled and danced on the back of my hand. The smell of HSS.

I was immediately awake, heaving, attempting to empty the contents of my stomach onto my lap and the back seat of a car.

Brakes squealed, movement stopped, my stomach didn't end its tirade. I flapped around for the door button until it was opened for me. I tumbled out and onto grass, expelling everything from my system onto the ground, between my hands. It splattered on my shirt and a bandage on my wrist. The stench only made me need to retch even more. Soon my body was spent. I sat back on my heels and took a deep breath of clean air. Trees surrounded us, and the highway we traveled was empty.

My eyes roved around until they focused on the man standing before me. I had expected another Emodiant henchman, or perhaps Dr. Rooken with his crooked grin and a frustrating lack of empathy. But my son was the man who stood before me. I burst into tears, sobs really. My cries tore at my throat and threatened to split my vocal chords, but I couldn't contain the relief flooding me.

I looked around for my daughter. There she stood, with her baby in her arms and a smile crossing her face. That wispy brown hair fluttered in the breeze and more gut-wrenching sounds came from inside me. Tears poured from her eyes too.

Miles knelt down, and I could see his face. His cheeks were wet. His arms encircled me. Aloisa came behind and hugged me as well, the baby cradled to one side.

Of course we didn't get much more than a minute before Jordan started screaming. He had wandered toward the trees as soon as Aloisa bent down on our side of the car and seemed to be lost in the shadows. We ran to find him. He sprinted in circles around the trees, like a chicken with its head cut off. Aloisa nearly dropped the baby as she set him down and rushed to contain her husband. I watched her calm him and felt the comforting presence of my son beside me. More tears rained from my eyes.

CHAPTER 41
aloisa

I chased my husband in circles until I finally caught up. Sweeping him into my arms, I shushed and squeezed and rocked. His screams lessened until they were only whimpers. Then he was silent, big eyes staring into mine, chest heaving. The Hormone Stabilizing Serum Dr. Rooken had given him to cope with the torture and surgeries had set him back a few days. The car ride so far had been interesting to say the least. We still didn't know the extent of what had been done. We hoped Elias could figure it out.

"Hi," I said.

"Hi," he said.

I cradled his head the way I did my son's.

"Get a room," Miles scoffed.

I kissed the top of my husband's head and walked back to the rest of my family. Jordan lay down, curled around his soul, hopefully on the path to healing but obviously in pain.

"What do we do?" I asked.

"I know where we can go," Elias said. He picked up the baby.

He was so sure of himself. Even his tone of voice and

the manner he now projected gave me confidence. He was changing, and it gave me hope for my husband, who still lay on the ground like a little child, sniveling. One day, perhaps, he could be back to the Jordan I remembered. I don't remember my father. I was only six and my brother four, but what I imagined him to be like from watching my brother and myself become adults, this was the man I pictured. Analytical, capable of taking care of us, logical, straightforward, capable of calming my baby boy with a few cuddles and humming a song.

"Dr. Wolff wrote about a cottage he had in Montana. He explained how to get there. But that's not the biggest issue. We can go off grid no problem, but do we tell someone everything we know so Dr. Rooken can be stopped? I wouldn't be surprised if he tries again. EMT is on the brink."

"If we keep quiet, he won't come after us," I said.

"You would leave the world to fall apart? What will your son see when he's grown?" Elias asked. He hugged the baby closer.

"My son won't grow if we say something. If we tell, we will be found. Emodiant is a dangerous enemy to have," I said. "Don't get me wrong, I agree that all of this is off the scale of sane, but we can't risk our lives on the chance that someone will figure out how to stop Dr. Rooken. Now, the risk that EMT will fall apart on its own, that I'll take a chance on."

"I'm not willing to do that." Elias fell to his knees, his breath shallow and the bandage on his hand turning a slight pink. I went to take the baby from him and sit next to him.

"What if there was a way?" Miles asked. "What if we could be anonymous?"

"That's not possible. Everything is trackable," Elias said.

"Not a paper letter. Why do you think the rebels always gave us paper?"

Elias's face brightened into a smile.

"That might work," I said. "But no handwriting. No DNA. Not sent from a place anywhere near us."

"I can do all that," Miles said. He started to help Jordan back into the car. "Where to, Elias?" Miles said, and tossed a clean shirt and towel to him.

Elias cleaned up and pulled out the tablet from the car console and started typing into it.

"Wait!" I cried.

I ran to my bag and dug through the contents with the baby balanced on my knee. I was up to my armpit before I finally felt wood. Most of my clothes spilled out as I yanked the gryphon from the pile.

I caressed the smoothness and cradled the creature in my palm as I walked back to Jordan. He perked up. His eyes were full of curiosity.

I placed the gryphon in his outstretched hand.

He studied it, and then looked up at me and smiled.

We all climbed back into the car, and Elias handed the tablet to Miles. Their hands touched and lingered for a moment. The map showed a route taking us farther into nothingness, into the state of Montana. From there we would make our way north, to the borders of Canada and the true wild.

Life hadn't come full circle. It wasn't pretty and tied up with a ribbon. It was a mess. My fingernails were broken and bloody, my back bent a little closer to the ground and ached every morning, my son was learning words like "vegetable" and "seed" instead of "computer" and "changeling." But my husband sat on the porch on a rocking chair that Miles had found in the old barn and fixed up. He had a blanket covering his knees, like a little old man, but his body was erect and growing stronger every day. Elias had found the stitches only led to replaced organs that still functioned normally without HSS. His hair had one tiny streak of gray left, the rest that had sprouted from the stress of getting his hormones back had grown out and turned brown again. That small reminder was the only sign on his calm and relaxed face that made me think of what we had gone through. Well, that and the cottage made of wood and pitch behind him with its tiny glass windows and the forest and mountains beyond that. Also the ground below my feet, dug up with the help of our computerized plow and being seeded by my father, brother, and myself.

I stood to my full height and let the sun warm my cheeks. My son, tied to my back, wiggled and giggled and squealed. He wanted let down so he could crawl, his new favorite thing. I trudged through the thick dirt, careful to avoid the new mounds with seeds nestled inside waiting for water and time. I pulled my baby from my back and set him on the grass in front of the house. Jordan looked up from the piece of wood he was whittling. For the longest time, he had made shapes out of the wood. We had blocks for the baby and bowls and plates for eating. But this one was different. In his hands I could see something forming. Something much more complex. But he covered it with a corner of the blanket before I could really study it.

"Come here," he said, omitting the name that hadn't been given yet. He reached for the baby.

My son crawled across the brittle, coarse green and contemplated the steps before attempting them. He must have calculated that he was capable because he went right up with no more hesitation and no problem. He cooed at his father and crawled right into his arms.

Jordan pulled him up and cuddled him. He looked at me and then waved his hand. "There's Mama," he said.

The baby turned and waved at me. The shape of his face was beginning to lose that baby look. He actually had his father's nose, his grandfather's cheekbones. His peach fuzz was still just that, but his eyes had a brightness to them I hadn't ever seen before. I didn't know if it was from living in fresh air or just the way a baby grows.

"Will you come here?" Jordan asked. He bounced the baby on his knee.

I left a trail of mud up the steps and sat down on the top one. I looked out at my father and brother in the field, both bent at the waist and toiling away in the cool Montana breeze. We had no idea how to farm, to survive the Montana winter. But I had my green thumb, and Miles had downloaded loads of information, and here we were planting our first crop of the spring with a variety of vegetables that grew well together and could be eaten right away, as well as preserved. We were determined.

I studied my fingernails, coated in luscious dirt. One seed clung to the edge of my thumb, and I pinched it between my fingers. From this minuscule thing I would grow something to sustain my body. I flicked the seed away.

"I've been thinking about his name," Jordan said.

I raised my eyebrows. Living off grid meant we had never registered him with the government, and we never would. Another layer of safety to protect him.

"I'm really not sure what to call him. I don't remember anyone important. I think naming him for your father would be a bit ridiculous as we would have to differentiate between them."

"We could give him a nickname."

"Why do you want me to name him?"

"Because. Well." I sat for a moment, trying to remember why I had thought it so important. He was Jordan's son. I wanted him to claim his boy. But there was more to it. I wanted his stamp, his approval. He had left me—us. Granted he hadn't known it was an "us" at the time, but he had left me when I had been against it, vehemently.

"It's a promise," I said. "That you won't leave again. That you're invested enough in your son to name him, to give him his first sense of identity."

Jordan thrust out a hand and grabbed my chin. He made me look him straight in the eye.

"I don't know why I did that," he growled. "But it won't happen again. I don't know how else to apologize. I won't spend my life apologizing, Aloisa."

My eyes stung. My chin throbbed.

"I'm not asking you to apologize anymore," I said. "I only want you to claim your son. He is yours. I want you to acknowledge it."

He gently removed his hand and then cupped my cheek. He smiled. His gaze drifted to the table beside him where the tiny gryphon sat bathing in sunshine. His free hand reached under the blanket for the new project, and I could see the beginnings of a gryphon. The barely formed claws of a lion's feet. The beginnings of an eagle's wings that needed patience and detail. Strong and powerful, full of potential.

"Then his name is Gryphon."

ABOUT THE AUTHOR

Amie McCracken edits and typesets novels for self-published authors and helps writers polish their work. She is an imaginist, with a lot of ideas floating around in her head and a long list of places still to visit. She's been swimming in books her whole life, therefore having a career as an editor and book designer was only natural. There's always a book or three on her nightstand and a manuscript in progress on her laptop. There's also a possibility she might be addicted to tea. This is Amie's debut novel.

Find out more about her at amiemccracken.com.

ACKNOWLEDGEMENTS

I've written an entire novel (and edited it 500,264 times) and I find this the hardest part to write. I am so grateful to so many people, and I'm not sure words can convey the extent of my gratitude.

Let's start with my editor, Paul Shortt, thank you so much for making me feel like I should give up on this whole thing and then helping me take it to a deeper level than I thought possible. Your intense editing was just what I needed, even if it did hurt like ripping off a bandage.

Then there are my beta readers (Lisa, Shanthi, Charlie), you all gave me confidence and humbled me and bolstered me, and I can't thank you enough. You were the first eyes to see this manuscript, and I thank you for being so kind.

I also want to thank Jessica Bell for the gorgeous cover she designed. Thank you so very much for everything we have collaborated on these past years. That cover is drool-worthy.

My husband, Albert, thank you for being the ears to read out loud to, the most awesome dad so I can get writing done, and an incredible partner in life. This might not be Harry Potter, but I'll try to become a billionaire some other way so you can play with cars all day long.

Thank you to my parents for always encouraging me to jump higher, follow my dreams, and excel at everything I do. You have let my imagination run wild my entire life, thank you.

To my grandfather (I'll try to write this part without crying), I miss you so much. I am incredibly sad that you can't read my first ever published book. You were always there with an orange slush drink and a pudding cup when I came over to show you my latest story. I would not have made it this far without your dedicated love of my terrible writing.

And finally, to the inspiration for this entire idea. My Type 1 Diabetes. A part of who I am every day; my life-long curse. I sat down thinking, what if I could, instead of curing diabetes, remove hormones altogether and continue on my merry way? If that was possible, then I wouldn't have to worry about insulin, let alone estrogen and progesterone and adrenaline and so many others that also plague me. Of course our bodies are not built to live without hormones. They are pretty important when it comes to survival. But what if?

If you liked this book, please help other readers find it by posting a review on any of the major retailers.

If you would like to find out more about Amie McCracken, visit her website amiemccracken.com.

If you would like to connect with Amie, and receive a free gift, sign up for her newsletter at amiemccracken.com/booknewsletter